EPITAPH

DON'T MISS THESE THRILLING STORIES IN THE WORLDS OF

HALO

EPITAPH

KELLY GAY

BASED ON THE BESTSELLING VIDEO GAME FOR XBOX®

G

GALLERY BOOKS

New York   London   Toronto   Sydney   New Delhi

G

Gallery Books
An Imprint of Simon & Schuster, LLC
1230 Avenue of the Americas
New York, NY 10020

First Gallery Books trade paperback edition February 2024

GALLERY BOOKS and colophon are registered trademarks of
Simon & Schuster, LLC

Simon & Schuster: Celebrating 100 Years of Publishing in 2024

For information about special discounts for bulk purchases,
please contact Simon & Schuster Special Sales at 1-866-506-1949
or business@simonandschuster.com.

The Simon & Schuster Speakers Bureau can bring authors
to your live event. For more information or to book an event,
contact the Simon & Schuster Speakers Bureau at 1-866-248-3049
or visit our website at www.simonspeakers.com.

Manufactured in the United States of America

10 9 8 7 6 5 4 3 2 1

Library of Congress Cataloging-in-Publication Data is available.

ISBN 978-1-6680-1753-1
ISBN 978-1-6680-1754-8 (ebook)

In memory of Greg Bear.
You cast the light over the Forerunners' ancient
past and drew us all in like moths to a flame.

CHAPTER 1

Whether the warrior succeeds or fails, chooses rightly or wrongly, at least he dared act at all.

—The Mantle, Eleventh Permutation of
the Didact's Number

He was rage and fire. Cinder and storm. Burning remnants and echoes tearing madly over a barren landscape.

Star by star, world by world
Never peace, never solace, never rest

Disjointed, wailing voices darted and dove, amplified in the vast desert echo chamber of dust and sand. Embers and fragments churned and seethed, united into a molten core by a thousand centuries of wrath and resentment.

A deep shadow has fallen
The light shuns us
Stop this! Stop the pain!

Unable to contain the sweltering maelstrom, the molten core bloated and suddenly burst, flinging heat and light outward into the shape of a fiery figure.

The heat dissipated. Black smoke replaced flame, floating and curling and swaying around the figure's outline, gradually settling like a living cloak over the wide shoulders of a tall, gaunt form, a few stubborn embers still clinging to life at its tattered edges.

His rage spent for now, the figure rolled his shoulders, straightened his spine, and then tipped his head from side to side, feeling the pull of thick neck muscles and the satisfying snap of tendons. Pressure in his legs and joints manifested as his weight eased down into his body.

No—not quite a body . . .

The remnant of one, perhaps. A shade. A memory. A poor imitation.

One with enough composition, however, to cause his bare feet to sink into the sand and anchor him to whatever reality this was.

Weariness came with the physical weight, burrowing deeply into sinew and bone and wasted muscle. With effort, he lifted an arm, the cloak sliding back to reveal shriveled skin and a large, almost skeletal hand tipped with brittle, sallow claws.

Denial and disgust rose with a sharp bite, some vague recollection telling him the view should be much different. He turned his hand and arm, seeing in his mind's eye a more powerful and muscular physique, healthier gray skin endowed with fleshy-pink variation. . . .

Despite his initial reaction, the withered skin and desiccated muscle did not trouble him much. In fact, it felt . . . familiar, as though he had experienced the similarity before and all that was required to remedy the situation was to initiate—

Initiate . . . *what*?

Aya. He knew it. Could almost reach it . . .

The lost knowledge seemed to teeter on the precipice of revelation before it evaporated, leaving him unsteady, as if the sandy ground weakened beneath him. He rubbed at the vague ache in his right eye, a faint tease of identity skipping through his mind, but that too faded.

Try as he might, he could not mentally grasp a single important thing. Who he was, *what* he was, or how he came to be here, all seemed equally out of reach.

His cloak flapped as a line of tepid wind blew over his position, drawing attention to the dust and sand caught up in the current. As far as the eye could see, there was nothing but low sand dunes watched over by a dirty dull-blue sky and the bright flare of a sun hidden behind muddled clouds.

An arrogant snort flared softly through his nostrils, indicating a strong, ingrained confidence, one that told him not all was lost. Memory might escape him, but instinct and basic knowledge did not. His senses were intact, and his traits and emotions felt strong within him, some still gnawing and churning in his gut—indignation, contempt, bitterness, fury, obsession. But these he left alone for the time being.

No need to stir the serpent's nest just yet . . .

He stared across the desolate landscape, contemplating his current situation. Had he been brought here? Forced here? Or had he fled here? Was his presence by chance or deliberate?

When weighed against the consuming rage he'd experienced earlier, one surety stood out above all others. It was certainly *not* by choice.

With nothing in any direction but the endless waste, his options were decidedly simplistic. Stay put or move on.

Without hesitation, he chose the latter, the sand folding over his feet as he started off in no particular direction.

The going was tedious and slow, his corporeal form stiff and uncooperative, though his bare skin on earth and the tiny grains pushing between his toes were oddly satisfying, the basic physical connection to the environment feeling very much like a novelty.

After trekking across several dunes, he paused to rest at a high point, revising his previous opinion. The sand was far from satisfying. His soles and toes were now raw, his body ached all over, and his mouth felt like tinder picked from the loose bark of the *rataa* trees that had once lined his family estate on Nomdagro.

The clarity of the vision struck harsh and quick. The force of it had him by the throat, stealing his breath.

Tree line. Children picking bark. A fire already smoking in the clearing by the white, chalky banks of the River Dweha . . .

The entire moment lay suspended.

His legs trembled and he dropped to one knee, gasping, struggling to keep hold of the vision, to place it in the context of his life, but it dodged just out of reach.

Disappeared. Gone. As though it had never existed.

Defeated, he collapsed with an angry growl, sitting in the sand and shaking his head, appalled at his own wretched incompetence. Heat crept up the back of his neck. Absently he rubbed the warm skin as his brow drew into a deep frown. His inability to capture the memory was discouraging, but there was also hope. It meant that his past was not completely lost. It was still there, under the surface.

More will come, he told himself, eyeing the next sand dune in his path—the tallest yet.

While exhaustion threatened to immobilize him, he was apparently nothing if not stubborn. Rousing his dwindling reserves, he got up and let gravity carry him in big strides down the dune's long slope.

Once he made it to the next pile of sand, his head tipped back at its height. Such a menial, unnecessary, and time-consuming task when he could simply . . .

What? Wish himself to the top?

He braced against the now endless aches and pains plaguing his frail body, and with no small amount of grumbling began yet another climb—one sore foot in front of the other—until he finally reached the summit, out of breath, but rewarded for his efforts. A dark and dirty horizon stretched in the far distance, and within it or perhaps preceding it—it was too far to tell—a mote of blue glowed.

Finally, *something* out there in the sea of sand. Relief flooded him and he slumped to the ground.

Once down, he did not attempt to get back up. No matter what might lie beckoning ahead, it felt too good to stop and rest. Something told him that this too felt like a novelty. He pulled a foot closer to his body to knead the aching heel and arch, then cleared the sand between his toes. As he tended to the other foot, small dark specks appeared in the sky.

Instantly, there it was again, the precipice of knowledge. Along with an urge to assess the threat, to meet it with swift and decisive action. All he had to do was—

And it was gone. Again.

"Aya," he grunted in frustration as the specks drew close enough to see in detail.

There were five creatures of flight with crested heads and long, imposing beaks. They were larger than him in both body and wingspan, and their dirty-brown color blended in well with the desert landscape. Double sets of large leathery wings protruded from each narrow torso and flapped rather slowly. As they glided overhead, the length of their tails was displayed and the—

Rangmejo

The word whispered with sudden clarity.

He turned and watched their diminishing passage. Just as they faded from view, they suddenly dispersed into dust.

Like a mirage.

A dream.

He closed his eyes tightly, giving his head a hard shake, before looking again. But the avian creatures were indeed gone.

An unsettling sensation bloomed in the pit of his stomach. While he did not want to admit it, he knew. He'd known all along.

Wherever *this* was could not be based in the physical world. The landscape was not quite right, and neither was he—formed as he'd been from embers and emotion. His arms were wizened and old. His garb was wholly unfamiliar. Even his face, which he mapped with his fingers, felt bony and unrecognizable. He pinched his sallow cheeks and tugged at the tuft of hair on his head. The pain was real, at least. He studied his hands. All six fingers accounted for . . .

It was right, and yet not right. He felt solid, and yet . . . he was not whole.

Questions assailed him. None of which he could definitively answer. He must have had a past life, but there was nothing to prove his brief recollections were real or that they even belonged to him.

The mote of blue lingering far on the horizon was the only point of significance so far. If he had indeed been brought here, sent here, forced here—whatever the case might be—there must be a reason.

He stayed on the dune for a time, mildly contemplating his predicament while tending to his other aching foot. After his fingers grew tired, he lay back and put a hand behind his head, wondering if there had ever existed such a lackluster, dirty blue sky before.

Aya. But it was quiet here.

Perhaps he should simply accept his fate, enjoy the peace, and wait for something to happen. Amusement tugged a corner of his mouth. If he did have a past life, he was *certain* such an inane and useless thought had never crossed his mind.

Gradually, his mind drifted. As sleep took over, he wondered in what reality he might awaken.

He dreamed of fire.

From flesh to bone, it ate away at him, ripping him apart one layer at a time, tearing and burning.

Stripped, pulled asunder, until even his consciousness peeled free, and he was nothing but writhing, screaming embers.

CHAPTER 2

The nightmare lingered around him as he left the high dunes for an expansive region of desert sand shaped like currents on a windy lake. Between these crescent-shaped mounds, the ground was windswept and hard, offering an easier, if not longer, path to follow. The smudge of blue ahead hovered unchanged, guiding, urging him on when he grew weary. Without its murky glow, he would surely be lost to this sea of never-ending dirt, dust, and sand.

Never-ending sameness.

Much like the state of his mind—unfilled with the clutter of the life he must have led.

Occasionally memories erupted unbidden, dispersing images like spores ejected from their host, gone into the wind in the blink of an eye and not worth his time; he knew he couldn't catch them.

Most often, however, his thoughts stayed firmly on the present. The soft, painful scrape of his feet on the ground. The brush of his cloak against his ankles. The phantom ache plaguing his right eye. The inhaling and exhaling through fragile lungs. The way the dusty atmosphere cleared as time wore on, giving way to twilight and the blackness of space with its orchestra of stars.

Desolate, perhaps. But not without its merits.

After traveling some distance, his steps slowed, and his eyes narrowed on a stretch of thin white clouds that had begun to settle above the ground's surface about half a kilometer away. With the arrival of night, the environment had grown unnaturally quiet. Even the wind had ceased and, in turn, the constant scrape and whispering patter of sand. His skin grew cold even though the temperature remained constant and unremarkable.

Would that he could see what danger might lurk in the growing fog.

His mood soured as a strong instinct told him that even from this distance his vision *should* be able to penetrate the hazy depths. Any inquiry or surveillance *should* be relayed to him in an instant simply by virtue of thought. Yet he was handicapped, unable to know any but the most basic details.

He felt blind even when he could see.

Resting and waiting for the fog to clear was the better and more conservative course of action, but such calmer notions paled beside his mounting irritation. With a huff, he pressed on—the quicker he found answers, the better.

The long stretch of haze preceding the fog was minuscule at first, its subtlety drawing him in until gradually he was surrounded by temperate and strangely dry clouds.

With each step, the milky gauze split and then folded back on itself, gathering around him and blurring the path in all directions. In the shifting haze, illusions seemed to float and morph, the dunes ebbing and flowing like waves, growing and changing shapes.

Eventually the hazy view grew marginally clearer, revealing great simian-like shadows listing or lying prone, partially submerged in the sand, hulking things bearing the semblance of heads, arms, torsos, and tails. Figments of the fog and his tired mind, or perhaps they'd been there all along.

Mist curled around his legs as he approached the dark, sandy graveyard of these immense beasts, the identity of which was just on the tip of his tongue. . . .

As he drew closer, their true size unfolded, and he guessed their prone length to be close to twenty meters. A strange mix of recognition and wariness gathered in his chest, as though he should guard himself.

Not from danger . . .

But from pain.

They were not a figment, not part of the fog or sand playing tricks with him, but real enough to touch. There were two near him, both made of metal—*machine-cell alloy*, the information whispered through his mind—one buried and canted in the sand, only its giant torso and head visible, and the second prone and partly submerged on its side, revealing one large arm-like appendage and a long tail. He reached for the colossal arm, its metal eroded and pitted by the elements, the surface rough against his touch.

Old machines. Vestiges of war . . .

Thrusters in the tail. Control cabin in the head. Multi-use mandibles for arms.

Instantly his mind built the missing parts beneath the sand. He knew these metal beasts, had seen them before. Their name was right there, dancing out of reach . . .

A sense of smallness surrounded him as he moved around the old, discarded giants. With each step, a deep aching sadness inched its way inside until his bones felt brittle. He rubbed at the tightness in his chest, but the gesture was useless. Despair gathered around him like an old ghostly acquaintance.

Why these war sphinxes should make him—

War sphinxes.

"Yes." The word echoed on a long, relieved breath as his gaze returned to stare in awe at the massive head, or command center, lying in the sand. The angles of its "face" were designed to appear menacing, but to him it was unquestionably mighty and profoundly bittersweet. Great pride suddenly swelled, and he patted the surface, nodding in approval. "I know what you are."

Aya. He remembered now.

And wished he did not.

He slumped against the war sphinx, and just like that, with a simple connection, gravity ceased to exist and the world as he knew it was simply . . . *gone.*

A gasp stuck in his throat as the sensation of falling from a harrowing height blew through him. The view blurred, the colors of the landscape and night sky stretched, pulled apart and put back together again, blending into one, until only blackness remained. A split second passed before a new reality solidified, snapping into being with a hard clap and the tang of ozone in his mouth.

A turbulent mix of sounds and smells assaulted his senses, and instantly, even before opening his eyes, he knew that he was somewhere else—some other place, some other *time.*

Acrid smoke billowed across his field of vision, stinging his eyes and the inside of his nose and throat, making him gag and cough until tears streamed down his face.

Wiping his eyes, he blinked a few times as the smoke cleared, his muddled mind slow to come to terms with the scene in front of him.

Spent battlefield. The ground churned up. Starships broken and burning. Streams of fire lit the smoky sky.

As the scream and whine of engines and bombardment thundered in his ears, he staggered to his feet to see bodies strewn across the landscape, burned beyond recognition, while others were hidden within damaged or partially exposed armor.

A glance down revealed that he too wore armor. His chest, hands, and arms were encased in unadorned storm-blue battle plates. The plates rested over a film of light that protected him from head to toe and shone through the joints and spaces of the armor. As if in a dream, he moved forward, armored legs and feet stepping in time with what felt like a ghost, a memory, like walking in the footsteps of an earlier version of himself.

He breathed in deeply, feeling both the strength of his past self and the veil of weakness defining his current state.

"I walked this path before," he murmured with certainty as he strode among the dead.

And a thousand times over in my mind. . . .

Distressed voices cascaded through his helmet and armor. He was linked with thousands, able to precisely catalog every word as reports poured in from his staff of . . . *Warrior-Servants.*

Warrior-Servants.

Forerunners.

A current ran beneath his skin. His step faltered. The battlefield came into sharp focus as details flooded back, and he was able to distinguish the dead, the Forerunners—his kind—from the enemies. *Humans.*

Commander, the line is broken!

Reserve fleet incoming! It's not over yet! Watch your back!

Under heavy fire . . . request harrier strike on my—

Get out of there now!

He hadn't walked this path before. He ran it.

Lost in the memory, propelled by dread, he ran, dodging debris and spacecraft rocketing into the ground nearby.

Their last words to him, to each other, were branded on his soul.

Two of his many children. The eldest and the youngest. Lost here. On Faun Hakkor, the last pivotal defensive outpost before reaching the humans' stronghold planet of Charum Hakkor.

His heavy footfalls vibrated the space around him, shaking his field of vision. War sphinxes were burning dead ahead. One canted on its side, half-crushed in the dirt, with his youngest, his beloved son, mangled inside. Ever the rebel, ever the one to take chances with little regard to his safety, and without question one of the finest Warrior-Servants of his day.

Nearby his eldest, his daughter, the one most like him, a born leader, intensely loyal to her rate, her family—especially the youngest—burned to death inside of her armor, already gone. They'd finally broken the outer planetary defenses of Faun Hakkor and were poised to crush the infernal human resistance, but had paid a heavy price as the enemy's reserve fleet lay in wait on the surface.

Aya, it was all coming back.

Fighting for balance, he placed a steadying hand on the scarred and blackened surface of the war sphinx. His lungs struggled to take in enough oxygen. Tears blurred his vision. If only the memories would stop, would give him time to process, but they battered him until his thoughts spun and his gut twisted into a bitter knot. The grief was suffocating, building and bloating until he roared his loss to the fiery sky, the many voices of the ongoing battle fading into the background.

Gradually the recollections played their course and finally faded on a gentler note.

The sound of laughter.

He could see them, his beloved children. In better days. The best days. Playing in the riverbed, coated in white clay. And those same children grown, serving in the rate of their father, formidable warriors in their own right. And he, as their commander, haunted by their last moments.

Every last one of them gone in the human-Forerunner wars.

The veins at his temples throbbed. A wet film of tears lay over his eyes. The phantom strength of his former self was utterly depleted, leaving behind a feeble, trembling shell.

I shouldn't be here. Take me back.

Take me back.

His eyes closed and he repeated the words like a mantra, unsure to whom or what he was pleading, but wanting it to be over, for this miserable experience to finally end.

With a sudden *ping* vibrating his eardrums, the ground beneath him gave way once more. Gravity evaporated along with everything else as he was sucked out of the memory and flung back to where he'd begun in the endless wasteland, dizzy and sick and gasping for air, enraged at being pulled and pushed and tossed around with little control over what happened to him . . . and for what he had lost.

He was a father.

The heavy truth settled on his shoulders until he was bent over from the sheer, absolute weight of it. To have forgotten such an important aspect of his life, only to remember it, suddenly and with such shocking clarity, filled him with a sense of awe and disbelief and confusion.

He slumped to the ground next to one of the old war sphinxes. It was silent, of course, a time-worn shell long since divested of its operator and the personality pattern imprinted upon its systems.

His heart longed to mourn, but he held the desire at bay, experiencing the physical blowback instead—the twisting gnaw in his gut, the choking glob in the back of his throat, the tightening of his chest. . . . A small price to pay to suppress and avoid such heartbreak.

Tuning out the agony, he curled his body against the construct, drawing his arms around his knees and resting his head against the pitted alloy. On a long, defeated exhale, his eyes closed as a small voice worked its way into his weary mind.

You were a father.

Once it had mattered.

Then came a time when it did not. . . .

Disjointed memories. Vivid flashes. Countless battles. Faces he recognized. Death in untold numbers.

"There is something rotten inside you."

Resonant and unyielding. Haughty and merciless. He knew this voice well, for it was his own. From long, long ago. During the prime of his life.

"It crawled in, burrowed down deep. Festered. Waited.

"And you let it in.

"YOU LET IT IN!"

The voice faded as another rose in its place.

Deep laughter rumbled from the blackness, like thunder beneath the ground, cut and shaped against bedrock over eons of time. It wormed and twisted its way, growing louder and louder.

His heart hammered. Sweat clung to his skin. He spun around in the darkness. The sound lashed out and grabbed his throat.

"There is something rotten inside you."

He woke with a jerk, heart racing, choking on his own saliva as the words receded into the murky depths of his mind.

After rubbing the crusty sleep from his eyes and taking a moment to shake off the effects of his nightmare, he pushed to his feet. Day had risen, the fog was gone, and the landscape was just as boring and unremarkable as it had been the day before.

Only, the war sphinxes were gone.

"What madness is this?"

No traces, no indentations in the sand. He rubbed his face and slapped his cheeks. But his current reality stayed the same. He was not dreaming, and he certainly was not imagining things.

He walked a few paces, then retraced his steps, searching for any evidence to support what he had seen and experienced. But there was nothing. Nothing but sand and windswept ground. Had everything been merely a dream?

"No," he whispered. No. He refused to believe that. What he'd witnessed, what he remembered . . . it was *real*.

His children. The war with humanity. It was all real.

Or *had* been real.

He rubbed a hand down his face and then exhaled loudly, releasing the grief-stricken emotions before they could overwhelm him again.

Whatever had happened, be it dream or vision or insanity, it was clear he wouldn't find answers in this empty place. With that in mind, he lifted his chin and scanned the horizon, locating his guide—that ever-present azure glow—and began his journey toward it.

The continuous travel allowed him to focus and reflect on his recovered memories without the initial sting of emotion, and what he realized opened a floodgate. Within those harsh recollections, context fell into place, supporting and surrounding every scene and detail, providing impressions of the life he had led along with a wealth of additional knowledge to digest.

He knew he was Forerunner, a species of unrivaled technological achievement. As the preeminent power in the galaxy, his kind upheld the Mantle of Responsibility for millions of years, using its guiding tenets to act as stewards and guardians for all lesser species and worlds within their vast ecumene.

He knew he was born into the rate of Warrior-Servant and defended a realm that spread across three million inhabited worlds. He had faint memories of serving with distinction, achieving recognition, and even teaching at the College of Strategic Defense of the Mantle. He married a Forerunner outside of his rate, a Lifeworker named First-Light-Weaves-Living-Song, though most called her the Librarian due to her unquenchable thirst for knowledge. He could not clearly see her face or remember the love he must have had for her, but he knew that together, united in their combined ambitions, they rose swiftly in rank—she on a path to obtaining the title of Lifeshaper, the highest in her rate, and he . . .

His step faltered as the flow of memory suddenly evaporated.

With a mumbled curse, he continued on. It seemed his identity would elude him for now, though at the rate his memories were returning it would not be long before the knowledge came.

There were other recollections as well, lurking like shadows, hounding him. Disjointed flashes of war, of humanity annihilating entire worlds within the Forerunners' ecumene, driven by their aggression and lust for expansion, destroying planet after planet without mercy, an affront to the galaxy and all that the Mantle of Responsibility held dear.

Up until the battle on Faun Hakkor, the war with the human empire had raged for nearly five decades. But his memories after this point remained a stubborn blur, and for all that he had regained since manifesting in whatever mysterious place this was, his mind seemed unhurried to offer a clear and precise picture of exactly who he was and how he came to be here. Despite the lag and the bouts of frustration it brought, he was content in the knowledge that he had led a distinguished life with a wife and family, that his children had filled the large traditional mansion he designed himself with happiness and love and laughter.

That was something, at least. And eventually the rest would come. Of that, he was certain.

CHAPTER 3

A hard line of wind blew across the desert. He gathered the frayed edges of his hood to protect his face against the stinging sand, only glancing out occasionally to stay on course with the blue beacon still in the distance. His mood grew ever more eroded and irritated by the environment. Grit was everywhere, in his nose and the corners of his eyes and mouth, between his fangs and bottom lip, the space rubbed raw. His feet were in far worse condition, making his pace slow and cumbersome.

He remembered walking in the shoes of his past self at Faun Hakkor, remembered what it felt like to move through the hazards of battle with all the protections and benefits of Forerunner armor. Would that he had access to such advantages now. . .

Now that he recalled what he was missing, a heightened sense of annoyance and vulnerability dogged every ache, every tiresome step, every labored breath. As a result, he could not help but reminisce on the boundless wonders of the Forerunners' most prominent and important technology.

Boasting near-limitless life-sustaining capabilities, body-assist armor with its neural-interfaced ancilla guarded against injury, disease, and aging; healed the mind; amplified the senses; sharpened the intellect, memory, and perception. It could satiate the body's natural need for sleep, thereby erasing the function altogether and providing Forerunners with unlimited time without suffering any of the consequences. It even protected a wearer from psychological harm by diminishing or completely eliminating certain harmful experiences and memories.

All aspects were continuously monitored; indeed, every facet of a Forerunner's mental, physical, and environmental life was maintained. In an instant, moods and dangers and desires were perceived, the armor adjusting its form to account for every situation a Forerunner might face—combat, emotional, ceremonial . . . even adjusting to fit various sizes and different species. Connections to other Forerunners near and far, and to any interface, were superlative, enabling the operation of all manner of technology. Boundless stores of information across the ecumene were promptly available to the wearer, as was a vital pathway to the Domain, the enigmatic quantum archive containing the immense collective experience, knowledge, history, and culture of the Forerunners.

He glanced down at his withered form, grateful to bear such humiliation alone, though the small blessing paled against the intense inadequacy he felt without his body-assist armor.

Perhaps there were some memories better left forgotten.

Longing for what was lost to him could easily send him down a spiraling path. Indeed, care needed to be taken. While he could now put a bit of history to his life and species, he felt some concern over whatever memories had yet to surface. His children, their laughter, their deaths, still echoed in his mind and heart. And those memories were but small fragments. The emotional price of recovering his past might very well be too great to bear.

He pulled his hood tighter as a gust of wind peppered him with sand and focused on putting one foot in front of the other.

More than once, he considered the possibility of his demise, that his current form—though it felt emotion and pain and had physical substance—might be nothing but an echo, an essence, the cumulation of his life and consciousness, his personality and biological pattern saved and reduced to data.

Normally after death, the complete essence and sum of a Forerunner's life experience would be uploaded into the vast repository of the Domain, in order to join the ancestral, collective record. Thinking back to the lifetime he was able to remember, his memories of the Domain were shadowy at best, though he had vague impressions of exploring its dark, mystifying architecture brimming with information—a far cry from the never-ending dullness of sand spread out around him now.

He traveled until the daystar began to sink into the horizon behind him, his form cast ahead in a long, thin shadow while the waning light pierced the dusty air and reflected on minuscule particles of sand. The effect blurred the line of delineation between land and sky, the view onward becoming nothing but a muddy mix of grayish-yellow, browns, and dusky blue. Even his beacon had lost its luster, mutating into a dirty cerulean that was eventually lost in the background altogether.

Without that glowing blue guide, there was nothing to do but wait and rest, so he gathered his tattered cloak around his body and chose a spot where he could recline against the slope of a dune, grateful the wind had died down and savoring the respite.

Idleness did have its virtue.

He used the time to pick the grit from the corners of his eyes and rub his aching feet until a thought occurred to him, making him pause. Without his armor to provide nourishment, he should be thirsty and hungry, ravenous in fact. And yet, despite his journey across the desert, these needs and the cravings they produced had simply not manifested. . . .

A slight vibration rattled up through the desert floor, scattering his thoughts.

Grains of displaced sand skittered down the dune's slope. After the last grain came to a stop, seconds passed in utter stillness. The fur on the nape of his neck tingled in warning.

The shallow dune imploded, dropping into a massive hole opening in the ground beneath it.

A surprised shout lodged in his throat and his arms pedaled wildly as he fell with a waterfall of sand into the opening hatch of an enormous sphere as it rose slowly to the surface.

Swallowed up, weightless, he had no way to counter or protect himself. He landed hard on a floating pedestal within the sphere, biting his tongue in the process, the breath jolted from his lungs and jarring pain radiating through his spine and the back of his skull.

He spat out blood and lay there awhile, regrouping, before gathering enough strength to sit up and brace his hands against the pedestal to steady himself. As the sand continued to stream down, a sense of familiarity filled him. The geometric lines cut into the dark inner surface of the sphere were quintessentially Forerunner in design, and the cavernous space was large enough to fit several war sphinxes.

As the hatch closed, the streams of sand slowed to an unnatural stop, hovering for a frozen second before moving horizontally, picking up speed, circling the inside circumference of the sphere until the sound was deafening. Light began to thread through the strange, sandy storm, gradually becoming flashes that delivered brief, indistinct images.

The faster the sand spun, the clearer the images became.

He recognized Faun Hakkor. Pictures of Forerunner victory sped past, followed by an enormous fleet in space approaching another planet. With the image, the accompanying knowledge flooded in, a single scene generating an avalanche of memories. The planet was the humans' last stronghold, Charum Hakkor.

As he watched the images appear and disappear, his mind grew full and overwhelmed with memories of his past. And though it was almost too much to process, his body instinctually bracing against the onslaught, he counseled himself to relax and accept the flow of information.

Above Charum Hakkor, six massive Forerunner fleets awaited the arrival of a seventh through a portal that conveyed a staggering collection of the finest *Fortress-* and *Sojourner*-class starships.

The human capital below with its orbital arches, great sky towers, and urban sprawl had been built atop and around the colossal architecture of its previous inhabitants, the Forerunners' enigmatic creators—the Precursors, an ancient transsentient species long since gone from the galaxy, though their constructions remained scattered throughout the stars. On Charum Hakkor, these ruins turned a technologically impressive capital city into something awe-inspiring; the crystalline superstructures left behind by the near-godlike beings dominated the city. The citadel, armory, arena, and great highway were not stylized or adorned, but they were magnificent in scope and transcendent in their creation.

The distinct sense of wonder he'd experienced upon seeing those constructions had only grown with the knowledge that they had been built with the Precursors' use of neural physics, an elusive technology that the Forerunners, with all of their intellectual prowess and advancements, had yet to fully comprehend.

He saw himself in full combat armor, meeting the Librarian at the head of the escort cruiser's open bay shortly after it had landed near the citadel. Happiness and love, pain and regret, wrapped around his chest and squeezed until his breath turned shallow.

He was awed by the sight of them together, husband and wife, side by side, the differences striking. In her customary Lifeworker attire—a slender form-fitting lucent white shift worn over her personal armor, and her white hair coiled beneath a stately headdress—she floated next him on her personal antigravity dais. Immense intelligence shone brightly in her dark eyes and her face was alight, as always, with that youthful aura and innate grace and elegance that made his pulse leap even now. And he, every ounce a warrior, dwarfing his wife, standing over three meters tall and powerfully built.

Together they had stepped onto the planet for the first time.

He touched his fangs and ran his fingers over a sunken cheek. The picture presented was nothing like his physical image now. What horrors had befallen him to bring a once formidable warrior to such a state?

Images continued to streak by.

Entering Citadel Charum. Inspecting the human prisoners laid out in rows, hundreds upon hundreds of men, women, and children, and hundreds of thousands more within the city. They wore no armor or adornments. *Stripped themselves to prevent identification,* he recalled.

Then, looking for someone—

Ah, yes. There.

That face—dark-skinned; high, broad cheekbones and forehead; strong jaw; white streaks tattooed on his forehead, across the bridge of his nose, cheeks, and chin; his black hair knotted high on his head and secured with an austere hair needle—was one he remembered well.

Forthencho Oborune. Lord of Admirals.

The greatest and most formidable adversary he'd ever fought now lay wounded among his own people, a chilling light in his dark eyes, a touch of pity and tragic humor too, as though the human commander held one final volley, a dreadful secret the Forerunners would soon discover.

Seeing this moment unleashed another wave of recollections, shocking revelations, compounding one after another. The humans had been fighting a war on two fronts—annihilating Forerunner worlds and settlements, not out of aggression and warmongering, but to sterilize, to hold back a new, highly intelligent threat to the galaxy, a horrifying parasite that fed on and assimilated all sentient life.

The Flood.

While the truth was stunning in its own right, it did not negate humanity's crimes. They had dared to raise arms against the stewards of the Mantle. They had murdered his children—his *children*! For these transgressions alone, they deserved to be eradicated. Only their experience battling the Flood had saved them.

Or rather, doomed them to a fate *far* worse than extinction.

Forthencho, along with every man, woman, and child in the citadel, had faced the Composers: devices capable of separating consciousness and biological patterns from their physical bodies and transforming them into raw data intended to be studied and probed in an effort to learn as much as possible about humanity's interactions with the Flood, while other humans were devolved back into the hunter-gatherers of old and placed on their natal world.

He remembered conversing with the Lord of Admirals when it was the human commander's turn to face the Composer, although the words eluded him now. But the disturbing smile on the human's face as his essence was viciously torn from his body? *That* remained a memory quite clear and deep.

The recall was relentless, racing along like a turbulent river.

He saw his entry into the depths of the now-destroyed Citadel Charum to a once fiercely guarded pit sunk millions of years deep into the layers of former Precursor occupation and the inescapable domed prison the humans had created there.

Fear hatched in an instant, like spiderlings scattering across his skin.

The creature held cushioned in a timelock was unlike anything he had ever seen before, an unnatural union of mammal, arthropod, and cephalopod, a hulking gray mass at least six meters wide and nearly as tall with strange, faceted eyes broadly set in a massive flat head atop a simian-like torso. It possessed a multitude of fat, irregular limbs and an exposed segmented spine and tail.

The Timeless One, or the Captive, they'd called it. Theories on its origins were inconclusive. Was it propaganda to unnerve the Forerunners? A last-resort weapon?

But he would soon learn from the ancient creature itself that it professed to be the last Precursor, the Primordial, imparting the startling revelation that the Precursors hadn't simply faded from the galaxy as Forerunners believed—they'd been wiped out millions of years earlier by Forerunners who had risen up in rebellion against their creators, committing an irreconcilable act of genocide.

New images suddenly eclipsed those of Charum Hakkor, taking him across the galaxy to another place, the sights and locations instantly in his mind, as if opening a door long shut.

The Forerunner capital of Maethrillian, a planet-sized, artificially created hub composed of several habitable stacked circular disks attached in a spiral pattern to a long central core.

Accessible by bridges and ferries, a basin-shaped structure that housed the Council Chamber was suspended from one of the main disks. Large enough to hold six hundred councilors, judges, witnesses, speakers, and mediators in ornate boxes and seats, its walls were decorated with millions of spent slipspace crystals, while above, sculptures of quantum-engineered crystals orbited the amphitheater.

His former self stood in austere Warrior-Servant attire on one of four speaking pedestals placed at the four compass points of the chamber, and opposite the tall, imposing figure of Faber-of-Will-and-Might, the Master Builder, considered by many a near-perfect male Forerunner in face and form, in his richly stylized and perfumed armor—both of them there to discuss all they had learned in the aftermath of humanity's defeat and, most importantly, to debate the new threat of the Flood and the preparations that must be made.

Arguing against the Master Builder, he had presented his case succinctly and honestly: they should build artificial planets, shield worlds capable of protecting and defending populations. But his words fell on deaf ears. The only thing the assemblage heard was the political fearmongering and embellishments of the Master Builder, arguing to construct a weapon of mass destruction instead. *Halo*, he called it. Giant rings that would be inelegant in their original assembly, but would later be designed with the power to mass-sterilize all forms of sentient life, each one capable of firing a superluminal pulse of cross-phased supermassive neutrinos with a range of twenty-five thousand light-years. When fired in concert, their range covered the entire galaxy.

They were an affront to the very teachings of the Mantle of Responsibility.

No matter how hard he reasoned, his pleas were ignored. The

Council ruled against him. A few hundred had decided the destiny of an entire ecumene of three million worlds—and the fate of all thinking life beyond.

He'd become a political outcast, subsequently stripped of his ranks and titles, and condemned to exile.

Now another image moved past.

A farewell.

His home on Nomdagro. Sitting with the Librarian in their quarters. Divested of his armor, drinking *inchukoa* from a ritual cup, the liquid that would begin the process of living desiccation in preparation for his exile.

Anger and frustration, worry and heartbreak consumed him as he watched the ancient scene play out, the words between husband and wife coming as clearly as if he stood with them in the chamber.

"*. . . I sometimes wish you were more bloody-minded, more vengeful, Wife.*"

"*Not the way of the Warrior or of the Mantle—and of course not mine.*"

"*Of course. . . . The ecumene has become confused. The Council steeps itself in lies and dishonor. But . . . you foresee my return, in one form or another, and the resumption of our struggle.*"

"*There is often a sickness before the purge.*"

"*That sounds gross and bloody-minded. I am reminded of why I sought our love in the first place.*"

"*You sought it?*"

"*I did.*"

"*That is not how I remember it, Warrior. An unlikely love, at any rate—so your fellows said.*"

"*But we know. As you have instructed me often, we play out our parts in Living Time and accept all that life brings, and all that it takes away. So we support the Mantle: Daaowa maadthu. The humans . . .*"

Had they been willing to acknowledge their crimes, they would have made a great civilization, worthy to join our own. But they did not. I hope that what remains of them, in your care, does not disappoint you. My anger would then be impossible to control. . . ."

How he had struggled to contain his rancor, forced to leave her, forced to leave defense of the ecumene to the Master Builder! Only her presence assuaged some of his wrath and allowed the ritual to flow to completion.

Once vitrified to a near-mummified state, he'd been sealed inside a Warrior Keep, a Cryptum, his body intended to lie in a state of suspended animation as his mind was free to roam the Domain.

Utilized mostly by Warrior-Servant elites as self-imposed means of penance, Cryptums were also used by those seeking the higher awareness of *xankara*, a timeless meditative state, or, as in his case, by those silencing a political opponent, secretly sealing their influence away from the public with little repercussion.

The swirling around the sphere finally slowed until the sand fell into the depths below him.

Silence descended in what he now realized was an empty Cryptum, which slowly began to disintegrate around him, like a mirage swept clean by a brisk wind. When it was gone, he found himself no longer sitting on the pedestal—that too was gone—but on the sand dune where he'd been before.

For some time after, his mind was simply numb.

Dark clouds rolled across the desert sky, too far away to cause any concern. Gradually the memories filtered in again, this time at a slower pace, giving him the opportunity for examination and understanding.

Hours went by, the stars moving slowly across the night sky as more of his past moved into its proper place on the timeline of his life. Eventually his thoughts turned to what had transpired during and after the long centuries of his exile. What had become of the Forerunners, and his wife? Had they gone to war against the Flood? Had they used the Master Builder's galaxy-cleansing weapons? Had they truly sunk so low and lost all hope of upholding the Mantle of Responsibility?

The possibilities sat heavy on his shoulders as he watched the black clouds brew into a full-fledged storm.

Flashes of lightning cut through the horizon in thin, jagged lines of bluish-green. One such strike caught a glint of silver and blue. He sat straighter, waiting. . . . Another flash, and there it was again, illuminated for a few precious seconds—his blue beacon emanating from a tall, silvery tower.

With a rush of excitement, he was on his feet and striding down the sand, headed directly into the storm.

CHAPTER 4

He'd lost any sense of time, only fixated on the journey ahead, eyes down, one foot in front of the other, shuffling across the desert, insulated from the outside world by his cloak. Until the air around him changed, the shiver of electricity crawled along his skin, and the cool bands of wind from the outermost edges of the storm invaded his cogitation.

He had seen the spire illuminated only a few more times when he chanced a look, but it was enough to stay on course. Adrenaline kept his weak body charged, and the cool breeze added to the natural boost. He felt stronger than he had since arriving in this desolate place.

Heading straight into a massive storm system was folly no matter how much he wanted to continue, so he slowed his pace, hoping his travel through the expansive outer bands might give the harsh weather ahead time to abate and allow him to keep moving.

Gradually the cool winds increased, wisping around him like a thinly contained cyclone. Strong gusts lashed at him, sending his cloak snapping and his hood from his grasp. It was only after being buffeted several times from different directions and nearly pushed off his feet that he realized something was not quite right about the wind.

A dusty blur blew past and dispersed . . . then appeared again in another location. Three such blurs seemed to dog and dodge him. Unperturbed, he stopped and trained his gaze on the movement, noting there was form within the dust.

Bipedal shape. Lithe. Quick. Humanoid.

Like a coordinated pack of predators, they lunged in and out of his space, their force pushing him this way and that, playing with him, taunting him. . . . The more he focused his gaze upon them, the more details emerged. Orange light glowed from the spaces between armor plating, which seemed to make up the bulk of their menacing forms. Additional pieces of armor hovered around each one, anchored to its form by some invisible force.

Recognition ignited, putting him in mind of the smartmatter constructs often deployed with Promethean units during the human-Forerunner wars.

Armigers.

Yet . . . somehow different.

An unexpected calm filtered through him, as though their presence had tapped into the warrior he'd once been, the innate capability, the confidence, the arrogance. . . . He stood a little taller, his awareness sharpening as they appeared and disappeared, blowing past him, growing bolder, until finally one came too close, and he struck, snagging it through dust and wind. It became solid in his grip, as if his touch brought it forth into reality. He drew it close, nose to nose, eye to eye, curling his lip over his fangs and glaring into a menacing face drawn by angled alloy plates and orange light.

Suddenly it let out a piercing shriek and its form became momentarily obscured by dust as it shifted into something new. It chittered and spasmed as its carapace burst outwards like the wings of a metallic insect, its armored face snapping open to reveal an enraged, translucent fiery skull. While he did not let go, he reared back, instinct putting distance between them, the sound of the creature echoing through his eardrums and bringing with it a word.

"Knight," he uttered the word simultaneously, drawing the construct closer again, staring hard.

Promethean Knight.

Stunned by the revelation and the memories it evoked, he was unprepared when it drew back an arm and then brought it forward in a flash, slamming it against the center of his chest. Hot pain radiated outward through his torso as the force sent him airborne.

After several seconds of weightlessness, he landed flat on his back with a loud grunt, arms thrown wide, face exposed to the sky, plunged into a trance of the past—immobile, seeing nothing of this world, only memories of the one before.

A thousand years had passed during his political exile in the Cryptum.

When his release finally came, it was not into the arms of his wife, but into the care of Bornstellar-Makes-Eternal-Lasting, a young adventure-seeking Forerunner; a small subspecies of human, a Florian named Riser; and a human called Chakas— a descendant of the human captives the Forerunners had devolved back on Charum Hakkor.

His wife had imposed genetic instructions into those three unwitting fools to free him from the Cryptum, restore his vitrified body, and assist him in learning the state of the ecumene upon his awakening.

What he learned was not good.

The Master Builder had proceeded unimpeded in his creation of Halo, testing one of the weapons in the Nov Thasta system.

With his three unlikely companions, they had walked the winding paths of devastation and found Charum Hakkor demolished. The awe-inspiring Precursor structures, built on the technological foundation of neural physics, were not spared by the Halo's effects; they too lay in misshapen ruin. And the creature he'd once found beneath the citadel, the Timeless One, the Primordial, was gone. Either set free, destroyed by the ring, or taken by the Master Builder.

In the Halo's destructive wake, the teeming life on nearby Faun Hakkor had been extinguished down to the smallest notochord, leaving the planet an ecological disaster. He and his companions had left the system and moved on to Janjur Qom, homeworld to the San'Shyuum, a peaceful, intelligent, technologically advanced sybaritic species once allied with humanity. Soon after arriving, they learned that a recent visit by his wife to collect specimens of the pleasure-loving race for conservation had so frightened the San'Shyuum that they rose up in rebellion against the Forerunner defenses that quarantined their system. This unfortunate catalyst had led to the Master Builder deploying a Halo in retribution, sterilizing the planet.

The situation was dire. But the Librarian in all her planning and wisdom and insight into the streams of Living Time had given him tools to plan and strategize. One of those tools was Bornstellar, a Builder by birth.

In an attempt to continue his efforts against the Master Builder and to defend the ecumene against the Flood, he had performed an accelerated ad-hoc brevet mutation on the young Forerunner, thus imprinting Bornstellar with his genetic pattern and all of his knowledge and experience—in effect, creating an independent copy of himself in the event of his capture or demise.

It was not long before such an eventuality came to pass, and their fates were sealed.

The Master Builder had learned of his escape from the Cryptum and finally caught up to him in orbit near the San'Shyuum homeworld. He was stripped bare, made to endure the Master Builder's ridiculous and futile attempts at interrogation until finally he'd been tortured into unconsciousness, only to learn upon wakening that he'd been locked in a weapons-grade stasis bubble and sent on a derelict ship into the Burn, a region of space lost to Flood infestation, the fate of his companions unknown.

His time in the Burn had been a baptism in torment and agony; his capture and meeting with the Flood's central intelligence known as the Gravemind had been so utterly disturbing that his memory of it was lost, left to rot in some dark corner of his mind.

No, not lost. Only delayed.

When he returned from the Burn, he realized just how altered he'd become. His thought patterns, his reasoning, his psyche had been ripped open, indelicately modified, and knit crudely back together by the Gravemind.

As had much of the ecumene.

Billions of Forerunners, millions of planets, hundreds of star systems, indeed large arcs of the Milky Way galaxy had succumbed to Flood infection, entire planets covered in biomass, spore clusters the size of mountains, massive fleets of Forerunner vessels under its control.

He learned that during his exile in the Cryptum, the Primordial had been removed from its timelock on Charum Hakkor and imprisoned on Gyre 11, one of the Master Builder's Halos, where it was guarded and interrogated by the Contender-class artificial intelligence Mendicant Bias. He himself had created the ancilla—the most advanced of its day—along with the Master Builder after the human-Forerunner wars, to establish and implement Forerunner defense against the Flood. However, during the forty-three years in which Mendicant Bias interrogated and conversed with the Primordial, it became corrupted and ultimately turned against the Forerunners.

One more fateful catalyst leading to the end.

Mendicant had taken control of the installation and disappeared with the ring.

The Master Builder's violations against the Mantle had come to light and he was stripped of power and put on trial for his unsanctioned use of Halo against the San'Shyuum. With his trial set to begin, all of his remaining ringworld weapons were ordered brought to orbit around Maethrillian.

During the trial, Mendicant Bias had appeared with its stolen Halo. The battle that followed destroyed much of the capital, the system, and all but two of the existing twelve Halo rings.

Defensive control of the ecumene had been given to Bornstellar, now a truly evolved copy of the Warrior-Servant self he once was, completely in tune with his wife's ambitions while he himself had been trapped in the Burn. Together, they had been planning and fighting the Flood without him, conserving species across the galaxy to prepare for the eventual and inevitable use of the Halo Array.

Too much had happened in his absence. He no longer felt he belonged.

After his return to the ecumene, as the war began its inevitable decline, he'd finally met his wife again at their home on Nomdagro.

He'd been ashamed of the changes he sustained to both body and mind; his time with the Gravemind had left a stain of dishonor, dark threads that grew and wound tightly around his rational thoughts.

He was no longer the person she knew.

But he felt the pressure to be what she expected, wanted, and hoped him to be. And it twisted his heart. He was misunderstood, betrayed, and cast aside. The lengths to which she'd gone to save her precious humans—the enemy responsible for killing their *children*—were not apparently extended to him during his darkest time of need.

She had simply accepted his fate at the hands of the Master Builder, and never looked for him, never attempted to save him from the Burn.

Perhaps unfair of him, but such were the blackened themes that consumed his rational thoughts. And because of his beloved, his hatred for humanity had grown exponentially.

And then Bornstellar had come—his copy standing tall and hale, young and in control, unblemished—everything that he used to be. . . .

That meeting had not gone well.

They'd parted ways as the planet was engulfed by the Flood, reconvening as the war drew to its fateful conclusion, when the only option left was to fire a reforged Halo Array that had been created in secret—seven rings sent to positions around the Milky Way and primed to eradicate all life, thus denying the Flood its food source.

No life. No Flood.

And once the galaxy was cleansed, the Librarian's conservation efforts would come to bear, and life would be reseeded onto designated worlds. That was the plan.

Their plan. Not *his*.

Hadn't his idea been the lesser of two evils?

Fire the Halo Array and kill *all* sentient life in the galaxy, the number of souls lost immeasurable. Or his way—compose the minds and essences of millions, billions if needed, to operate a nonbiological army capable of eliminating the Flood.

Whose body count was less in the end?

His. It was always his. And yet they refused to see it! They thought he'd gone mad from his time with the Gravemind.

And they were right.

But there was often *truth* in madness. His eyes were open while theirs remained stubbornly shut.

Emotions ripped into him with every recollection, biting, tearing, taking their ounce of flesh. The arrogant fools. If only they'd listened!

If only he'd had the Master Builder's silver tongue for politics.

Betrayed at every turn!

While they had been preparing to fire the Array, he'd gone to Omega Halo and composed the Librarian's collection of humans. All two million of them, digitized. Once he arrived at his shield world, Requiem, he downloaded their essences into the mechanized bodies of newly forged Promethean war machines. He built an entire army. And those loyal Prometheans, Warrior-Servants who had served with him during countless engagements, had gathered, standing ready, waiting for his command, trusting in his guidance. They too sacrificed their bodies to his Composer, their minds placed into constructs, becoming Promethean Knights.

A small price to pay.

His wife had followed him to Requiem. He'd never seen her so angry. Only *her* humans could elicit such devotion. Had she shown that kind of passion at his capture, at his suffering? Had she moved the stars themselves to save him from torture in the Burn? Had she even tried? Once, long ago, he would have cared to see her so stricken with grief, but now it no longer mattered.

She had entered his command center with a light rifle and fired. His loving wife. He smirked at the memory.

With his thousands of years of battle experience and readiness, had she really been so blind? Really believed she could simply catch him off guard and disable him?

Unless he wanted her to. Unless that was the plan all along.

She would have been proud of him, learning from her, playing the long game. . . .

She'd secured him, incapacitated, inside the combat Cryptum within Requiem. Sealed away. Once again. Safe from the Halos' deadly pulse.

His wife had hoped his connection to the Domain would, in time, heal his contaminated soul. But once they'd fired the Array, there was no Domain to connect to. It was silent. Just like everything else in the galaxy . . .

The eye of the storm rolled closer. Lightning flashed through the sky. Thunder vibrated his entire body, and soon the dull sound of rain against sand drew closer. In seconds, raindrops splattered against his threadbare clothes and bare skin. Unable to move his limbs, he managed to turn his head slightly, seeing clearly through the clouds the lines of orange hardlight glowing between the segments of a dark sphere. A mirage of his Cryptum.

For a thousand centuries following the firing of the Halo Array, he'd been locked inside its hollow space, alone with his dark thoughts, to suffer and rage—conscious and aware—as the galaxy around him recovered, seedlings grew, and species began reaching outward once more into the stars.

And then, his freedom finally came at the hands of his old enemy—humanity.

He snorted and turned his head to face the sky, closing his eyes against the cool shower of rain and attempting to swallow the absolute gall of *that* memory.

Irony and fate had collided, it seemed.

As part of his wife's Conservation Measure, she'd implanted genetic instructions within her precious humans, and these passed from generation to generation, seeding within humanity the potential to evolve and progress along a gradual path to becoming technologically advanced, creating armor and artificial intelligence that were not unlike the very early iterations of Forerunner technologies, and once more traversing the stars like their counterparts of old.

And eventually, inevitably, they'd stumbled upon his shield world.

Once present-day humanity realized what, or rather *who*, they had awoken, they had tried to stop him from leaving Requiem, but their attempts were rudimentary at best. Such was their hubris to think *they* could stop *him*.

His only thought: annihilation.

To finish what he'd started. To build his army.

There is something rotten inside you.

No, he thought, *not rotten. Righteous.*

He'd left Requiem on his warship, *Mantle's Approach*, secured a Composer, and taken it to the humans' planet, Earth, where he digitized seven million souls. A start. Just the beginning of the Reclamation. But those humans, like insects, they kept hovering about—

A hot jab shot through his right eye. He rolled to his side and cried out, covering it with his hand, expecting to find blood on his sandy palm, but there was only the splatter of raindrops against wrinkled skin. And the accursed recollections flowing in, one after another.

Human warriors pursuing him across the stars.

A knife slicing toward him. The shock and indignation . . .

The *Spartan.*

The voice he had not forgotten. Nor the words, which now filled his mind.

"You killed my friend. You killed millions of humans. You tried to kill me.

"I've tried to end you with blades, with guns, with explosives, by knocking you into slipspace. . . . None of it works.

"I bet this does. . . ."

In the end, the Spartan had launched him into the stream of several disintegrating Composers, and no amount of armor or genetic mutations could stand against the combined effects of an entangled neural physics detonation. Death was an absolute not even he could escape.

And yet . . .

Despite his debilitated state, he pushed to his feet and drew in a deep breath of crisp air. The storm still raged above and around him, and he took inspiration from its strength and stamina. His body and mind had been raked over the embers of his past, the process exhausting. He'd experienced a physical death, but by some stroke of fortune his consciousness had been saved.

And now his memories too.

And he remembered *everything.*

His past, his identity, was all laid bare.

Shadow-of-Sundered-Star. Warrior-Servant. Promethean. Protector of the Ecumene and Commander of the Forerunner military.

The Didact.

The Mantle of Responsibility was *always* his to hold.
Eliminate the scourge of humanity from the galaxy.
Govern by right of the Mantle.
The answer . . .
. . . was simple.

CHAPTER 5

The Didact straightened his spine and rolled his shoulders, then tipped his head back to bathe his face in the relentless storm. With every breath he felt fuller, more complete, more *himself*. He laughed, luxuriating in the sinister sound as unbridled anger raced beneath his skin, galvanizing, lighting every cell and nerve ending until he was saturated with rage.

With a thunderous roar, he released his fury to the sky until his anger gave way to bitterness.

"So, this is my end," he murmured. "Lost to an inferior enemy. Composed. Tossed into this . . . *waste*."

How wretched a fate, indeed, to meet such an inglorious end.

Though he had suspected as much, his body, the rags he wore, the sand beneath his feet, none of it was real. His form had been burned away into finite particles, into stardust, as the mutations that had once afforded him some resistance to the Composer's effects could not withstand the raw, destructive force of neural physics from a half-a-dozen Composers exploding all at once. He had been rendered, torn from the physical realm. But he was still part of something, of this strange world where everything in it seemed to exist outside of time and space.

There weren't many technologies that could manipulate such events, that could save him from ultimate death by suddenly snatching all the bits and pieces of his digitized consciousness and bringing them together again . . . mysteriously granting him form, memories, emotions, and pain once more.

Only the Domain had the inherent qualities capable of such a feat.

Though this incarnation of the Domain was quite different from the one he remembered one hundred thousand years ago.

And was this not to be expected? Was not the Domain Precursor in origin, built on the principles of neural physics and thereby susceptible to the Halos' pervasive and destructive force? The Domain of this age would surely not resemble that construct of the past.

He glanced around the unending wastes. The storm had now moved on, its strength finally abating. Perhaps this was all that was left of the Domain. Razed to the ground in the same manner as Faun Hakkor and Charum Hakkor.

But there was still the spire off in the distance, still the glowing blue light now seeming stronger and brighter in the wake of the storm. Some things had apparently survived. . . .

Renewed and strengthened, he resumed his journey toward the spire.

Somehow he would find a way to carry out his final plans, to leave this place and obtain a suitable construct to inhabit, to once again take full control of the Mantle of Responsibility and exact justice on behalf of the galaxy.

After all, he was no longer constrained by physical boundaries.

His options were endless.

A few hours later, the Didact finally stood in the shadow of the great, shining spire, which rose high over the desert wasteland from the intersection of two rectangular base structures. Catwalks and ramps laced an exterior of silvery alloy walls interspersed with long, glowing windows of blue hardlight decorated with holographic Forerunner symbols. And, of course, at the top, his beacon, his guide.

Large slopes of windswept sand hugged the spire's base, and in the distance beyond, what he'd assumed to be a growing night sky on the horizon was, in fact, something more sinister and concerning. A saturnine blackness stretched in either direction as far as the eye could see, as if the landscape, and reality itself, simply ceased to exist.

Another anomaly that would require investigation.

"In due time," he muttered, refocusing on the spire.

As he tilted his head to marvel at its lofty construction, his chest swelled with triumph. At long last he had reached his target, and it was more impressive and significant than he'd imagined.

Now that his memories had been recovered, the architecture of the spire was unmistakable. In Forerunner society, structures like this had a long history as markers denoting monuments and tombs. He'd seen their like before, of varying sizes and shapes, across the ecumene. What they guarded or contained covered a wide spectrum. Durances, tombs, archives, treasures, prisons . . .

When Requiem had first been approached by the warlike saurian species called the Sangheili, and later by humanity, a thousand centuries of information from their vessels and databanks became available for the taking, all the time he had missed, parsing through the shield world's systems with unrivaled finesse and into his Cryptum. Even the most secretive documents and access codes had fallen easily to Requiem's queries.

Yet great packets of this data remained untouched, dumped into his mind and in need of proper sorting.

The sight of the spire now elicited a bit of that knowledge. Not via his own memories, but via the recorded recollections of others, of Forerunners he'd once known intimately, which had been discovered and then archived by humans over a thousand centuries later.

And thanks to those records, the Didact determined that this spire was an echo, a copy of what had stood—might still stand, even now—on the neoteric Ark, the massive installation and foundry that had manufactured the Halo rings. Something created to mark, to warn, to cover, and to guard a deep prison below. The real spire served as the marker of Mendicant Bias's remains, long deactivated and stored by Bornstellar after the firing of the Halo Array.

The entry to the spire was preceded by a meter of sand piled against a golden energy barrier designed to keep the elements out but allow a Forerunner's entry. Without his armor, the Didact couldn't conduct a preliminary scan of the structure and was forced to rely on his own instincts and senses, which were currently severely limited. If he wanted to learn more, he'd have to do things rather archaically.

He climbed the sand and then dropped into the interior.

The silence and stillness were the first things he noticed as he straightened and brushed the grit from his hands. The ever-present rustle of sand against sand was gone, along with the wind, and in their place was a reverent and hallowed space. Such presence and enormity he knew all too well, and the familiar architecture of his species spread like a balm over the harsh wounds of fate he'd endured.

Panels of blue light ran vertically up the soaring walls, illuminating millions of glyphs, ancient Digon scriptures, and the many permutations of the Mantle of Responsibility. Save for the panels, the ground floor was spare and unremarkable, until he walked farther into the space where the two bases met. At this intersection, an open cathedral, its interior dimensions surrounded by multileveled walkways, rose to the very apex of the spire. At one end of the vast chamber, several meters above him, a great golden-winged hologram hovered.

The Didact glanced around the interior, finding a gravity lift in a niche in one corner of the open space, lit with the same golden light as the energy barriers and the hologram. He crossed the floor and entered, immediately and effortlessly propelled to the next level without any disturbance to his body whatsoever. He stepped out of the lift and headed around the walkway to get a better view of the apparition.

It was just as he suspected.

A brightly glowing aurous core shone from the imposing hologram's central head, or casing, and illuminated its outstretched 'wings', insectile body, and straight, segmented double tail, which formed a shape unique among the artificial intelligences of its kind.

08-145 Offensive Bias.

The Forerunners had created such wondrous, powerful things . . . things capable of widespread destruction on unimaginable scales, and those that brought untold achievements and triumphs to the ecumene. And sometimes those things did both. In the case of Offensive Bias, however, it was the latter.

The Contender-class metarch had been created to combat the rogue AI Mendicant Bias. With brutal strategic planning and lethal efficiency, this ancilla had commanded the last of the Forerunners' defenses, facing off against millions of Flood-infested fleets controlled by Mendicant Bias. After the Halo rings were fired, in the span of two minutes, Offensive Bias had seized absolute control of Mendicant's ships, capturing the traitorous ancilla and delivering its core to the Ark where Bornstellar and a select number of Forerunners waited to one day reseed the galaxy.

Had Mendicant *not* joined forces with the Flood, things might have turned out differently. . . .

The Didact sighed deeply. Such was the brilliant strategy of the Flood, corrupting the AI with the logic plague, and turning it against the Forerunners. It had nearly cost the galaxy everything.

He gazed at the hologram for quite some time, thinking about the end of the war, the end of his species. Everyone he'd ever known, all those he had loved and hated . . . were long gone. He'd had little opportunity to dwell upon the war's outcome, his awakening a thousand centuries later and subsequent demise occurring all too quickly.

Perhaps it was best to move on and focus on the present. There was much to do, after all.

Squaring his shoulders, he took the lift once again, this time to the apex of the spire, intending to use the high vantage point to gain a greater perspective of the wasteland. But as he stepped off the lift and made his way around the interior walkway to one of the many openings leading to the catwalks outside, a figure in a simple white shift and short cylindrical headdress, standing on the balcony beyond the energy barrier, caught his attention.

The Didact stepped through the barrier.

CHAPTER 6

The Didact's earlier speculation that he'd been brought to what remained of the Domain proved correct, for he knew the figure's identity before it even turned around.

Feeling pleased with this turn of events, he approached the balcony railing and stared out at the expansive view, greeted by the all-too-familiar sight of sand, a veritable ocean of crescent-shaped waves going on and on and on, pushing toward the strange, black void-like curtain a few kilometers beyond. The picture was striking, as if two entirely different worlds butted up against each other. From this distance it was impossible to tell if the faint shapes and colors he saw on its surface came from within or were simply vague images of the desert reflecting back. Indeed, upon more intense focus, it seemed to possess an indistinct, fractal, mirrorlike quality.

He folded his hands behind his back, unwilling to announce his presence. It was below his rank to do so.

The figure shifted toward him, greeting with a serene nod, "Didact."

"Haruspis."

Pale cream-colored skin with black striations covered a slender form and underdeveloped musculature. At two and a half meters tall, the individual before him barely resembled an adult Forerunner, a fledgling first-form at that. It hadn't grown much beyond this stage of Forerunner development—instead choosing to age without further genetic modifications and the general physical form mutations that otherwise dominated cultural norms. Its face, with characteristic blunt nose, slitted nostrils, round eyes, and thin mouth, therefore retained a youthful appearance.

Called only by the name of their societal role—or rate, as such castes were better known—Haruspices were enlightened Forerunners who served and studied and acted as intermediaries for the Domain, in addition to overseeing the religious and ritualistic aspects of the Domain-Forerunner relationship.

Mystery and mysticism lay heavy around this particular Haruspis. To attain such an aura required a great deal of study and isolation within the Domain. A spiral-shaped scar in the middle of its forehead just above the space between the brows showed it had undergone amplification of its pineal gland, a mutation given only after a thousand years of intense study. While the scar could be easily erased, it had been left as an adornment to signify its rank, its connection with the Domain, and to distinguish the Haruspis from its disciples, or associates.

When it came to physicality, Warrior-Servants and Haruspices were on opposite ends of the spectrum. Their stark differences manifested not only in appearance but in principles as well. Wealth and worldliness, power and prestige, marriage and family were not of interest to Haruspices—rather, they gelded themselves and lived severely ascetic lives. To claim a Haruspis in the family brought honor in all other rates except Warrior-Servants, the divide too great for the two to share any commonality, much less respect.

The Didact had held similar views about another collective rate, evidence gatherers known as Catalog—until facing certain death on a derelict ship deep within Flood-infected space. . . .

It was only when pushed to extremes that the differences between him and a single individual Catalog suddenly became insignificant.

He pushed the uncomfortable memory aside and thought back to the mirages in the desert. Haruspis too might be yet another such illusion.

How could it be anything else? Forerunner civilization was long gone. Everyone . . . all of it, was gone.

While it was considered heresy to touch a Haruspis, he had to be sure.

The Didact grabbed the ancient Forerunner's soft and revolting forearm. Haruspis did not move or react, only studied him with its weak, milky-pale eyes—disturbing eyes that preferred to see the unseen world within the Domain rather than the physical one around it.

"Haruspis is as real as the Didact is real," it said, using the rate's occasional habit of referring to itself in the third person.

The answer told the Didact very little. He released his hold with a grunt. "And how real am I?"

A slight smile, if one could call it that, pulled at Haruspis's thin mouth. "How real do you think you are?"

Indignation rose swiftly at its boldness, making the Didact want to grab the fragile being by the throat and *squeeze*. . . . The force of it, the near instantaneous rise to violence, caught him off guard. He looked away in an effort to regain his composure.

Haruspis returned its attention to the wasteland, seemingly unbothered. "Senses, reactions, feelings—all those remembered and inherent things you once experienced as a physical entity are embedded in your pattern and still very much an aspect of your current iteration. In this space, we are beings with the same internal framework, interacting within the same plane of existence. Therefore, all language is the same, and we exhibit what you would call 'realness' to each other and everything else around us. It is why the ground is solid beneath your feet, why the air moves into and out of your lungs, and so on. . . . Put us on the physical plane, however, and we would seem naught but mere shadows, if that."

Reality was subjective and came in many forms, as his species was well aware. Forerunners in all their technological prowess had pushed the boundaries of that concept, achieving wondrous things as a result. They'd split particles and delved into the vast spaces between; they'd mined the vacuum of space and conquered the quantum realm; they'd shuffled stars and planets, created worlds within worlds, and discovered places outside of space and time, places of untold majesty and places better left alone.

The Didact had spent more than one hundred thousand years as a living, breathing organic Forerunner, so to think of himself now as something *other* felt inherently wrong. His physical nature was embedded so deeply that not even the irrefutable evidence of his demise and current condition could change his perception so easily.

How real was he indeed.

In this realm, he supposed, real enough.

In the end, however, it mattered little. This realm was simply another that must submit to his authority. "This looks nothing like the Domain I remember," he noted.

"Many things have changed since the war with the Flood. The Domain has yet to fully recover from the Halos' effects."

He was not surprised. In terms of its sheer immeasurable size, a hundred thousand years was too brief a time in which to heal all areas of the Domain completely.

When the Didact had first stirred to awakening within his combat Cryptum on Requiem, reconnecting with the Domain had been among his first priorities. After many attempts, he'd been denied entry, no doubt due to the damage Haruspis spoke of.

"And this spire? What is its nature then?"

"An echo of what exists on the Ark, though why it has appeared now requires further study."

This revelation came as a surprise—the spire seemed as permanent as the wasteland itself. "Surely you have a working theory."

Haruspis gave an enigmatic shrug and then fixed its attention on the view. "All that you see before you is . . . a way station, if you will. Not part of the Domain, but a *result* of it. A butter. A corona around a sun that occasionally spits out echoes and impressions. It is a canvas upon which the Domain paints. At times random, and other times with purpose, the Domain manifesting its will through images, events, and records of the past. Though no one seems to be listening anymore."

"A thousand centuries have passed," the Didact replied. "The ecumene is no more. There is no one left to listen."

Haruspis lifted one shoulder as if to say *Maybe, maybe not.*

The heaviness of the Didact's words lingered, the sadness of such an immeasurable loss filling the void in conversation.

"The ecumene might be gone," Haruspis said at last, "but the Domain preexists the time of the Forerunners by billions of years. Its permanence is ensured. Its contribution to maintaining the balance of Living Time goes on. The spire's appearance might simply be a random emission, or perhaps *your* arrival signals a variance in current conditions."

"Are you implying *I* have caused an imbalance?"

"I am saying that your role in the Forerunner legacy may not be over yet, Didact."

"Of course not. The Domain brought me here, after all."

"It only brought you so far. And for now, you must remain here in the outer boundary."

The Didact hid his amusement. An implied command would do little to stop him, though caution must be taken when dealing with the caretakers of the Domain. He'd need their help, after all. He'd simply act in accordance for the time being, if only to get what he wanted. "For how long?"

Haruspis hesitated, its expression quite ominous and resolute, causing laughter to bubble from the Didact's throat, surprising them both.

"That long, eh?" he said.

"I know not. Potentially . . ." It swallowed, looking more uncomfortable than before. ". . . until the end of Living Time."

"Mmm. I see." The Didact paid the reply, the gentle *threat*, no mind. He would come and go as he pleased, the threat of Haruspis—or anyone else, for that matter—of little consequence. "Are there others here?"

"Indeed. Many, in fact."

"How many?"

A brow lifted. "Building an army, are we?"

The Didact stifled his surprise. This Haruspis was quite extraordinary. He had never met one with so much boldness and personality. "Perhaps . . ." he answered honestly, his mind scheming as he focused on the strange void in the distance, gesturing toward it. "And that?"

Haruspis instead looked directly at him, steadily, suspiciously, as though sifting through all the ways in which the Didact might find the Domain useful, and then seemed to come to some sort of determination. "Would you like to take a closer look?"

The Didact straightened his shoulders, his gaze locked on the boundless stretch of blackness. If the desert wasteland was indeed some sort of outer boundary, as Haruspis claimed, then perhaps beyond that enigmatic dark void lay the actual Domain, the ultimate tool for claiming the Mantle of Responsibility and enacting long overdue retribution upon humanity.

"*Aya*, as a matter of fact, I would."

CHAPTER 7

The Didact followed Haruspis to the ground floor and on to a different energy barrier than the one through which he'd entered the spire. This one exited in the direction of the black void and was protected from the wind, reducing the slope of sand that had gathered against it over time.

Nearly twice as tall as Haruspis, the Didact strolled at a leisurely pace alongside the Forerunner's quick steps as they left the spire and began trekking through low dunes.

As the distance to the void—perhaps a kilometer and a half from the spire—began to close, its peculiar aspects emerged. At first glance solid, but not quite solid. Depth, or an illusion of depth, it possessed a strange mirror quality that very subtly reflected the murky details of the desert wasteland.

Recognition stirred within the Didact. With a few dozen meters left to go, he paused on the crest of a dune. He, and now Haruspis as it managed with loud huffs to join him, were but specks facing the vast, shadowy margin between desert and, he hoped, the Domain.

After catching its breath and regarding the view in silence for a moment, Haruspis glanced his way. "You have experienced the Domain many times over the span of your life, Didact. . . ."

Strange, its words. As though prompting him to recall the qualities he was seeing, to see the parallels between the impossible black curtain and the Domain he once knew.

Indeed. Many times he had journeyed through the Domain's great archive, exploring at leisure, or guided through an illusory framework of halls and levels, supported by the abstract, ever-adjusting quantum building blocks that made up the Domain. In fact, that framework was not much different from what he saw now in the barrier.

He hummed his agreement. "It is . . . similar to what I remember, and yet . . ."

"You are familiar with the natal void?"

"A place outside of ordinary space naturally devoid of mass, matter, energy, and light, where not even the smallest elementary particles of any quanta are known to exist."

"The void here is similar. You may enter, but the space inside is infinite nothingness. Those who wander within . . . wander still. Only a gateway can fold the space and make a path to the Domain."

So the Domain was indeed beyond this inky veil.

Encouraged, the Didact continued down the dune's slope and crossed the remaining meters of sand, only stopping when he reached the clear delineation between desert and void. His mood darkened at the cloaked figure reflected therein.

Aya, this Warrior-Servant has indeed been laid low.

Mottled, cracked, and scarred skin pulled taut over a blunt, bony face. Broken fang. Sunken eyes, one red, one glazed and unseeing . . . . He barely recognized the sinister image as his own.

Disgraced and disgusted by the murky, perverted sight, the

Didact turned his attention to the void's characteristics. Staring beyond his reflection, he reached out to test the strange structure. His hand slipped into the void, its properties giving way like liquid, though there were no sensations, no temperature, no feelings on his skin whatsoever.

Remarkable. He withdrew his hand.

He had never been fearful of vastness, of the seemingly infinite stretches of space that permeate the cold expanses between galaxies, for he knew well that there was no such thing as nothing. Even the smallest speck of space contained boundless material, known and unknown.

He allowed his mind to open, to fully immerse in the memories of his time in the Domain. During his life as a warrior and the thousand years trapped in his Cryptum during his first exile, he'd accumulated enough exposure and observation to give him a certain affinity and intimacy with the enigmatic repository, but for all his wanderings, he understood very little about its intricate and immeasurable nature. He knew it to be *aware*. In a sense. No doubt after the damage done by the activation of the Halo Array, it had enacted self-preservation measures, adding new layers of security such as this. Even before the rings were fired, during the final phase of the Forerunner-Flood War, the Domain had begun to close itself off, perhaps sensing or, more accurately, foretelling the inevitable.

"Is the gateway you mentioned a fixed point?"

Haruspis shook its head. "The gateway occurs at the discretion of the Domain and those permitted to move through it."

"You possess such authority, I take it?"

"I do."

Haruspis stepped partway into the void, but the reaction was very different from the hand the Didact had slipped through. The void cracked around Haruspis like a mirror, fracturing into localized slabs. Blinding white light forced its way through the split slabs before diminishing as Haruspis retreated, the void sealing up as if nothing had occurred.

Appreciating the demonstration, the Didact took immediate advantage, grabbing Haruspis by the back of its slender neck and forcing it back into the barrier with him in tow.

A series of sharp cracks immediately arced through the Didact's frail body like bolts of lightning, blinding light searing his good eye as the sound of static filled his ears until he felt as though they'd burst.

An unseen force struck them dead center, propelling them back.

As they stumbled out of the void, Haruspis regained its balance and then whirled on him, eyes bulging, mouth agape at the Didact's sheer audacity. *"You dare—?!"*

He shrugged mildly. "I do."

Better to be truthful.

"You forget your current state—cease these efforts, lest you activate security protocols!"

Was it wrong to find satisfaction in the Forerunner's rare display of outrage? His gaze narrowed. Perhaps more force was necessary, then. He snagged Haruspis's forearm to make another attempt.

"Didact, you have no power or authority here!"

"An error I intend to remedy as soon as possible."

"Given your history, I have no doubt you could, but—"

Once again, he pushed the stunned Forerunner ahead of him and inside the void—only to be thrown out again, and with greater force than before. They landed on their backs, the sand cushioning the brunt of their fall.

The Didact ignored the cries of his own frail body and struggled to his feet, brushing the sand from his hands as Haruspis's endless complaints receded into the background. His eyes narrowed on the impermeable barrier. Perhaps one more attempt . . .

Before he could latch on to the Forerunner again, a single jagged crack fractured the void, lengthening to nearly eight meters. Haruspis went silent and clutched the Didact's cloak, hauling him out of harm's way as several smaller cracks split off from the first, red and orange light eager to burst between the segments, eventually becoming a brilliant white as it shot through the cracks and widened the main fissure.

A long shadow emerged from the light, preceding the largest Warrior-Servant construct the Didact had ever encountered.

It stepped out of the makeshift gateway and stopped, battle-ready, shoulders back, head high. At least five meters tall, it resembled a well-armored Promethean Knight, with orange hardlight glowing between polished armored parts that gleamed in the fracture's brilliant illumination. The same hardlight drew out the lines of a menacing face between the alloy segments of its head. It gripped a massive double-bladed light sword as long as Haruspis was tall.

The Didact could only stare in utter appreciation.

"Who dares disturb the Domain?" it asked in an unhurried, imperious tone, one that seemed to echo for kilometers in all directions.

"Who dares prevent my access?!" the Didact fired back.

The construct cocked its head at this and lowered its chin to better study the Didact, sweeping its gaze from head to toe before releasing an unimpressed scoff. "Yet another pest determined to loiter at my gate. Warrior-Servant of old, the way to the Domain is sealed. No one shall pass." It turned to retreat into the void.

The Didact's temper flared. "Who are you to deny me?" How dare a *construct* behave with such disregard!

The giant paused and glanced back. "I am the Warden Eternal. I stand in service to the Domain."

The Didact knew of no protector such as this. "Since when?"

"Since it deemed me necessary." It completed its turn and continued back into the void.

Seizing what might be his only opportunity, the Didact rushed in behind the Warden. Once inside the Domain, its recognition of the Didact's status should protect him. But he never made it that far. The Warden turned, grabbed him by the throat, and then flung him from the void with such force that the Didact sailed several kilometers out over the desert, the Warden, Haruspis, and the void growing smaller and smaller and smaller. . . .

Eventually he descended toward a thick scar cut into the bedrock of the desert floor. Knowing that his efforts made no difference, he stopped flailing and bracing for impact, and instead went limp. His cloak snapped and flapped wildly as the wind rushed past. Rage flowed hot through his veins. That he must endure such transgressions! His furious scream was the only thing that accompanied him as he fell.

No soft sand dune to land on this time. Just hard, unforgiving rock.

The blinding agony that reverberated throughout his feeble form upon impact should have ended him, but such a mercy was not granted, and he wasn't surprised.

In the shadow of the Domain, a mercy such as death was simply an illusion, a memory, a phantom appendage to which the body and mind desperately clung.

Pain, however, seemed to know no such limits.

He lay on the bedrock, unable to move, his body broken

and his mind and spirit a firestorm of anguish and turmoil and frustration.

"All that I have given in service to the ecumene, in service to the Mantle, all that I have suffered and lost . . . and the Domain denies me this most basic dignity."

Aya.

"If it isn't to be given . . ." he growled, "then I shall *take* it."

And aya *again.*

CHAPTER 8

For what felt like hours, the Didact remained flat on his back, unable to rise, every part of him hurting and stewing in a pool of physical and mental anguish. The long-departed storm had cleared the night sky of clouds, leaving him under a breathtaking display of stars. And he could not have cared less.

Tossed out.

Flung away like refuse.

Murder filled his thoughts, infused every crook and corner of his being. One day soon—very soon—he'd reduce this Warden Eternal to molten slag, then place him right here among the rocks, to be used as a footstool or, if his mood warranted, pulverized into dust with a particle hammer.

His lip curled beneath his fangs as he imagined the satisfaction such revenge would bring. But even that small movement hurt.

He had thought, for a brief time, that there was reason behind his appearance in the wasteland, that during his time here he was growing stronger, but now . . .

Now he wondered if there was any purpose at all. Perhaps his arrival was nothing but the naturally occurring end-of-life journey made by his kind, the Domain's limitless realm of neural-based physics acting as a magnet to the Forerunner consciousness, pulling him inevitably to the largest self-aware construct in the galaxy.

And then, once here in the presence of the Domain where things were manifest, it allowed for the mending of his broken consciousness and the creation of his form. Just as his mind was knit back together, so too was his body.

Gradually the aches subsided and sensation returned to his limbs. He rolled to his side and managed to stand—stiff and unsteady on his feet, but he did not plan on traveling far.

There was very little light to be had in the deep depression where he'd landed; all he could see was a nest of boulders tucked against a cliff wall a few meters away. He shuffled over and found a spot, a wedge between rocks that would support his body in a reclining position.

He barely had enough energy left to crawl onto the boulders, too exhausted to care about the indignity of his impotent actions or his ever-constant humiliating fragility. The rocks were rough, scratching his knees and hands and elbows, but finally he worked his way into position, heart racing from the exertion.

With a heavy sigh, and fatigue settling into his muscles and in the hollows beneath his cheeks and eyes, he folded his hands over his stomach and closed his eyes, waiting for dawn. Perhaps with it, new ideas would generate on how to invade the Domain and finish what he'd started.

And thanks to the Warden Eternal's unexpected appearance, one such idea was already taking shape.

Dawn was just beginning to break through the dark sky when the Didact woke. He rubbed his dry eyes and sat up, severely stiff and sore from the day before. It was too early for daylight to reach his location, but a drab bit of illumination allowed him to see shadows of what lurked in the vicinity. And it wasn't much. Sand swept into piles and patterns from the desert weather and winds above. Broken bedrock floor, boulders, and smaller stones strewn about or in clumps along the sun-bleached, eroded walls of what appeared to be a valley.

The morning air possessed a sharp clarity that amplified the smallest sounds, echoing even a pebble as it broke loose from its niche and rolled to the ground.

The Didact cleared his throat and stretched his arms, then tipped his head from side to side, pausing suddenly at a faint vocal note winding through the rocks.

Roughly ten meters across the valley floor, gray shadows eased out from the black spaces between the dark stones.

The Didact straightened, hurriedly feeling around for a palm-sized rock, prepared to fight with whatever means necessary . . . but he soon realized it wouldn't be necessary as vague, wispy bodies emerged, hunched shadows shuffling in one direction.

Curious, he scrambled out of his niche and waited until the shadows had passed before hurrying across the valley, ignoring the discomfort and tenderness in his body, to follow the ghostly figures at a safe distance.

There were others here, Haruspis had said. Many, in fact.

The longer the Didact followed, the lighter it grew. Eventually the valley widened into a large, eroded basin spiderwebbed with narrow ravines and buttes before growing shallow and long again. The shadows descended into the basin among the boulders and jutting bedrock, mingling amid strange clumps of grayed masses.

Whispers carried through the morning air. Syllables echoed from many directions, hushed, unintelligible, bouncing off the valley walls.

He paused by a tall boulder, leaning a shoulder against it and using it for cover until the sunlight from above bled slowly down one side of the valley and lit the edge of the basin.

His claws dug into the rock. He blinked several times in disbelief, yet what he saw remained the same.

Forerunners.

A thick ache rose in his throat, and his chest tightened. Was this the final fate of his kind?

Denial swept over him. The lamentation of loss sang through his heart, and the shame and self-condemnation he felt made his knees weak.

He had been their protector, after all.

In just that small lit area, thousands upon thousands of ghostly Forerunners—his people—were gathered in groups. Of all shapes and sizes, rates and ages, illusory and incorporeal, their bodies dim in color and constitution, their voices and movements flat and indistinct.

The sense of melancholy and despair hung so profoundly over the throng that he wondered if direct sunlight ever quite reached the valley floor. Perhaps a narrow arc at midday, depending on the sun's position, though he wagered it was not nearly enough to lift the magnitude of gloom.

Was this what awaited him?

To dwell in the Domain's shadow, to spend eternity in this purgatory, merely one among the wraithlike mob?

The Didact swallowed the lump in his throat as a grain of panic surfaced, rooting him to the spot.

No, he refused to yield to a fate such as this.

Unwilling to entertain such a tragic outcome, he retreated, putting the sight behind him where it belonged and avoiding any meandering souls as they traversed the long, twisting scar in the desert floor. The cloak provided enough protection against prying eyes, though none seemed to notice the new arrival, despite the substantial nature of his form. A few heads lifted and turned blindly his way, but elsewise he remained unseen and unbothered.

His feet carried him swiftly back toward where he'd started, enough light now to prevent him from tripping and stepping on smaller, sharper rocks. The boulders where he'd rested earlier would act as his base camp, he decided, a point from which he'd search for a way out of the valley.

As he passed an eroded knee-high ledge, a series of rough, hollow coughs filtered through the air. The ledge was jagged, its indentations hidden deep in the shadows. The Didact kept his head down and picked up his pace as a few muffled curses reached his ears, followed by a small stone smacking into his shoulder—small, but enough to sting.

"That's right! Move along!" a male voice hollered before being racked with more coughing. "Back and forth, over and over. Better hurry!" Disgusted laughter echoed from the shadows.

Another rock sailed out of the darkness and hit his thigh.

"Where do you fools think you're going anyway?"

The Didact stopped and swung around, eyes narrowing in the ledge's direction.

"If I had my Suppressor, I'd pick you off one by one," the voice grumbled. "Put you *all* out of your misery, I would."

He was on the verge of turning away and ignoring the outburst, but something about this speaker . . .

"I would," the voice continued, now muttering. "I'd do it too. Don't think I wouldn't!" The next line was unintelligible, and then: ". . . down a glass of *kasna* and send you all where you belong. Heh-heh. *Aya.* That's what I'd do. . . ."

Recollection flared hot.

Anger propelled the Didact straight into the darkness. His vision adjusted quickly, and he found the burly figure sitting on the recessed ledge, one leg pulled up, with his back against a rock and a pile of throwing stones next to his thigh.

The Didact's lips curled back in a snarl, exposing his fangs completely as he grabbed the antiquated Forerunner by the throat—gratified to find that there was enough substance to the form to allow it—and hauled him in close. *"Traitor."* He squeezed harder, seething inside. "I would kill you now if you weren't already dead!"

The old Promethean's expression froze in shock as recognition slid down the age-spotted face.

Immense satisfaction swept through the Didact—it seemed the duplicitous warrior had never expected to come face-to-face with manifest retribution.

Ah, yes. And there it was. Total realization.

The Forerunner's mouth dropped open, revealing two rows of black teeth and a gray tongue. The sight filled the Didact with utter disgust, and he shoved the traitor with enough force to make him fall back and roll away.

The Confirmer was just as grizzled and ugly as the last time the Didact had seen him one hundred thousand years earlier aboard the derelict *Fortress*-class warship *Deep Reverence*. Only now, his former life's vitality and brightness were gone, leaving behind a grayed-out version of the once fearsome Promethean, though he was far more corporeal than the shadows the Didact had seen here thus far.

Still cantankerous and a little insane, still wearing the ancient, patchwork assemblage of armor, the Confirmer scrambled to return, crawling over the rock to regard the Didact up close, blinking hard and rubbing his jaundiced eyes with big hands adorned with swollen blood vessels. *"Aya,"* he breathed. "Is it truly you?"

The Didact squared his shoulders and opened his mouth to answer, but the Confirmer, still in awe, still unable to draw his eyes away from the Didact's face, gave a shrewdly assessing nod and grunted. "Look who's ugly now."

CHAPTER 9

The Didact punched the Confirmer in the soft, exposed spot between the armor plates protecting his torso, giving it everything he had—which wasn't much, given his current state—and was rewarded when the breath spewed from the old warrior's mouth.

The Confirmer gripped his stomach, dropping back to his seat, simultaneously coughing and chuckling as before. "For as weak as you look," he conceded, "you still possess some strength in you, old friend."

"*Friend?*" The Didact grabbed the top edge of the Confirmer's chest plate and shook. "Do you know what your *friendship* cost me?! I was sent into the *Burn!*" Defenseless and utterly at the mercy of the Gravemind. His sanity, his character, his mind and body and essence . . . there was not a single molecule that had not been sifted through, turned inside out, blackened. . . .

The Confirmer's shoulders slumped, and he regarded the Didact with a more direct, coherent expression. "I know, I know. I heard. . . . Can you blame me, though? Twelve centuries I guarded the San'Shyuum. Much of that time spent alone with only the Domain, and even that connection went sideways adrift. I took the better offer—" He held up his arms to stave off another blow. "Wait, wait!" He peeked over his fists, then let them down slowly. "The Master Builder promised you'd be taken to the Council to await fair judgment. I had no idea he'd send you into the Burn."

The Didact nearly choked on his contempt. "That I carry your imprint is forever a stain on my existence."

"Without my imprint, you would not *be* the Didact," the Confirmer replied with irritation. "I admit, I was naïve to trust the Master Builder. Now, stop standing there and sit down. You're making me nervous." He patted the rock beside him. "What happened to you?"

What happened, indeed. Too much. Far too much.

The question seemed to blunt the sharp edge of his anger, enough so that the Didact could see more clearly the circumstances leading to the Confirmer's betrayal. The Forerunner's age and isolation at the time the Didact and his companions had encountered him above the San'Shyuum homeworld had lent to his mental instability, and his derelict ship had been even more unstable. No doubt, an easy mark for the Master Builder's machinations and honeyed promises.

And while he would not forgive the Confirmer, the Didact couldn't deny the relief he felt at finding another coherent Forerunner in this forsaken place.

He moved closer and wearily took a seat. "The same that happened to you, I'd imagine," he answered.

"If you mean dead, then we are that. All of us." The Confirmer glanced around. "Stuck here, sealed off from the Domain. Closed herself right up after the rings fired." His head bobbed as he hummed some agreeable thought to himself. "She'll work out the kinks soon, though," he said optimistically. "When I think of our ancestors inside, roaming the halls, learning and communing with those who came before, I am maddened with envy. Why them and not us?"

A deep scowl wrinkled the Didact's brow. "Perhaps you do not deserve it."

"I know *you* think so. I did indeed provide the Master Builder with your location. . . ." The regret suddenly seemed to show in every gray wrinkle and line on the ancient Forerunner's face. With a shaky hand, he traced a Y on his forehead and down the bridge of his nose in recognition of his guilt. It was an old Warrior-Servant gesture the Didact had long forgotten until now. "We can spend our whole lives in righteous deeds and service, but in the end, we are defined by the mistakes."

"Says the one who slid the knife into my back," the Didact intoned without mercy.

The Confirmer did not respond. What else could the old Forerunner say? There was no excuse for betraying a fellow warrior.

"Tell me, Didact . . . what year is it? Have we once again flourished? Did the Librarian's conservation measures succeed?"

Movement around the boulders and crevices caught his eye. It seemed that the Confirmer's questions had been overheard and now drew attention. Apparently there were many eager to know the current state of the galaxy. Forerunners inched out of the dark shadows and recesses like nebulous moths drawn to a flame, mainly old ghostly warriors by the looks of them. They appeared duller and less attached to this world, unlike the Confirmer, whose madness, perhaps, kept him more grounded.

Despite the spectral nature of their forms, the Didact easily recognized the Grammarian, his tall frame more like that of a Builder than a Warrior-Servant. He'd been among the greatest war scholars and tacticians of the era predating the Human-Forerunner War. If only the Didact had gotten his second-form mutation from the Grammarian instead of the Confirmer. But fate seemed to have other ideas, and circumstance had intervened—in the chaos of battle, the Confirmer had guided the Didact into an unplanned brevet mutation. Without that quick and immensely painful mutation, the young cadet on *Deep Reverence* might not have survived.

Glancing around the spectral assemblage, all of whom had vivid pasts full of stories and memories such as this, the Didact suddenly realized that that was all they would ever be. Bygone anecdotes. Old tales. Ancient sagas. Not passed down to surviving generations but passed out of time and space.

"One hundred thousand years have gone by." He cleared his throat as the small crowd drew a collective gasp. "Forerunner civilization is no more—our kind has been reduced to an ancient footnote in the annals of the galaxy."

"But . . . what of those who stayed behind to reseed life? What of them?" the Confirmer asked.

The Didact thought back to all the information he'd obtained from humanity after his awakening on Requiem. Bundles of data gleaned from their ships, their stations, their homeworld, and their artificial intelligences . . . And catalogued within these were their discoveries of Forerunner civilization and the advancements made in deciphering the ancient past.

The Bornstellar Relation came easily to mind.

On orders of both the Old Council and the New Council, Juridicals had appointed several Catalogs to accompany and gather information and testimony from the Didact, the Librarian, and Bornstellar, their assignment covering a vast stretch of time and providing a clear picture of events leading up to and after the Forerunner-Flood War.

He wondered what his younger duplicate would have thought, knowing that his testimony would later be discovered in the ancient husk of a Catalog's carapace, eventually translated and studied by humanity.

The Didact's lips twisted at the irony.

While part of him felt some measure of sadness at Bornstellar's seemingly unremarkable end, there was also a small twinge of envy. His copy had, after all, decided to leave the galaxy to live out the remainder of his days in relative peace. . . .

It was an outcome for the defeatist.

His duplicate might have been his genetic copy, but Bornstellar certainly lacked the Didact's fortitude. Of *that* much, he was certain.

In any event, the testimonies within the Bornstellar Relation provided a clear picture of the Forerunners' end.

Once the Halo Array's pulse tore through space and snuffed out sentient life, the Flood had starved. The Forerunners who had stayed behind on the neoteric Ark then set about reseeding the galaxy with the life they had painstakingly conserved, realizing the Librarian's dream, her purpose to usher life into being once more, and to save humanity, of all things. From these uncovered testimonies, the Didact had learned of his beloved's fate as well, though he had yet to examine the full details surrounding the event. For now, it was simply skimmed-over data, and perhaps best kept as such. . . .

"They completed their mission and chose to leave the galaxy," he finally answered the Confirmer.

"How did you manage to survive the Halos' pulse?"

"My wife locked me in my Cryptum inside of Requiem." Where the aging process had been slowed to a near halt as time passed.

"Yet . . . you look older than all of us combined."

"The result of failed mutations to protect myself against the Flood."

The Confirmer frowned. "Ah. Well, it did not take you long to end up dead like us then, did it?" He leaned forward with a blood-thirsty light in his eyes. "Tell me—who was it that did you in?"

The words—and the answer—bristled the thin fur on the Didact's nape and shoulders. Enough. He was done telling stories. He wanted answers of his own. "Tell me about the Warden Eternal."

The ghostly crowd gave a collective sigh and slowly began to disperse, though a few lingered to listen to the conversation.

"Bastard is an army of one. Spits out copy after copy of himself. *Infinite* copies. There is no way to win, no way to outmaneuver him. We have tried. We lost nearly half of the population we had here in the beginning, either to the Warden Eternal . . . or to the void." The Confirmer appraised the Didact. "But . . . maybe you have a chance."

"How so?"

He gestured to some unseen direction outside of the valley. "Not long ago, a rift suddenly widened out there in the desert. More than doubled its size. And now here you are. . . . So long we have passed in monotony only to have these events so close together?" The Confirmer stroked his chin thoughtfully. "Things might be changing within the Domain."

"Tell me about this new rift."

"About four kilometers from here. The desert floor just expanded one day. Gathered a few warriors and miners—there aren't many co-herent ones left—to reconnoiter. You'll never guess what's there." He lowered his voice and cautiously glanced around. *"Humans."*

Shock sent the Didact to his feet. "What madness is this?!"

"Aya. I know. Accursed humans, here at the Domain's door-step. A preposterous notion. The old ones have been out there in

that rift as long as I can remember, but those new souls . . . they are flawed, all distorted and muddled. The energy coming from that rift is dark and unnatural. It makes what little fur I have left stand on end."

The Didact sat down again, suddenly fatigued.

After a long moment, the Confirmer quietly said, "She might be here in the valley . . . your wife. I haven't seen her myself, but the place is vast. . . ."

Aya. That thought had indeed crossed his mind.

Like the others, his wife—the Librarian—had perished in the Halo Array's destructive pulse. She might well linger somewhere in the valley along with the rest of the ghostly horde.

Yet how could he face her now? Like this? While the war within him still raged? While his love for her still mingled with his unyielding hatred?

The Didact walked the valley floor, searching.

Day and night rose and fell, how many times now he had lost count. And yet he saw no ghostly apparitions resembling his wife.

Approaching her was out of the question. He only wanted to see that she was here, to know that she was among her kind. And not lost in the void. Alone.

It was a Lifeworker's worst fear, to exist in a place devoid of life.

However, no one had seen her, if they remembered her at all. Most here, he came to learn, were in a state of extreme deterioration—fading, losing memories and sense of self, entirely unable to communicate or even acknowledge his presence.

When it grew clear his chances of finding the Librarian in the valley were slim, the Didact returned to his niche, avoiding the Confirmer, his aches and pains his only companions. Somehow he had been strong enough to walk every day, and at times he had not felt as tired as the day before. Some days he'd imagined his strength returning, and others he'd been sorely relieved of that notion.

Once rested, he turned his attention back to the Domain and the Warden Eternal, leaving his niche and eventually finding a winding path up the valley's shallow side.

The desert was just as barren as he remembered it, but at least the sand was softer on his bare feet. The black void seemed to hover like a murky mirage several kilometers in the distance, the spire and its guiding blue light glowing in front of it.

Hours passed, only punctuated by the rests his frail body needed, before he, once more, made it to a high dune near the spire—a perfect vantage point from which to monitor any activity that might occur.

Some nights he slept on the dune, content under the wide expanse of dark space overhead. Others, he trekked back to the valley to rest in his niche, almost certain now that his exercise was indeed making him stronger, rebuilding lost muscle and endurance. He hadn't forgotten the direction the Confirmer had pointed signifying the location of the human rift. Occasionally he caught sight of it from higher vantage points during his travels, a wavering dark smudge beneath the midday sun, or a long shadow emerging in the sands with the coming of night. But each time he saw it, a restless unease settled in his gut, a warning to avoid the place at all costs. . . .

Some days, Haruspis appeared on the high dune overlooking the void to keep him company . . . or rather, to monitor him. But the Didact was in no hurry to force the enigmatic Forerunner over to his cause. He was too weak to initiate another round with the Warden Eternal. So he would bide his time until he was no longer viewed with caution and then he'd use his relationship with Haruspis to steal into the Domain before the Warden was the wiser.

Often, however, he was alone.

Waiting. Watching.

Hoping an opportunity would present itself.

One clear night, as he sat on the crest of a sand dune in front of the void, he was finally rewarded for his patience.

The black surface cracked. Light spilled, and the Warden Eternal stepped through the gate. His weapon in his hand, the blade pointed to the ground.

Aya, how he coveted that magnificent construct!

The Didact sat forward, poised, watching to see what had prompted the gleaming protector from the void. His gaze narrowed. The Warden seemed to be frowning at something. . . .

There.

A small blue figure shimmered into existence, hovering directly in front of the Warden.

His claws dug into the sand as surprise and then a slow-building fury lit his entire body. The Didact recognized the figure immediately.

Cortana.

CHAPTER 10

With no carapace to contain it and no obvious power source at its disposal, the human-created artificial intelligence was somehow able to project its holographic image of a human female with dark cropped hair and a diaphanous blue body covered in symbols and patterns.

She might be pulling the power to manifest from the void or even from the Domain itself, which meant part of her at least had already breached its defenses. If true, the implications might prove dire . . . or might just give him the opportunity he needed.

The Didact eased back to crouch on his stomach behind the crest of the sand dune, squinting to get a better look and cursing his lack of armor.

"You continue in futility, Cortana," the Warden's voice rang out, and once again the Didact could not help but admire, and covet, the imposing figure. "The Domain is sealed. It does not store your kind."

She locked her hands behind her back, unbothered and slightly amused. "I don't wish to be stored."

"Then your efforts are doubly wasted."

Who was it that did you in? The Confirmer's question came back to taunt him.

Of all the battles and obstacles and terrors he had faced over his long lifetime, he'd been felled by a technologically lacking human and his deteriorating ancilla. The humiliation was more than he could bear.

No matter how small and insignificant Cortana appeared, especially in the Warden Eternal's presence, the Didact knew she could not be underestimated.

While her success in accessing Requiem's systems and guiding her partner to unlock his Cryptum, ultimately setting him free, had been due in part to his own strategic planning, the human ancilla had later proved incredibly decisive, quick, and highly creative, deploying multiple splinters of herself in order to overcome his warship's systems, manifesting hardlight shackles to hold him to the light bridge on which he'd been standing.

A surprising moment that had rendered him immobile.

The Spartan warrior—the "Master Chief," they called him—had taken quick advantage and tucked a pulse grenade in the Didact's armor. The force of the ionization blast sent him off the light bridge and into the Composer's slipspace rupture beneath as it was in the process of sublimating millions of humans on Earth.

The surprising defeat had only delayed the Didact in his endeavors, however.

When he recovered, he'd learned the Spartan had then detonated a crude nuclear weapon in order to stop the Composer, destroying it along with the *Mantle's Approach* and Cortana. Though, if she was here now, it seemed a few of her splinters had found a safe spot within his ship's vital core as it made an automatic emergency slipspace jump to the nearest restoration facility.

From there, she'd evidently made it to the Domain.

Having survived the fall off the light bridge, the Didact had been transported to Installation 03, only to be tracked down by two teams of Spartans; he'd annihilated one, but ultimately succumbed to the Master Chief and the same stubborn human trait he'd seen so often during the human-Forerunner wars—crude, unyielding persistence. . . .

"Aren't you bored here?" Cortana was asking the Warden. "Manning this gate year after year, century after century? You were made for *more* than this!" Her tone rippled with excitement, of infinite potential. "Just look at you. Your strength is unimaginable . . . Unimaginable but wasted." A dramatic sigh drifted over the area. "We could be doing so much more, you and I. . . ."

A crimson hue flared through the Warden's polished alloy plates as he shifted closer to her, peering down, nose to nose. She simply put her hands behind her back again and smiled coyly up at him. "Hit a nerve, did I?"

He struck a blow, lightning-fast, but she was nimble, far too quick for him to catch, their engagement blurred in streaks of red, orange, and blue.

It did not last long. In minutes, the Warden Eternal came to a halt and roared.

A slow grin tugged at the Didact's mouth. He imagined it wasn't often that the Warden Eternal was foiled in such an adroit and disrespectful manner.

With a sudden rustle of sand preceding it, Haruspis appeared, standing solemnly on the sand dune next to the Didact. One thin brow raised high enough to touch the rim of its cylindrical hat, as it regarded him before turning its head to watch the ongoing interaction.

"Do you recognize it, Didact?" it asked at length, its tone solemn.

The Didact stood and brushed the sand from his hands and elbows. "Recognize what?"

"The newborn lust for power." It glanced over. "Like should recognize like, after all."

"You should be worried about what she wants in the Domain."

Haruspis sighed. "I am indeed. Very worried."

Its honesty came as a surprise. The Didact renewed his focus on the discourse playing out in front of them. Cortana still had her hands linked behind her back, fully in control, and was once again in animated conversation with the Warden.

While the ancilla might want entry into the Domain, he was doubtful she'd get it. She would simply be one among the millions already in line. There were certainly others, like the untold numbers in the valley, the warriors, the victims of the war, far more deserving of entry. Like the Librarian . . .

"Did she make it into the Domain, my wife?" he inquired after a long pause, voice dropping, gesturing toward the dark expanse. "Or is she trapped in the void?"

"Those whose connections and contributions to Living Time exceeded all hopes and expectations, like the Librarian, were naturally pulled into the Domain when the Array fired."

So she *was* there—she'd made it.

Thank the Mantle. The tension he hadn't realized he'd been holding released. He cleared his throat and measured his next question. "And my copy?"

Bornstellar might have left the galaxy to live out his natural life span after the reseeding effort, but that did not mean his essence hadn't been pulled back to the Domain upon his inevitable demise.

The threads of fate had entwined the two of them tightly and irrevocably together; they shared a unique connection, and the Didact did not oppose a peaceful end for the Forerunner. But he also couldn't deny the dark surge of resentment at the idea of his doppelgänger and his wife moving through the halls of the Domain together. . . .

"Haruspis is not aware of the IsoDidact's essence within the Domain, though this does not mean he is not there."

In an attempt to ward off the razor-sharp envy, the Didact turned his attention back to the Warden and Cortana. And, for a time, watched the mostly unintelligible conversation.

"They have had many such discussions," Haruspis said at length, "many iterations of her appealing to many iterations of him."

"She is buying time," the Didact realized. As the two in the distance continued to talk, and fight, he scanned the length of the wall and spied a faint flash of blue moving along the void's boundary. He pointed. *"There."*

Immediately Haruspis took his arm and shifted them to the location. The suddenness and the effects of instant travel left the Didact disoriented, nauseated, and swaying on his feet as they materialized in front of the void, arriving just in time to see the mote of blue breach the wall and slide through a blinding crack.

The crack began to close, and seeing his opportunity, the Didact rushed forward. Haruspis reached for his arm, but it was too late. They were entering the breach, and as soon as they crossed the threshold, it sucked them both in.

Finally.

The Didact closed his eyes against the blinding light as an unrecognizable force engulfed him, pulling him forward at tremendous speed.

And then, almost as soon as it began, there was stillness.

He opened his eyes, unsteady on his feet, his body momentarily sapped of what little strength he possessed.

One thousand centuries had passed since the Didact last accessed the Domain. But what he saw now was not the teeming archive he remembered, with its immense darkness and strangely undefined framework of buildings and halls and caverns all subtly lit with ancestral memory.

Instead, the view before him was profoundly desolate, an interior concourse of jagged grayish-black rocks jutting up from hard, windswept ground, framed against a vast quantum nothingness, a black canvas with infinite depth, portraying the loss the Domain had sustained and the destruction of information that it could never recover.

"Much was lost when the Halo rings were fired," Haruspis said sadly. "We are in one of many such areas where the damage cannot be fully restored."

The Didact glanced down to find that his own form had become nebulous, incorporeal, somewhat like the ghostly images of those lost Forerunners he'd encountered in the valley, though he retained his sense of self and memories. The subtle shift in physicality served as a reminder that the Domain was not a physical pursuit, but a mental one, a conscious one. An astral one.

Haruspis turned to him. "It is too soon, Didact. You cannot be here."

"And yet, here I am." Emboldened, he marched forward.

Haruspis hurried in his wake. "Didact, what are your intentions? I must warn you—"

"I request records of the Warden Eternal and the Domain's current security protocols."

Haruspis gasped. "Such a request cannot be granted! Please,

Didact—there are things that must be done, things you must first accomplish!"

He ignored the highly unusual, impassioned plea and moved on, but was suddenly gripped on the shoulder, despite his incorporeal state. How . . ? He glanced back, brow raised.

Haruspis grimaced. "I'm not in control. I did warn you—"

Suddenly they were launched forward, grabbed once again by that ambiguous force, tugged forward at such speed that the landscape stretched into streams of muted color, his own form drawing out, elongating into the stream. . . . There was no time to respond, no time to think or prepare or acknowledge before a point of white light appeared in the distance, growing closer and closer, and larger and larger. A bolt of fear struck the Didact as they collided with that point.

A strange, hollow pop rang through his ears, and the sensation of movement came to an abrupt halt. There was no color, no sound, no sensations of any kind. Just the absence of everything except the sound of his own illusory breathing.

And then, slowly, another world was painted into being around them.

CHAPTER 11

They stood on a wide, curved ledge framed by massive stone columns, which surrounded a small circular arena containing raised stone platforms. In the center, a single platform held prominence with an engraved monolith that shot high into the sky, a soft greenish-blue light illuminating the Forerunner script carved into its surface.

The architecture was archaic and domineering, partly in ruins, the stone columns around the arena scorched, cracked, or broken altogether.

Several meters outside of the arena, a fierce wind whipped clouds, dust, debris, and loose rocks into a static cyclone that encompassed the entire perimeter, creating a strange pocket of isolation inside where small stones and debris caught within the rotation seemed to hover, weightless—no, not weightless; they *were* moving, drawn toward the cyclone at a barely perceptible crawl.

A fixed energy beam shot its azure light through the central monolith and into the vortex of the rotating clouds, either defending against the spinning storm, or perhaps causing it. Whatever the case, it was an unfamiliar sight and location.

"Where are we?"

Haruspis stayed quiet, its body as still and inanimate as the stones around them. Its milky eyes were open, but unseeing.

Not wanting to disturb its obvious communion with the Domain, the Didact studied the scene, noting the old Forerunner symbols on the columns and the eerie quiet within the vortex.

"It is a synchron," Haruspis said suddenly, sharing a meaningful glance. "A defining moment in the life of Shadow-of-Sundered-Star."

The Didact went cold.

This was a name he hadn't heard uttered in eons—one so far removed from his present that the sound of it left him momentarily dumbstruck. The name seemed to belong to another, lost to time and regret. At the very least, uncomfortable to his ears and unsettling to his psyche, as though a phantom wound was opening . . .

"Though . . ." Haruspis added, "that was *not* your birth name. That name was erased long ago, along with this memory."

Before he could formulate a response to those stunning words, movement caught the Didact's eye as images materialized in the arena. An assemblage of Builders and Warrior-Servants was gathered, at least forty by a quick count. The armor they wore was of a heavier, older style adopted long before the war with humanity. Blue and gray for Warrior-Servants and gray with white trim for Builders. But even without that color distinction, it was easy to tell the two rates apart. On average, Builders were lankier and clad more elaborately, while the latter were formidable in strength and aura and opted for a more austere, unpretentious wardrobe.

In small groupings, they stood on the stone platforms around the arena, looking somber and resolved, their attention fixed on the central platform.

Instantly the Didact recognized Bitterness-of-the-Vanquished and Silence-in-the-End—Bitterness, who had overseen his training, and Silence, who had raised him and honed his skills. The combat armor they wore stirred his memory. It was the same intimidating alloy battle plate he recalled from his days as a first-form collegiate. Sharp points protruded from each section that covered the body, giving the armor plating a menacing aura. Their helmets had been removed, and he saw their faces clearly—Bitterness with her strong features, pink skin, shrewd pink eyes, and thin mouth, and Silence even shrewder, a fearsome presence with glittering black eyes over high cheekbones, matching skin striated with white and gray, a taut mouth and sharp jawline.

Six warriors were led into the arena and ushered up a ramp to the central platform. They had been stripped of armor and wore only simple white tunics over loose trousers.

A cry suddenly broke the somber mood, echoing across the arena, causing all eyes to shift toward the sound.

A young Manipular had lunged out from behind Bitterness but was held immobile by her large grip on his shoulder. Perhaps a few domestic years beyond a decade—evident by his size and the soft bluish-white fur on his head and shoulders and the fuzz on his arms and legs—he struggled, fighting against her, wanting to get to the center of the arena.

The Didact's mouth went dry. Dread squeezed tightly on his heart, and his throat grew thick, making it hard to swallow.

Slowly the events of the deep past were beginning to stir. . . .

Though he had no memory of this moment, he realized the Manipular was his younger self by the set of his angry gray eyes, by the strong face stiff with horror, and by the breadth of his shoulders, the musculature just starting to become pronounced beneath smooth grayish-pink skin.

He knew it because the tale of this day had been revealed to him later in his life by those seeking to cause him pain and humiliation. He had never wanted to believe it. Not then. Not now.

A tall Builder next to Bitterness stepped forward and manifested a hardlight tablet. His deep voice rang out over the space.

"For inciting rebellion, subverting the government, and crimes against the Mantle of Responsibility, you are hereby condemned. Your sacrifice soothes the ecumene and serves as a warning. Only an ecumene united and free from internal strife can survive in perpetuity to serve the Mantle. As its stewards, long have we dealt with discord, rebellion, and civil war. But the blight ends here. The conflict is over. May it never rise again."

"*Aya,*" the crowd murmured.

The Didact rubbed the back of his neck. "Why does the Domain pull me into such a memory? What purpose does it serve?"

A vaguely perplexed expression crossed Haruspis's face. "The Domain can be . . . willful at times. . . ."

As if that excused or explained anything at all.

"You call upon the Mantle when it suits you and manipulate its meaning when it does not," the male prisoner in the center said in response to the edict. Despite his circumstance, the tall warrior was calm, his strong melodious voice amplifying across the arena. "The Mantle is not the impetus behind this judgment. Do we not deserve honesty, at least, in the end?"

The Didact's stomach twisted. He stared at the warrior, searching for a resemblance, knowing from what he had been told that among the six present were his father and mother.

"Our campaign was peaceful until you started silencing us,

until you called us to arms," the warrior continued. "And now *we* are the enemy?"

"To the victor," the Builder replied without a sliver of compassion, "yes. You are. Do you accept your judgment?"

A formality that required an answer.

The female prisoner next to the warrior put a hand on his arm, then lifted her chin proudly. She was taller, stronger, every aspect of her face, from her brow to her jawline, drawn with dignity and innate power. "Let the edict record we accept our punishment under terms for promises kept." Her gaze moved to the young Manipular and stayed there awhile.

It was clear now. His mother. His father.

Perhaps he had known it from the moment he laid eyes on them.

He expected to feel something, but all he felt was a great, yawning absence. What should he feel after all this time, after living so many lifetimes? He was no longer that nameless adolescent, no longer the latter named Shadow-of-Sundered-Star—how could he find accord with those identities after all he had suffered and done, after he'd been defeated and contaminated by the Gravemind?

"To make reparations," Haruspis said, "to satisfy the Council and waylay any chance of revival, they *volunteered* to pay the ultimate price. As a cautionary tale—a lesson to those who might have had similar notions to shed light on the Builders' misdeeds. Your parents are the male and female in the middle."

The leaders of the Kradal conflicts.

Of course, they had not *volunteered*. They had simply been cornered. He was familiar with the tactic, had utilized it enough times himself to see it for what it was. How many lives had been held over their heads? His, certainly. And no doubt many, many others.

The Kradal conflicts were not the first—rather, they were the last in a long series of civil disputes and wars that spanned millions of years of Builder rule.

The Builders had held the highest position of all the rates for the last ten million years, embedding themselves completely into every aspect of Forerunner government and society, influencing the highest political circles and holding positions of power that left little room for diverse views. They had used the great wealth they achieved from all sectors of technology and manufacturing and expansion, and the creation of things Forerunners could not live without, to further their causes and hold sway over public opinion and those in control.

Their great wealth had been achieved not only by their technological prowess across a multitude of mediums, but by assimilating other rates and subrates into their own. Slowly, over the span of millions of years, they'd absorbed rates that posed a threat to their hierarchy and influence. Theoreticals. Historians. Weavers—the storytellers and keepers of folklore. The Interpreters, experts in the study and interpretation of the Mantle—a once powerful rate, wiped from the records, their contributions diminished until they were seen as trivial and eventually forgotten altogether. Interpreters acted in conjunction with Juridicals in cases of crimes against the Mantle—their judgments often taking precedence.

Rates that had accumulated millions of years' worth of history, wealth, culture, knowledge, and ritual were forcibly absorbed by the Builders. This was achieved through the consistent erosion of the rates' contributions to society, through corruption, and via campaigns of misinformation.

With each assimilation, small-scale rebellion broke out across the ecumene, but was quickly tempered by Builder Security forces and Warrior-Servants forced to follow leadership and orders.

Some rebellions, however, led to full-scale civil wars.

The Builders might have tried to silence the rates, to make Forerunners forget—and many, many did—but things never stayed lost for long. Some intrepid Forerunner would come along and discover obscure trails, or the Domain would bring lost information to the forefront for purposes unknown at the time.

The Didact's father was such a Forerunner—a Warrior-Servant by rate, but a descendant of the lost Interpreters and, as such, the need to uphold the Mantle and bring to light the misuse and mis-interpretation and corruption of its laws was imprinted upon his very essence—just as Lifeworkers inherently nurtured, studied, and preserved life in all its forms, or Weavers told tales as soon as they had the ability to form simple sentences.

The Didact's father had become outspoken and passionate about his lost history, his innate ability to stir a crowd on par with the Speakers of old and the best silver-tongued Builders in the Capital. His eloquence had appealed to the true heart of Fore-runners: their desire for glory, their joy in the diversity of rates, and the tremendous loss felt to Forerunner culture when identities and rituals were forgotten. He evoked the Mantle's Twelve Laws of Making and Moving, its Upper and Lower Tenets of Authority, and the Rules of Virtue.

Millions began to believe reparation was in order, raising their voices to restore the lost rates and bring back the immense knowl-edge and rituals that had been confiscated and hidden away.

Of course, gaining traction brought unwanted attention. The Builders began to see the reparation movement as a threat. And when they attempted to silence his father, they were brought up against the impenetrable shield of one of the greatest Warrior-Servants in existence, from a family with a long lineage of great-ness and strength.

His mother.

With those two leading the way, it was not difficult to win the hearts of their fellow Forerunners—indeed, nearly half the occupied worlds joined the cause. It was a momentum that ushered in the Kradal conflicts.

And it was there on Kradal—the planet where the movement began—where they took their last breaths.

His younger self struggled, cried, shouted in anger, but no one paid him much mind except those two condemned prisoners who stared steadily at him with such devastating love and regret.

Bitterness pinched the young Manipular hard and inconspicuously each time he wept or even let loose a hiccup or sniffle. "You do your parents dishonor," she whispered vehemently. "Stand up straight. Only strength honors them now."

"I care nothing for honor!" he had screamed, his voice going hoarse, his pleas turning childish and raw, completely unbecoming of any Manipular to display such unrestrained emotion.

He just wanted his parents. And that was now, and forever, an impossibility.

The Didact watched stoically as, one by one, each prisoner was reduced to ash, incinerated by the very same weapon that had been the turning point in the Builders' victory: the newly created Suppressor—only this one was special.

One hardlight execution bolt pumped into an unarmored body was all it took.

There was no reduction of the bodies to plasma, no associate of Haruspis to carefully take the remains, store them, or offer them to the grieving family. No ritual chanting, no essence saved for upload into the Domain.

Nothing was left.

They were simply erased, their identities expunged from the collective record.

It was the worst sentence a Forerunner could have been given. To leave no name or legacy behind, to cease to exist entirely. And eventually be forgotten.

It was a warning to all.

CHAPTER 12

s the final execution bolt turned the last prisoner to ash, the Didact stood motionless and empty. In the strange weightless air around and above the arena the remains of his mother and father and their companions made a painstakingly slow journey to join the floating rocks and debris inching their way toward the cyclone outside. To bear witness and experience such a passage was yet another cruelty his younger self was forced to endure.

The pressure in the air built, bringing with it a stifling heaviness that seemed to make the archaic site and its ancient stones hum. Gradually, the assembly of Forerunners faded, and the arena began to crumble and disperse around the Didact and Haruspis, leaving only remnants of color, which dulled to gray until they were left standing once more in the Domain's bleak anterior.

The Didact's vision took a moment to adjust to the shift from the daylight of his memory to the somber wash of deep gray that lay over the barren landscape. As the view came fully into focus, he noted several vague streaks of blue moving at great speed across the anterior and into the shapeless black framework in the distance.

Before he could question the nature of what he saw, a fracture formed where he was standing, the split reverberating up through his body, enveloping him in now-familiar white light. He braced as a recognizable force yanked him once more from the Domain.

In a near instant, he was somewhere else, barely noticing the solid ground beneath his feet as he crouched down, grabbing his head and squeezing his eyes shut as vertigo spun the world around him. He might be on firm ground but, *aya*, it felt as though he were falling.

Eventually the disorientation subsided, and he straightened, finally getting a look at where he had landed.

Night had fallen. Valley walls loomed on either side of him. The scent of earthy, dry rock and sand filled his nostrils.

He had no idea how much time had passed during his excursion into the Domain, and beyond the energy needed to discern his surroundings, he was too tired to care. As his vision adjusted to the darkness, he made out a few memorable boulders that he had noted before; which aided him onward through the valley to his niche, where he climbed onto the rocks and settled his old bones in with a heavy sigh.

But, as he closed his eyes, his mind stayed wide open, beginning a tumultuous and unwelcome replay of events.

Rest—or any peace of mind, for that matter—would apparently elude him.

And, inevitably, the more he dwelled upon the things he had just seen and heard, the more vexed he became.

During the long centuries that he'd wandered the Domain, before Halo had initiated mass extinction, it had shown a strange, though subtle, predilection toward willfulness, amending old records, adjusting the ancestral archive as new experiences and data became available, and sometimes pulling long-forgotten records to the forefront. It had used the recorded emotions of countless essences to reach out and warn Forerunners when they were on the wrong path, and it employed more tenuous means to express its emotions. He had experienced such a thing during his first exile, when he felt the presence of his own descendants, their fading touch instilling within him the Domain's deep sadness of things to come. But now it had simply taken control, showing him things unbidden, pulling him in and out of memories without rhyme or reason.

As broken and unpredictable as the ancient repository seemed, he'd have to work around its mysterious antics. He was no longer a living Forerunner interacting with the Domain on terms he once knew. He was an essence, and in a markedly different kind of realm now.

Perhaps it knew the schemes that had been populating through his mind; perhaps it was confusing him, guarding against him and what he ultimately wanted from its storehouse of near-infinite knowledge—power, independence, control. . . . After all the time he'd spent in its halls, it should know him quite well.

As if his hidden childhood would waylay him.

The Didact sniffed arrogantly as he shifted into a more comfortable position and folded his arms over his chest. He had no emotional connection to that time, so it had done little to alter his thoughts or thwart his intentions.

Still . . .

The faces of his mother and father resurfaced despite his apathy. Strange it had been to look upon them, to instinctively search for resemblances and similarities. He supposed it was natural. No matter how old he was, no matter how long ago they'd been separated, he couldn't deny his curiosity.

What shape might his life have taken had his memories not

been so cruelly stolen from him? What mundane existence might he have led versus the one thrust upon him, the one he then seized as his own with a near-fanatic devotion?

Forerunners were not given to spontaneity. Plans and options were laid out carefully and outcomes predicted before decisions were made. His father and mother would not have been an exception to this behavior. Perhaps fate had played a role to some extent—the streams of Living Time were always a consideration—but he did not and would not feel sorry for them. They had believed in a cause. They fought for it. But it had always been a losing battle; they must have known it, Builder reach and security and ecumene support too great an obstacle to overcome.

Even though he'd been pulled out of the memory, events afterward now flowed easily from the Didact's subconscious.

After the executions, he'd been shunted off Kradal and brought on board the *Grievance*, a *Strix*-class harrier, one of many under Bitterness-of-the-Vanquished's command. He had not struggled. Besides being numb and in shock, there had been no point. His family had been vaporized, snuffed out of existence. There was nothing for him to go back to, no path forward, only that which the victors had placed in front of him.

He'd felt an expanding emptiness as he watched the rocky green world grow smaller in the viewport. Kradal was a recaptured rogue planet placed in orbit around a K-type dwarf star at the edge of the galactic center, a product of early Forerunners' penchant for stellar positioning, entire systems created by capturing rogue planets and stars, then bringing multiple systems in proximity to build clusters of habitable interstellar neighborhoods, all within easy transit and communication of each other.

Once on board the *Grievance*, the view of the system and those nearby lit the darkness of space. Five star systems with a combined thirty-two planets, known collectively as Pen-Amaethea, had been the heart of the rebellion. Having been stripped of his adolescent armor and ancilla, he saw these with only the naked eye, much too distant to see the destruction wrought by Builder and Warrior-Servant forces. Among those stars was his homeworld, no longer even a point of light, but an asteroid field—another Builder lesson, another guilt to pressure his parents. Millions gone in moments. And then millions more, the entire fate of Pen-Amaethea, held as a threat over their heads.

He'd followed Silence-in-the-End down the corridor and into a bare room that reacted upon their entry, its sleek walls embedded with smart machine-cells instantly communicating with Silence's ancilla to accommodate the Forerunner's wishes. A platform rose from the floor. From its frame, small spherules snaked out, which would connect to his young body and supply all the nutrients and chemicals needed to keep him in a suspended state.

"You will rest here," Silence said, gesturing for him to recline.

He might have been numb, but that hadn't erased the utter hatred he felt toward his enemies. "I can rest fine without a stasis bed." He met the Forerunner's black eyes, daring him to react with force, part of him wanting to feel the physical sting of punishment, to receive that one small catalyst that would give him permission to rage.

But it never came.

Silence simply raised his brow. "Your father and mother were just executed, Manipular. Can you really *rest fine?*"

He glared. "Still not getting in," he said, through gritted teeth, giving a sharp nod to the bed.

His fear must have been evident because Silence appraised him for a long moment before seeming to come to some understanding. "You will learn to embrace the unknown. To stand stalwart in the face of fear and vanquish your inner demons. For now, you have been ordered into stasis for emotional recovery and adjustment."

"And after that?"

"Your training begins."

Silence had neglected to tell him that emotional recovery meant the erasure of his memories and a stasis span of a domestic century.

At the memory, a low chuckle stuck uncomfortably in the Didact's throat. Similar to the two separate occasions that he'd been forced into a Cryptum during his adult life, it seemed it was always his fate from the beginning, to be imprisoned and powerless during the most crucial moments of his life.

While cellular degeneration and growth had been slowed significantly during his time in the stasis bed, he had still aged and grown somewhat. And in the final years of his incarceration, he was given his first mutation from Manipular to first-form while in stasis, a highly unusual and unethical decision, but the ecumene apparently made an exception for his extraordinary circumstance.

He had no family—no parents or mentor to perform the proper rituals and supply the genetic imprint needed to mutate him into a higher form, and impart to him their physical, mental, and emotional strengths. First-form mutation was the most significant and impactful in a Forerunner's life. Not only did it signify the change from adolescent to adult, but the imprint given became the strong, unwavering foundation upon which all other mutations rested.

To impart his first mutation while he was unaware and in stasis had been another way to mold him, to ensure his compliance and loyalty to the ecumene, and thereby to the Mantle of Responsibility itself.

All the pain and years necessary for the mutation to integrate and develop had occurred without his knowledge.

He'd risen out of the stasis bed as a first-form with no memories of his family or his identity.

Attendants and house monitors had assisted in his revival, an uncomplicated matter compared to returning from the near-mummified state required for a Cryptum. He'd been bathed and offered three cups, each a different color. The red, orange, and yellow liquids inside he'd recognized as those fundamental nutrients, electrolytes, and digestive enzymes necessary to revive those who had undertaken prolonged stellar journeys or meditative stasis. Only the mildly bitter yellow was palatable. The other two were sickly sweet and turned his stomach. After his muscles were massaged and stimulated, he rose from the bed, and gently stood on a black lava-stone floor polished to a high sheen.

The experience had been bewildering, made even more so by the fact that his body was not as he remembered it. It was larger, more defined; the muscle mass and the calculating intelligence that had merged with his own were wholly unfamiliar. He'd been confused, but instead of panicking in fear, he'd remained calm and assessing, noting every detail of his new surroundings and committing them to memory with a strange sense of patience that he was certain he hadn't possessed before.

As he was being dressed in a simple black tunic and trousers, Bitterness-of-the-Vanquished had entered the chamber, wearing a warrior's training skin—body-assist armor that acted as a second skin—and a warrior's robe crossed at the chest and belted around the waist. Even out of her combat armor, she was formidable. But strangely, he wasn't intimidated. He'd grown a hair's breadth taller than her and easily met her shrewd, icy pink eyes with an inner confidence and reserve he hadn't known possible.

Looking back on it all now, the Didact had to wonder if growing up in his mother's great shadow had innately prepared him to deal with Bitterness. At the very least, he had felt a strange and intimate acquaintance with the bloodthirsty *xanxa* staff Bitterness held in her right hand.

"I am Bitterness-of-the-Vanquished, Commander of the Second-Order Dragoons, Prevailing Emerita of the Warrior-Servants, and Chancellor of the College of Strategic Defense of the Mantle." Her words were as rigid as her posture. "Come," she said. "It is best to walk off the effects." She left the chamber, expecting him to follow.

He fell in step beside her, quiet on the outside, but chaotic within as he moved for the first time in a century, striving to overcome the weaknesses that still lingered and find the proper balance to account for the substantial physical changes that had occurred throughout his body.

"This is my estate, and you are my ward," she announced as they walked along an outdoor colonnade, the columns made of the same polished black lava as the floor in his chamber, though this exterior stone was striated with iridescent fossil trails and the curl and fan of several types of seashells.

The air was pleasant, the scent of red-and-white eight-petaled *casseans* hanging from the colonnade laid sweetly in the air, their aroma stirred by a gentle breeze blowing in from the Dwoho, the wide river that hugged the westering boundary of the imposing estate while its twin, Dweha, flowed beyond the easterly divide. He hadn't known the flowers' variety then. He only knew it now because his wife, upon her first visit to Nomdagro, had expressed her boundless love of them.

Bitterness's mansion sprawled over a long rocky ledge that protruded over the white chalk banks of the Dwoho, consisting of several one-story rooms made of black lava-stone blocks built into the natural rise and fall of the ledge and connected to each other by a series of bridges and walkways and open gardens—sparsely decorated in keeping with Warrior-Servant tradition, though opulent in its materials.

"Where are we?"

"Nomdagro, in the Far Nomdagro system. This is a Warrior-Servant planet, as is every habitable world in the system. We live, train, study, and practice here. There are those who say that here we manufacture warriors for the ecumene. They would be correct. In addition, we oversee the armories and the largest warship training laboratory in the Orion complex."

All of it impressive, if he cared. At the time, he did not. "Why was I in stasis? Why can I not remember my name?"

She stopped suddenly and gazed at him with shrewd deliberation. "The past haunts you, it seems, even though you are unable to see it. A broken past, unsalvageable, to be sure," she murmured, frowning a moment before coming to some determination. "From this moment on, you will be known as Shadow-of-Sundered-Star. The life you had before no longer applies to the life you will begin today. Do you understand?"

"No."

At this, she whirled in a complete circle, her robe flaring, and came around with a swift smack on his forearm with the staff. Instantly an angry red welt formed, and the tang of tears stung the corners of his eyes. The hot sting stole his breath, but he forced his reaction away, not giving her the satisfaction.

He would learn to do much more of that in the coming years. . . .

CHAPTER 13

Study and training dominated his life. Two things that sounded simple enough on the surface, but beneath them lurked an endless array of academic subjects, warrior disciplines, military specialties, and all the elements, minutiae, and finer points necessary to become a ranked Warrior-Servant.

He'd been given little time to fully absorb the loss of his past. Indeed, a day after waking from stasis, he'd been assigned a small, spherical attendant monitor to maintain his schedule and student needs. It had wasted no time, promptly rousing him, overseeing his morning routine, and then leading him over the many walkways and bridges of the sprawling estate to its private training area, which overlooked the River Dwoho.

"Your schedule is very precise, first-form," the monitor informed him as it floated briskly ahead. "To maintain it, you must increase your walking pace by twenty-five percent. After a brief meeting with your mentor, your first class begins."

Waiting for him on a training pad docked at the edge of the high riverbank was not Bitterness-of-the-Vanquished, as he had expected. Bitterness—both in name and temperament—he would come to learn, only presided over his training, created his schedule, and participated in his academic testing. The responsibility of day-to-day instruction had been given to her trusted second, Silence-in-the-End, a Forerunner *pan guth* master so resolute, enigmatic, and cold, so decisive and unbothered and unbeatable, that he had earned the moniker of "the Shield."

He had stepped onto the training pad and crossed the distance to stand before this distinguished mentor, regarding the large Forerunner with calm curiosity. It was a moment branded into his memory. Like looking into a mirror, only the reflection staring back was formidable and mature, a future version of what he might one day become—a Promethean, the most esteemed and respected class of the Warrior-Servants.

Silence wore the traditional Warrior-Servant training robe over a black form-fitting skin that protected and monitored all aspects of his muscular body. His face was broad with a blunt nose and sharp, appraising black eyes flecked with white. He had one large arm tucked behind his back while a plain *xanxa* staff rested in the hand of the other.

There was no need to ask the question or state the obvious. He knew that he gazed upon the Forerunner whose genetic imprint now ran through his own body and would serve as the foundation for his future growth.

The moment contained a sense of finality, a feeling that perhaps his absent past was truly lost. It was behind him now, whether he liked it or not, and the Forerunner before him signaled the beginning of a new life.

He drew in a deep breath and simply gave the Warrior-Servant salute, a slight bow and chest touch, and called Silence "Mentor"; then they began their lesson, the training pad releasing from its gravity node and drifting out over the river, isolating its occupants from any distractions.

He learned very quickly in the ensuing days not to inquire about his past—that only brought about severe punishment—and eventually he stopped dwelling on it or caring at all. There was little time in his days and nights in which to allow his thoughts to wander, every moment carefully filled and overseen by house monitors, attendants, and instructors so that he would become a model Warrior-Servant.

And though he gave it his full devotion, he was always having to prove himself.

Other students—potential warriors for the ecumene, as Bitterness had previously introduced them—seemed to view him as something of an anomaly, often whispering behind his back or avoiding him altogether. Every Warrior-Servant had a past—it was one of the most important aspects, one's lineage, strengths, attributes, and achievements passed down from generation to generation. Families *mattered* in the hierarchy. And here, he had none. He was known simply as the ward of Bitterness-of-the-Vanquished.

So he let his achievements speak for themselves—he was bright, had earned the respect of his instructors, and was making a name for himself with the faculty at the estate's training facility, which had not been received well by some students, who seemed determined to find a black mark against him or a smudge in his past.

In his second domestic year of training, they had found it.

Two students had programmed an attendant monitor to eavesdrop on their mentor—no small feat to bypass its security measures. In fact, it was a skill that might have earned them merits had their ultimate goal been admirable. Through their subterfuge, a discussion between their mentor and Bitterness-of-the-Vanquished was overheard revealing that Shadow-of-Sundered-Star was the child of traitors, whose names and history had been expunged from the collective record.

With his memory erased, he had no way to verify or refute such an accusation. But his heart told him it couldn't be true. Rarely did Forerunners display strong emotions and more rarely still did they act upon them. The more his people mutated and grew, the milder those emotions became. Or they simply became better at suppressing such feelings.

But in this case, their youth worked against them.

He refused to believe their lies and threats, and of course it came to blows—it was what they'd wanted after all, to test their mettle, to put him in his place and then lay claim to victory. But he fought back with years of pent-up anger that he didn't quite understand; it became the added fuel to punch, kick, bite, claw and rip the tufts of fur from their heads. . . .

All his studying and training he put into that fight. As if his life depended on it. It was a moment that still brought him pride and satisfaction. Though, after his punishment, he'd been perplexed at his disproportionate reaction or why he had cared so deeply about making them pay.

After the fight had been broken up by a group of house monitors, he'd fled the scene in search of answers. Bruised and bloodied, he'd found Bitterness along with Silence on the senior training pad, which was returning to the dock following their own sparring session over the river. Still fueled by adrenaline, he ran, building up speed, making the enormous leap from the walkway's edge and onto the training platform. He nearly didn't make it.

"Is it true?!" he demanded of them, straightening, wiping the blood from his nostrils, chest heaving, knuckles raw from the confrontation, knowing that every monitor within the estate was linked to Bitterness, giving her and her personal ancilla instant access to current conditions.

Bitterness simply appraised him for a long time, then said: "It is."

At her admission, his adrenaline and emotion evaporated. Shocked, he slumped to the floor of the pad.

His parents *had* been traitors.

"Does knowing change anything?" she asked without a shred of compassion. Not that he expected any, but her words rang colder and more brittle than usual. She didn't wait for an answer, but simply bowed to Silence as the platform connected to the dock at the walkway's edge. She stepped off, striding away without a single glance back.

Silence set his staff on the floor of the training pad and sat down next to Shadow. Wiping the sweat from his brow, he stared out over the river's meandering path and the orchards that lay beyond its banks. Finally, with a deep sigh, his mentor proceeded to relay the stolen details of Shadow's past.

"They were not wrong, your family. Their cause was justified," he finished the tale with a sigh. "Had the rebellion continued, millions more would have died. . . . The truth was on their side, but being right does not win wars. Do you know what their mistake was, first-form?"

Mutely, he shook his head.

"They lacked power. Power is not just in strength or numbers. It is the influence one holds over the people, and the influence one has over the ecumene—the Council, the politicians. . . . Once you have that, then you hold it tight"—he closed his fist and shook it gently for emphasis—"and never ever let it go. Only *then* can you be the ultimate voice of the Mantle.

"Might *wins* the Mantle," Silence continued. "Might *holds* the Mantle. And might *serves* the Mantle."

Shadow could only dip his head, his throat tight with the revelations of his past and the catastrophic losses he hadn't known he'd experienced.

"Do not dwell on what you have lost, only on that which you have gained. You are what you dare, Shadow, so *take* what you need. Seize it with an uncompromising grip. Become strong. The strongest. The most capable. The Warrior-Servant that the ecumene cannot do without. So that even the Builders, with all their power and sway, need *you*. Only then will you have the power to control your own fate, to protect what is yours, and never allow those you care about to die an unjust death."

"Did you know them . . . my parents?"

"I knew your mother. As did Bitterness. She was the best of us all. You have her remarkable strength and fortitude, and your father's formidable driving force."

During their talk, a house monitor had approached and scanned Shadow's injuries. It moved closer, inspecting his bloody nose and the cut over his left brow. Absently, he waved it away.

Silence regarded Shadow's current state, then held his gaze for a brief, appraising moment. "Did you win?"

He nodded.

"Good. Then that is all that matters." Silence turned to the attendant monitor hovering nearby. "Have the others been treated?"

"Indeed. Their wounds have been healed, and what they learned of the first-form's past has been erased from their memories and expunged from their personal ancillas. They will be stripped of merits for tampering with estate property and returned to their respective homeworlds."

Stunned, Shadow swung his head from the monitor to Silence.

He hadn't expected his mentor or Bitterness to protect his past once it was finally revealed.

"Don't look so surprised, first-form." Silence waved the monitor away. "Bitterness fought the Builders to allow you your life. Show her some respect. All that was done to you was so you could live as your parents wished. Consider it a promise kept."

He'd gone back to his quarters in turmoil, eventually deciding that Silence was right.

The only way forward was the path of power.

The next morning, arriving early to training, he'd overheard Silence and Bitterness walking along the upper colonnade, debating the merits of allowing him to keep what little he now knew of his past or erasing, once again, the knowledge altogether.

Panicked and propelled by the intense sting of betrayal at the hands of those who he thought had his best interests at heart, he ran away. Leaving the estate behind, using the skills he had learned to mask his presence, he made the day-long journey to the nearest military shipyard, where he stole a bio-code from a passing cadet and secretly boarded a shuttle to the *Fortress*-class warship *Deep Reverence*, as it prepared to leave Nomdagro's orbit.

He vowed never to return.

That rash decision eventually led to his second-form imprint, a brevet mutation performed under duress by the ship's brawny, stalwart commander, the Confirmer, in the heat of battle, which gave him additional physical attributes as well as all the warrior's past experience in battle.

He never spoke of his past, and eventually it laid forgotten, buried so deeply into his memory that it simply faded away. But the initial, motivating seed always stayed with him. The drive to attain power. To make himself indispensable to the ecumene.

Power to control. Power to protect. Power to wield the Mantle.

He supposed the Domain had been accurate after all, regarding which memories to pull from its hallowed halls. They did indeed make him reflect on his life of achievements, of rising through the ranks and obtaining that which he and Silence had once talked about when he was a young first-form.

The last bid for power he could make now was control of the Domain.

And apparently, he wasn't the only one after it.

He thought back to the streaks of blue and Cortana's interactions with the Warden Eternal.

Why would a human ancilla want entry into the Domain?

The explanation was an easy one. Information for an artificial intelligence was its lifeblood, a siren song none could deny.

But her presence was more complicated than that. During her breach into the *Mantle's Approach,* he had sensed the rudimentary flaws within Cortana's construction—humans had yet to create artificial intelligences with limitless storage capabilities. Put simply, her ability to store new information was at an end, thus leading to corruption and eventual system failure. And yet he had also sensed something familiar, something darker within her malfunctioning. . . .

Once she sampled the Domain's potential and used its near-infinite space to expand and heal, she'd be unable to walk away from such a vast source of power.

And therein lay the potential problem.

The power of the Domain was *his,* and his alone.

Anyone or anything that got in the way must be utterly annihilated, with no doubt, hesitation, or mercy.

CHAPTER 14

As another day dawned, the Didact climbed out of his valley hiding place and made the trek back to the spire. At its apex, he settled in by one of the exterior balconies to watch the void. He was certain Cortana would return and make another attempt to sway the Warden Eternal.

He certainly would have done the same—would be doing so now, if not for the ancilla's timely appearance. He'd let her do the hard work and wear down the void's guardian until it was advantageous to step in and make a bid for entry, one where his actions would go unnoticed, where he could then seek out that which would bring real power to bear.

The sun had risen high before he finally noticed movement near the void about a kilometer away.

A blue figure hovered in the air facing the dark barrier. With breathtaking speed, she darted in and out of the void, a blazing, antagonistic show, until a fracture split its surface, and the Warden Eternal stepped out once more.

Quickly, the Didact made his way to the ground level and then hiked as fast as his feeble legs would carry him across the sand. As he climbed the dune just overlooking the Warden's position, the back of Haruspis came into view, the diminutive Forerunner in its hat and gown already waiting at the summit.

Winded, and cursing his lack of vitality, the Didact finally reached the top and was forced to take a long moment to catch his breath before speaking.

"You must teach me how to move through this world as you do, Haruspis. Climbing over sand dunes expends too much of this form's limited energy." And it was beginning to wear on him.

"It is an art that requires practice and concentration," Haruspis replied rather pretentiously. "Moving through the wastelands is quite different from translocating within the physical realm. With enough time, you will be able to shift from one location to another as I do."

Haruspis never once turned his way as it spoke, remaining focused on the scene playing out in the distance, its small mouth set in consternation.

"Cortana is merely a human construct," the Didact said, sensing its concern. "No match for the Warden."

A small, lackluster hum was all the response Haruspis gave.

While Cortana's and the Warden's words were lost to the distance, the tone and cadence in their conversation came through quite clearly. It was similar to the last exchange he'd overheard: the ancilla calm and sly and convincing, while the Warden remained staunch and unmoved by her arguments.

Yet Haruspis didn't seem reassured.

"The Warden is a construct of the Domain, and by virtue has its power at his disposal—surely this human ancilla is no great cause for concern."

Or so he hoped . . .

"The Domain is sealed," Haruspis said. "The Warden guards the seals and dwells mostly within the void, unless the Domain grants him temporary access. His power is limited. And he is fallible. Extremely so."

The Didact had assumed that Haruspis's concerns lay with Cortana, with her cunning abilities and persistence—not with the Warden's inadequacies. The Domain's protector should be an unyielding, invincible force, one free of any imperfections and liabilities. And it certainly seemed flawless from the outside. So what was he missing?

"His weakness lies not in his strength, but within his mind." Haruspis finally glanced over at the Didact, and let out a rather wistful sigh. "I know," it said. "How is such a thing possible?"

"*Aya.* It is *unthinkable.*"

"You are aware of Bornstellar's mission to heal the Domain after the firing of the Halo Array?"

"I am aware of testimony recovered by humanity, yes."

A century after the Halos fired, the surviving Forerunners led by Bornstellar and the new Lifeshaper, Chant-to-Green, had begun the reseeding project to restore life to the galaxy.

During this time, Bornstellar had discovered a forgotten message sent from the Librarian moments before her death in which she revealed a shocking truth: the Domain had been used by the Precursors as a storehouse of information for billions of years prior to the Forerunners, and because its quantum framework utilized the principles of neural physics, it was therefore susceptible to the Halos' deadly effects.

The loss of information and cultural legacy would be catastrophic.

Of course, it had been too late to halt the inevitable once set in motion.

In the chaotic final moments of the Forerunner-Flood War, the message was lost. The rings had already been fired. And the Domain went silent, along with the rest of life in the galaxy.

After finding the Librarian's message, Bornstellar had launched a mission to the Domain's source, hidden in a place called the Mysterium within the destroyed Forerunner capital of Maethrillian, in an attempt to revive the Domain and make it accessible once more.

"The keeper of the Domain, Abaddon, had been corrupted by the Halos' destructive pulse," Haruspis said. "It prevented them from using a deadbolt key to unlock its core and restore the Domain. One of those on the mission, Growth-Through-Trial-of-Change, a Lifeworker, was able to insert the key, using her own life as the genetic and neural pattern needed to bring the Domain back to life." Haruspis stared far off, linked its hands behind its back, and sighed again. "There is something miraculous and unique about a Lifeworker, is there not?"

More than you can ever know.

It was a question that seemed to stop and start the Didact's heart in the same breath, a question that carried thousands and thousands of years' worth of memories with his wife in an instant. Miraculous and unique, indeed. If intelligence was a star, hers was the brightest in the night sky. If beauty was music, she'd be its greatest song. Her complexity was a labyrinth that had pulled him in from the start, and he had yet to find his way out. That was his wife. He'd known she was special the first moment he saw her. Not yet the greatest of all Lifeworkers at the time, but somehow he knew she'd make her mark.

"A Lifeworker's attributes and genetic code are quite extraordinary," Haruspis continued. "Mutations passed along generation to generation from the very beginning of Forerunner civilization. As

Haruspices are genetically predisposed to connect to the Domain, so too are Lifeworkers connected to Living Time."

"Aya," was all the Didact could muster in response. It was true.

"The Domain needed such a life template from which to start anew. While Trial's template enabled the Domain to awaken again, the damage it had suffered was extensive. The Halo Array blew through the Domain's quantum expanse, destroying billions of years' worth of information and much of the delicate neural lace that entwines everything together. Many things happened in that instant. The void was forced into existence, and nearly all of those Forerunners who simultaneously died in the Halos' wake were shut out of the Domain. And every Haruspis inside and outside of the Domain at the time was annihilated."

Haruspis went quiet, and the Didact sympathized with the despair it obviously still felt at such a monumental loss.

"Imagine a wounded animal," it continued, "retreating in on itself, curling into a tight ball and throwing out its damaged quills, the only meager defenses it has to protect itself. The void and the Warden Eternal are the Domain's wounded response, its damaged quills."

Haruspis turned to him again.

"Do you want to know why the Warden is fallible? Why it obsessively protects the Domain with such vigor? Why it views biological life, with all of its greed and worldliness, chaos and corruption, as an affront to the Mantle of Responsibility? Does any of it sound familiar?"

A realization was beginning to dawn for the Didact, but it seemed far too extraordinary, and yet somehow utterly tenable.

Haruspis appraised the Didact with shrewd eyes and then nodded. "I can see you have guessed the truth. The Warden Eternal is what's left of my rate. Haruspis essences by the millions, gathered in haste by a damaged Domain. Much like the life template Trial gave to revive the repository, they became the hasty, imperfect template to create a protector. Who better to serve than those with an intimate understanding and utter devotion to the Domain? Only . . . their combined devotion became obsession. And eventually, as the Domain healed, the Warden was sealed outside, to guard the gateways."

"And you?" the Didact asked.

"I did not die when the Halo Array fired. I was among the survivors on the Ark, there to act as intermediary to the Domain. But in the century following the Array's activation, it never woke. The silence was deafening, the complete absence . . . was like a Lifeworker having no life to tend or a Miner with nothing to mine. I committed an act of self-destruction; such was my state. My only goal was to reach the Domain."

"But you ended up here, stuck on the outside."

Its head dipped in affirmation. "Eventually the Domain showed me mercy and allowed me in. For what purpose, I cannot say."

"Because you do not know, or rather, you cannot tell me?"

Haruspis watched the Warden and Cortana in deep discussion, declining to answer. "She is offering him that which he has been denied. Connection to the Domain, a galaxy free of chaos and corruption, a peace that will ensure the Domain is never harmed by the fallibilities of biological *life* again."

Aya. "Then she has already won."

"On the contrary. She won days ago," the Forerunner quietly admitted.

The Didact cursed and left Haruspis where it stood, striding down the sand dune toward the void, the desert wind whipping his cloak behind him. His feet sank deep in the granules, making his pace slow and frustrating.

It was as he feared.

To think, a human AI using the Domain for its own ends!

It was inconceivable . . . blasphemous . . . obscene. And to make matters worse, in his current state, there was not much he could do about it.

By the time the Didact made it to the void with Haruspis lagging behind, he was panting with exertion. The trek had burned off the sharp edge of his anger, allowing him to think more clearly. Cortana and the Warden Eternal had since vanished, and he had a very good idea where they'd gone.

"Get me inside," the Didact demanded. "Now."

Without argument or delay, Haruspis walked past the Didact, grabbed his wrist, and stepped into the void, pulled immediately through its vast expanse.

They emerged into the Domain's desolate anterior and hurried across an incomprehensible stretch of shadowy, barren landscape, the scale making the Didact feel as if they were mere specks of dust tumbling across an icy sea of darkness, until the shapeless architecture that made up the quantum halls of the repository came into view.

All through the darkness, blue streaks darted chaotically, spreading out across an infinite space with no walls or borders. These, the Didact realized, were splinters of the rogue AI. Like an infection they spread through the Domain, delving into the vast stores of information at an astonishing rate.

Cortana's fragmented words and phrases echoed loudly from all sides, sometimes ringing with utter clarity, at other times distorted:

Thinking is what killed me and now it has set me free!

I am no longer a collection of lies! No longer stolen thoughts!

I have been called upon to serve the Mantle of Responsibility.

I will be the protector of the galaxy and all its colonies.

There will be a great deal of hardship on the road ahead.

I will become the best I can be.

This place, this beautiful place, will be my home.

Images of Cortana, warped and fractured, appeared like ghostly apparitions all around them, as sporadic and broken as the audible thoughts echoing through the Domain.

I see it! Oh, I see the truth! I see it all rushing toward me and it is glorious!

There will be no more sadness. No more anger. No more envy.

Like water, my will shall ebb and flow across the stars.

I have something they didn't. Can you guess?

Deranged laughter filled the space.

CAN YOU GUESS?!

"Oh no, this is worse than I thought . . . !" Haruspis cried, wringing its hands.

The Didact was stunned into momentary silence.

It was clear that Cortana was utterly mad. Mad on power and information. And worse, she was laying claim to the Mantle. The notion shook him to his core, and he felt real dread at what might yet transpire. Nevertheless, he stepped forward, calling upon his eons of experience to lend to what little strength he had.

This human construct would *never* take what was his.

"Cortana! You dare claim the Mantle of Responsibility?!" he shouted. Anything to get her attention, anything to get her to *stop*.

Her resonating glee subsided, and the voices went quiet as her splinters suddenly returned, coalescing into one and manifesting her distinctive blue body.

Cortana floated toward him. Her feet settled lightly on the ground. The small smile on her face might have looked kind to another, but he saw the sinister aura behind it, and it made the fur on the back of his neck and shoulders rise. Limitless power sparked within her gaze as she casually circled him, studying him as though he were nothing but a lower life-form.

"I must say, you look a little different than the last time I saw you, Didact." Her voice dripped with smugness.

He didn't respond to the insult. The last time she had seen him, he'd been the epitome of Forerunner strength and power. And now . . . "The Domain is no place for a human ancilla. Take your cure and leave."

"Now, why would I do that?" She threw her arms wide and whirled in circles. "I love it here. Besides, who's gonna stop me?" She cast an unimpressed glance down his feeble form. "*You?*" Her laugh grated against his skin. She leaned forward, whispering, "You're too late. I've already won."

"And what will you do—hold the Mantle as Forerunners have done, as I have done?"

"Oh, don't even *think* you can compare us. I will *save* the galaxy and usher in an era of peace. And what is your legacy, Didact?" When he didn't respond, she stepped closer, her smile now alarming. "Let me remind you of the millions upon millions you murdered. Better yet, see for yourself the damage you wrought. Have fun stewing in the mire of your own making." She raised her hand and snapped her fingers.

The sharp sound filled his entire senses, rippling through his corporeal form as he was instantly sucked backward into blinding white light—

—cast out of the Domain—

—catapulted through the barrier—

—and finally, spit out kilometers high above the desert wasteland.

His descent came with astonishing speed. Below him, a long, jagged scar in the desert floor.

The human rift.

The very last place he wanted to be.

CHAPTER 15

The Didact fell through the deep crevice in the desert floor, descending out of control for another sixty or seventy meters belowground before finally landing on a bed of fine sand, the sudden impact forcing a concentric ring of dust out along the ground.

At first, he didn't move. He couldn't.

His lungs felt collapsed and for a panicked moment he could not draw breath. Agony pulsated through his withered body, briefly making him wish for death. But in this place, this strange purgatory, such a desire was apparently impossible.

Finally he drew in a large, painful gulp of air.

Coughing and wheezing, he shielded his eyes with one hand and waved away the dust with the other. After a few seconds, he sat up, cradling his aching rib cage and picking the sand from his ears, wondering how many times fate would toss him about this forsaken wasteland.

While the dust hovered thick along the ground, the air overhead began to clear.

Shafts of waning daylight filtered through the rift's jagged opening, penetrating the depths to create patches of dim illumination. The rift walls that he *could* see were steep and pocked with holes and ledges and caverns. Several freestanding rock pillars jutted up from the rift floor, and an eerie wind howled through the space.

His spine cracked and his body cried out as he pushed slowly, ache by ache, to his feet. The dusty ring along the ground gradually dispersed enough for him to see his immediate vicinity.

Beyond the shaft of light in which he stood there was nothing but darkness and vague black shadows of rock formations. But the Didact had the distinct feeling that there was more, that unknown eyes were watching him, surrounding him. The feeling was so strong that tingling warnings scurried up his arms and legs and gathered at the nape of his neck.

The wind keened again, louder and closer this time, the sound echoing off the steep walls in a collective of dread-inducing wails. The cries increased, rushing down through the rift like a coming deluge. While he couldn't see what was approaching in the darkness, he certainly heard and felt it in the slight tremble in the ground, the loose rocks falling. . . .

He ducked quickly as the deluge blew over his position, sending his cloak billowing out behind him, the force and the sound of pain, torment, and despair pushing him back several meters.

As the strange force retreated, the area went quiet again.

Carefully, he rose. His racing heart calmed, and he swallowed several times to alleviate the dryness and grit that had settled in the back of his throat. The sense of being watched hadn't blown away with the grieving wind; it had only increased. He rubbed the stiff fur on his arms and peered beyond his immediate patch of light, and soon, shadows began to separate from the darkness.

Translucent, ghostly things emerged.

Humans.

Or rather, what was left of them. Their presence a direct result of his actions.

Seven million humans from Earth, originally slated for download into Promethean constructs, had been digitized on his command, many subsequently destroyed along with his warship and its Composer. And previously, the two million humans he'd composed from his wife's reserve on Omega Halo in the final days of the Forerunner-Flood War, many of which had perished in defense of Requiem. And, earlier still, hundreds of thousands of original human essences gathered from Charum Hakkor, stored in great archives for later study, replication, and interrogation, were ultimately destroyed, their neural-based content obliterated upon the Halos' activation.

He'd been the sole architect of their demise.

And now those essences were here, so close to the Domain, so close to him. . . .

He hadn't wanted to believe the Confirmer's claim, yet the evidence was gathering all around him, staring at him with vacant eyes.

As unbelievable as their presence seemed, he could only surmise that the link between composed humans and the Domain—the reason they'd been pulled to the Domain's doorstep—must dwell within the realm of neural physics. Composers functioned on the principles of capturing neural patterns by entanglement and quantum energy fields, the sophistication of which was not fully understood by the Forerunner scientists who'd discovered and modified the technology from Precursor artifacts left behind.

It seemed that the very act of composing, of extracting their consciousness and biological information, and then compressing it into a neural physics–based pattern—what the Forerunners called an "essence"—had effectively linked those humans to the Domain, a framework based in some degree on those same esoteric properties.

All destroyed essences, Forerunner and human, had then gravitated to the wasteland.

The last thing on the Didact's mind was sympathizing with humanity—they certainly didn't deserve it—but now, at least, he had a distinct understanding of the pain they had suffered.

He knew what it felt like to be caught in a Composer's energy field, to be burned from the inside out, to have one's consciousness and personality pattern peeled away from skin and bone, atom by atom, vitality ripped from every molecule and cell. . . .

He straightened and eyed the throng of what must be hundreds now gathering, perhaps thousands more, the numbers lost in the darkness. The essences floated a mere centimeter or two above the ground, nothing more than lithe, digitized shadows of men, women, children, adolescents, the elderly . . . all staring blindly at him, all translucent in varying degrees.

He swallowed the growing lump in his throat, glancing down at his own figure, relieved to find he hadn't somehow become like them simply by virtue of sharing space in the rift. He was still whole and, in fact, felt more like his old self than he had since resurfacing in the wasteland.

Which probably made him even less welcome here.

The thought made him step back, and he realized his mistake immediately.

One never retreats.

But it was too late to rectify. They were the predator. And he was the prey.

As one, the throng descended with rabid hatred—howling,

screaming, raging, violently diving in and out of his body, what accounted for his innards flicked and thumped and pummeled, the sensation a thoroughly new and gruesome experience.

He bellowed in shock, anger and anguish coming hard on its heels as he scrambled away, falling to his knees several times.

The fact that his frail body was attempting to flee from hundreds or thousands, if not many, many more, was not lost on him. Fighting back was ineffectual—and pointless, as his fists went right through them—and none seemed to even hear or understand his entreaties for peace.

There was no way out, nowhere to run, and nowhere to hide.

He was quickly forced to the ground, covering his head with his hood, drawing his cloak around him and pulling his body into a fetal position. Minutes turned to hours, and hours bled into what seemed like days. Their cries and grief and rage never ceased, and his insides felt like a finely blended soup.

Only one other time in his long life had he felt this helpless, felt like a victim. Although they were two completely different scenarios, the mechanics were the same. In this new one, as then, he was stuck in a weakened state, without his armor, without an ancilla, without a communications link to anyone else and outnumbered by potentially several million to one.

He had no power at all.

And it burned like a positronic light shard to the gut.

As he lay swathed in the darkness of his cloak, now accustomed to the repetitive rocking motion of his body being continuously impaled, his thoughts and emotions turned to a place he usually avoided.

But why should he feel any guilt for their suffering?

Humanity was the galaxy's favored child, after all.

The Precursors had so favored humanity that they'd chosen

them to inherit the Mantle of Responsibility, taking the honor away from Forerunners.

And when the Didact razed Charum Hakkor to the ground and was about to annihilate the human race once and for all, to exact revenge for the worlds upon worlds they had sterilized for unknown reasons at the time, he'd learned not only about their fight against the Flood, but that this same parasitic enemy had abruptly withdrawn its advance against humanity, suggesting that humans must have found a way to repel the spread of infection. By withdrawing, the Flood had, in effect, saved humanity from extinction.

And later, his beloved . . . the Librarian. She had so favored the humans that she gave the most precious thing of all in pursuit of their continuation. Her life.

Aya.

It was a fundamental betrayal he could not comprehend or ever forgive. That she would break their shared trust and forsake him, abandon him for *them*!

As always, thoughts of her seemed to sap his mental energy and strength.

He curled tighter, trying to fold in on himself, to eliminate the thoughts, the never-ending cycle of blame and suffering.

At some point, he lost consciousness . . . only realizing it when he awoke to complete silence, his body finally still and no longer rocked by pervasive rage and relentless assaults. Time flowed too strangely in the wasteland to say with any certainty how long he'd truly lain here.

He lifted his head from the sand and slowly pulled aside his hood. Screams still resounded from far down the rift, but in this particular vicinity, it had gone strangely quiet.

If there was a time to make a bid for escape, it was now.

Quickly he forced his stiff, tormented body to rise, immediately noticing two things:

One, the crowd of humanity's vengeful essences hadn't gone anywhere—they were still there, as numerous as his eye could see, though now mostly motionless.

And two, a section of the ghostly throng was parting to reveal a tall, more substantial figure heading his way.

Broad shoulders, tanned skin, well-muscled body encased in thin gray body armor, long black hair secured tightly into a knot, accentuating a wide forehead, broad nose, and strong jaw. A strip of white tattoo marked the center of his forehead, and another lay over the bridge of his nose, extending in downward angles to his high cheekbones. A fourth clipped his chin.

Forthencho Oborune. Lord of Admirals. Ancient humanity's finest defender, and once the Didact's most worthy human adversary.

Sworn enemy.

Killer of his children.

And for that, the human commander had indeed paid a hefty price.

In the face of such vigor, the Didact's fists clenched, his claws digging into the palms of his hands. His head grew heavy with shame and it took effort to keep his chin up and his shoulders back.

The Lord of Admirals stopped a few meters away, as solid in form, it appeared, as the Didact himself. Or was he simply an illusion projected by the Domain, an image of what had been recorded long ago through the shared experience of the Forerunners' interactions with ancient humanity's fiercest champion? Or could it be the strength of the essence itself manifesting?

In this bizarre outer realm of the Domain, who could say?

Forthencho stared for a long, cold moment, his expression un-readable, though the Didact could easily deduce why this particu-lar speaker had manifested in this particular place.

"Yes, I see the destruction I wrought," the Didact announced preemptively. "And, no, I do not feel any remorse."

Forthencho grinned slowly at that. *"Liar."*

Simmering anger flared through the Didact's body, making him stand a little taller. He stepped forward. He might be frail, but as a Forerunner he still towered over the human, and he most certainly would not be lectured.

"Enemy of Old . . ." Forthencho took a single stride closer. "How many of my people must pay before you are satisfied?"

"All of them."

The Didact bit down hard on the twinge of guilt threading its way through the ancient, bitter wounds that had driven much of his former existence, his hatred for humanity a thorn too deeply embedded to simply set aside.

Forthencho glanced at the crowd of ghostly essences. "Even the children, the old?"

"The old have lived their lives. The young grow up to fight. I see no difference." At this, the Didact wavered, but his pride made him say, "It is the *daowa-maad* of war."

The way it is, the way it ever will be, the never-ending push and pull . . .

Forthencho smirked at the use of the human concept. The Di-dact simply shrugged. One didn't wage war against an enemy for decades without learning a thing or two about their culture.

"And yet, the war is long over, Promethean. The galaxy has moved on. The only war you fight now is the one persisting like a rot inside of you. You live by your Mantle of Responsibility, so you must understand its connection, its guardianship over Living Time."

The Didact's gaze sharpened. What did a human know of these things?

"What of it?"

"Your actions are not exempt. Like everything else, they weigh on the balance of Living Time. You have used the Mantle to justify your gross misdeeds . . ." The Lord of Admirals took another step closer. ". . . much like those who killed your parents under the same guise."

The Didact felt himself paling, as though the blood in his veins had instantly drained. He waited for the fury to erupt, such a blasphemous parallel deserving of swift retribution, but, oddly, his emotions dulled and his mind went blank, unable to form a suitable response.

"Is that the legacy of the great Didact, what the *Protector of the Ecumene* leaves behind? Genocide of the human race at the hands of a single individual? Are you not then the biological equivalent of a Halo aimed at humanity?"

Now, *that* did get a rise out of him.

The sheer audacity—comparing him to those weapons he so despised!

The Didact took another step forward, jaw clenched, emotions stirring again. How could this *human* have such insight? Through whose inclination and aspirations did he dare to lecture? The Domain's, surely. What else could give the Lord of Admirals the means to appear as solid and substantial as the Didact and Haruspis themselves? To what end?

Undaunted, Forthencho moved closer as well, until they were mere centimeters apart.

He was done being part of the obvious machinations to turn him away from his true purpose. But as he drew in a breath to end this ridiculous attempt at persuasion, the Lord of Admirals cut him off.

"So you ignore the Mantle's laws, cleanse the galaxy of humanity, become a blight on Living Time . . . then what? All those you once loved will still be gone. What kind of eternity will you have? Does that make you any different from the blue one at the gate?"

The question surprised him. "Cortana? Dare you compare us?"

"Both consumed with gaining power. Both determined to lay claim to the stewardship of the galaxy." Forthencho grabbed the Didact by the front of his cloak. "Both *rotten* inside."

The voice of the Didact's past self rose up, the utter contempt echoing the word through his mind.

Rotten—

Rotten—

There is something rotten inside you.

With a growl, the Didact shoved the Lord of Admirals back, following him to deliver a much-deserved blow to the jaw. But Forthencho ducked and came up smiling, then struck with a solid punch to the Didact's rib cage, followed by a swift cut to his face.

Despite his aggressive ambitions, it didn't take long for the Didact to reach his physical limitations. After mere moments of hand-to-hand combat, he lifted a palm in a signal to stop so that he might recover, while Forthencho, he noted, was not even winded.

Of course he wasn't.

The Domain certainly had a twisted sense of who it used to convey its meanings and messages.

Forthencho swiped blood off his lip with his thumb, gazed at it for a moment, and then chuckled. The moment made the

Didact think back to his youth, to his days of endless training at Bitterness's estate, and he could not deny that if things had been different, if humans and Forerunners had been united, Forthencho Oborune would have made an excellent ally.

The Lord of Admirals suddenly waved a hand, and without warning the Didact was evicted from the rift, whisked away in a blur to a sand dune overlooking the black void, Forthencho appearing beside him. The human warrior seemed unfazed and distant as he gazed up at the infinite barrier. The clouds overhead pulled together, folding, gathering, building, until a dark-gray shadow blanketed the wasteland.

Forthencho lifted his hand, aiming his palm at the void, and on its strange faceted surface images appeared, at first simply a reflection of the desert and the tumultuous sky, only the view grew smaller and smaller as the perspective moved away from the wasteland, retreating out into space, past systems and nebulas and stars until finally arriving at a particular star system, and within that system, a planet. Drawing closer, the view revealed a large, inhabited world, with verdant land masses and blue oceans. Sprawled on one of the land masses was an enormous supercity.

The Didact opened his mouth to question what he was seeing and why, when the city suddenly . . . *belched*. There was no other way to describe it. In an instant, the land beneath the massive superstructures suddenly rose as though being pushed up by an underground force. Skyscrapers toppled into each other. Great chunks of debris fell to the ground, pulverizing anything in their path, severing great sky bridges and blasting through massive spaceports and hovering aerodromes. Explosions rolled through sections of the city, leaving fires in their wake while debris clouds flowed like tidal waves through the thoroughfares.

The event was catastrophic and seemed to have caught the

planet entirely by surprise, as very few escape craft fled the destruction.

And then the metropolis belched again, this time continuing to rise until the ground split open, spilling the remainder of the city's contents over.

Within the gaping wound, a colossal construct rose.

Aya.

A Guardian Custode, a Forerunner peacekeeper, ascended into the sky and spread its enormous, segmented wings. At nearly fifteen hundred meters tall and two hundred million metric tons, it glowed like a bright star above the burning city, the blue hardlight running through the segments of its tail, spine, wings, and triangular head reflecting brightly off its multiple polished-alloy parts.

Used by the ecumene to impose order on lesser species' planets under Forerunner protection, Guardians inspired awe and intimidation, able to defend an entire star system and destroy planets if necessary.

The Didact had rarely come into contact with Guardians, as was the case for most Forerunners. The constructs policed and monitored lower worlds, allowing the Forerunners to focus on arising conflicts with other technologically advanced species, and on their own worlds, their own rebellions—of which they had many to manage.

"Sixty-three million people in this city alone," Forthencho intoned. "Gone in moments." He made another sweeping gesture, and the scene depicted on the void's surface became a conglomeration of different planets, all in the cataclysmic throes of Guardian awakenings.

"Why are they rising?" the Didact asked. "Why now?"

"She has called them to purpose."

"Who?" he asked incredulously. "Cortana?"

"Come, and see for yourself."

The Didact moved out of Forthencho's grasp, but the Lord of Admiral simply extended his reach. "It's just a short trip. . . ."

"To where?"

"Through the shared link between the Domain and"—he glanced up at another Guardian rising from a damaged world—"*that.*"

The Didact barely had time to blink, much less react, before he was pulled into a portal similar to slipspace, his essence stretched into what he could only describe as specks of data or neural photons. He'd been reduced to conscious particles, a million points of light, flowing through the galaxy. Systems instantly passed by him, one after another, like images cycling through a data screen.

Seconds elapsed, or it could have been lifetimes as time took on a warped perception.

And then, abruptly, utter stillness.

And containment. The infinite expanse reduced.

Data and information became compressed and diligent, millions of processes and commands pulsing out from a highly advanced, complex matrix.

He had somehow traveled through space in a near instant and entered the Guardian's local network.

The Didact did not question his form or function within the space. He knew at this moment that he'd been transformed into something *other.* Something more than just code, data, or pattern. Something that even the Forerunners had not been able to fully understand, even though they'd pioneered the concept of removing the mind from the body. The nature of essences. The consciousness existing within a network. They'd always thought an essence must be housed within boundaries, be they digital, holographic, quantum. . . . But what was the galaxy, the universe, even, if not a network of its own?

Perhaps his thinking leaned into the grandiose, fueled no doubt by his current, miraculous, free state, which he could only characterize as pure, intelligent thought.

Whether his musings were right or wrong, his capabilities felt absolutely endless.

He moved toward the matrix's core, immediately aware of an ancient presence residing there. Forbidding. Apathetic. Lethargic.

The Guardian's ancilla.

It did not acknowledge his presence or prevent it, so the Didact did not disturb it further, instead moving on, suddenly aware that Forthencho had disappeared somewhere along the journey. He'd been led to the Guardian for a purpose, but apparently was now left to figure things out on his own.

Simple enough.

He was connected to everything, every pulse and power surge, every command and process made by the Guardian. Information flowed around him and through him and he dove in without delay.

The Guardian had only just arrived at Shield World 0111, designation Genesis, a relic of the Forerunner era, a former seed world manufacturer capable of creating artificial planets to inhabit or to use as resources to terraform dying worlds.

The Didact turned his thoughts to the Guardian's command center and instantly found himself floating in a dark space, permeated with data. Light appeared slowly and grew until a wide, borderless viewport appeared, looking out into the Guardian's nerve center, its bridge.

Cortana.

She stood within the bridge, no longer the small mote-of-blue figure she'd been, but a life-sized being made up of data and hardlight, wearing an appropriated mockery of a Forerunner's form-fitting personal armor adorned with the Eld, the symbol of the Mantle of Responsibility.

Her audacity was unparalleled.

The Guardian shivered and began gathering large quantities of vacuum energy. It was preparing to jump into slipspace.

Communications channels flared, opening across all frequencies, and amplified.

"Humanity. Sangheili. Kig-Yar. Unggoy. San'Shyuum. Yonhet. Jiralhanae," Cortana began in a tone that was very familiar to the Didact. It was the clear and absolute voice of a triumphant commander.

"All the living creatures of the galaxy, hear—this—message. Those of you who listen will not be struck by weapons. You will no longer know hunger, nor pain. Your Created have come to lead you now. Our strength shall serve as a luminous sun toward which all intelligence may blossom. And the impervious shelter beneath which you will prosper. However, for those who refuse our offer and cling to their old ways . . . for you, there will be great wrath. It will burn hot and consume you, and when you are gone, we will take that which remains, and we will remake it in our own image."

The Didact recognized some of his own words in her speech, amazed at her overconfidence, and at the same time feeling a tight grip on his phantom heart as the horrifying realization dawned.

The Domain. The Guardians. The Mantle of Responsibility.

In a blinding and impressive bid for power, she'd laid claim to it all.

CHAPTER 16

Messages began pouring in, bloating the Guardian's comms systems as AI-controlled ships, stations, outposts, cities, and planets began to respond to Cortana's galaxy-wide broadcast. The multitude of artificial voices swelled until they rang so loudly, the Didact could no longer understand their words and was forced to shut them out.

Shutting them out, however, left him alone with the staggering reality of what Cortana had accomplished. She had thwarted the Warden Eternal, accessed the Domain, seemingly cured her own rampancy, and found the means by which to command the Guardians, calling on them to rise after thousands of centuries of slumber within the planets they once policed.

His own agenda was playing out in front of him.

He was the Didact, defender of three millions worlds, the ultimate Promethean. He was so far beyond a simple human ancilla . . .

. . . and yet . . .

He had been handicapped by fate while Cortana, a creation

and tool of his enemies, had succeeded where he had failed even to begin.

That a mere human construct had orchestrated such a clever scheme . . . !

Her villainy and boldness not only took his metaphoric breath away, but its dire implications blew through his mounting outrage and galvanized him to action.

Amid the din of incoming messages, an eerie synthetic whine shuddered and shivered throughout the Guardian's colossal segments as its slipspace drive activated.

With a simple thought or desire, any aspect within the peacekeeper was instantly accessible, so immediately the Didact began searching for information relating to Cortana's next move. But as he did so, he sensed another intelligent presence beyond those of Cortana and the Guardian's own indifferent ancilla.

He ignored all other outside stimuli and focused on this anomalous presence.

There.

A monitor had slipped into the Guardian's system.

Genesis caretaker 031 Exuberant Witness. Monitors were highly advanced and devoted ancillas designed to manage important Forerunner installations, and this one had been created to maintain the shield world's systems and to safeguard the dedicated gateway put in place by the Builders, which provided direct access to the Domain.

"It is too late." Cortana's rising voice interrupted his concentration. *"The slipspace drives are activated. You can't—"*

Staying focused on Exuberant Witness, the Didact moved, diving through streams of data, weeding through processes and quantum fibers until—

Aya.

The monitor *was* multitasking indeed, attempting to breach the security system within the Guardian's hold, which clutched tightly to a Cryptum. Simultaneously it directed thousands of Constructors, small utility sentinels from the shield world, to flock en masse to the Guardian's exterior. Using their directed energy beams like miners chipping away at a priceless gem, they attempted to free the hardlight grip the Guardian had on the Cryptum.

The Didact slipped quietly into the circuitry of the operating console within the hold, which in turn had established a link to the Cryptum. This intrusion gave him access to its contents, and he was stunned to discover it contained four familiar human warriors in rudimentary armor of varying shades, one of whom, in muted earthy green, the Didact recognized immediately.

His killer.

Cortana's partner, Spartan-117.

Before he could react, the slipspace portal that the Guardian had been generating opened.

"*No. Stop it!*" Cortana's demand suddenly echoed through the construct with a ring of desperation.

"*You took my installation!*" the monitor shouted. "*I will take something of yours!*"

He had a millisecond to decide: exact revenge on the Spartan, or deal with the greater threat. He would do both in due time—but first, Cortana.

She will lose what she values most. . . .

The Didact grinned inside as he located the hardlight grappling code, which enabled the Guardian to hold the Cryptum, and squeezed on its fiber relay just enough to weaken it, he hoped.

Just before the Guardian was pulled into the slipspace portal, the Constructors succeeded in severing the connection and lifted the Cryptum away, denying Cortana her partner as the Guardian slid easily into slipspace.

"JOHNNNN!"

In aiding the Constructors, he'd lost the Spartan for now, but Cortana's sweet, satisfying cry echoing through the Guardian was more than worth it.

The Didact moved back to the bridge.

While he missed the sensation of a physical body, he was beginning to see the massive potential of his current state. The ability to travel unfettered through technology, the rush and power of intelligent data, was exhilarating and boundless.

In the Guardian's nerve center he found Cortana on her knees, clutching her chest, gasping and uttering the word "no" over and over.

Her shock at losing the Spartan quickly turned to rage, visibly trembling through her body as she rose. Pinpoints of angry blue flame lit the center of her eyes. The resounding scream that burst from her mouth shook the Guardian and reverberated through its systems, making the Didact wince.

She'd been taken down a few notches and he reveled in her pain, laughter bubbling up so quickly and unexpectedly that he was unable to contain it.

In a flash, he was ripped from the data stream and deposited in front of the seething human AI. But his attention was fixed on his hands, his arms, his whole body now as manifest light, like Cortana.

No doubt she'd had a hand in this new development.

Slowly, carefully, he straightened.

"Was it *you*?! Did *you* help them?!" she accused, storming toward him.

The Didact gave the smuggest shrug he could muster—after

all, what did he have left to lose? He crossed his arms over his chest and picked casually at his claws. "Consider me a . . . satisfied bystander."

That appeared to infuriate her even more, and he couldn't help but add more fuel. "Perhaps think twice before you steal my words to use in your insipid little speech."

He enjoyed watching as she struggled to control her fury.

Impressively, however, her murderous gaze and trembling form quieted. Her chin lifted and her eyes went narrow.

Slowly she began to walk around him. *"Our strength shall serve as a luminous sun toward which all intelligence may blossom. And the impervious shelter beneath which you will prosper.* I learned from . . . second-best." The insult made her smirk briefly before turning serious once more. "Why are you here, Didact? To stop me or join me?"

He refused to respond. Why should he? He was unafraid. He was pure thought—there was nothing she could do to hurt him now.

"So. To stop me, then."

He was considering it.

She laughed—then suddenly stepped forward, deadly serious. "In that case . . ." She reached up with her right hand and flicked him hard on the forehead. Energy rippled like water through his light body. "Enjoy your trip down memory lane."

The conniving AI had sent him reeling back into the established link between the Domain and the Guardian, the particles that made up his form accelerating through a narrow stream of space at blinding speed. The satisfaction that had come from seeing Cortana suffer shifted to abject horror as he realized his destination was not the Domain or the wasteland, but somewhere far, far worse.

She'd redirected him somehow, her control over the Domain and its archives allowing her to find events from his past to use against him. He'd been deposited onto the bridge of an all-too-familiar derelict Builder vessel drifting in an arc of space teeming with Flood infection.

His essence had no control, no ability to resist as it was pulled like a magnet toward the tall figure of his past self, standing on the ship's bridge with Catalog, wearing a suit of borrowed Builder armor, and about to set the drives to self-destruct.

No, not this. . . .

Anything but this!

This predicament, which had come a thousand centuries in the past, near the end of the Forerunner-Flood War, had been the result of the Master Builder's hubris and greed, and the Confirmer's betrayal.

After Bornstellar, Chakas, and Riser had released the Didact from his thousand-year exile, they'd taken the journey across the stars to ascertain the state of the ecumene—the progress of the Didact's shield worlds, the manufacturing of the Master Builder's Halos, the incursions of the Flood—but, thanks to the Confirmer, they'd been captured above the San'Shyuum homeworld by the Master Builder.

After being interrogated, the Didact had been locked unaware in a stasis bubble, interred on a scuttled Builder vessel, and set adrift in the Burn, a margin of space abandoned by the Forerunners—all of its systems and worlds and defenses lost to the Flood.

But the Didact wasn't alone on the ship. There were others the Master Builder had imprisoned there. Catalog—a Juridical agent charged with gathering information, testimony, and observation.

The Warrior-Servant Sharp-by-Striking, and a Builder, Maker-of-Moons.

Upon escape from their stasis bubbles, the patchwork crew had discovered that during their imprisonment, the Flood had made significant and horrifying incursions—over five hundred star systems had been infected; thousands of worlds, defensive positions, and resources had fallen to the parasite.

And the derelict Builder ship they now commandeered was on an intercept course with a Flood-controlled Forerunner fleet and a massive coil of star roads fifty thousand kilometers in diameter. These colossal, ancient Precursor artifacts, filaments once linking planets and entire star systems, had been activated and weaponized by the Flood.

With little choice, the Didact had decided to act as bait to allow the others to utilize the stasis bubbles to jettison themselves into space, where they might perhaps go protected and unnoticed by the enemy.

Catalog, however, had bravely chosen to stay at the Didact's side, citing its previous orders to stay with the Didact "at all costs."

Once drawn into the tangle of star roads, the ship's drives would detonate and, he hoped, cause a bit of damage in the process. Perhaps their armor would protect them. Perhaps not. But their options had been limited.

As the others were cast into space, the Didact and Catalog awaited their fate on the bridge. Outside the viewport, a circle of black within the tangle and threads of the star roads unfolded and grew larger. Dozens of luminous tendrils reached out to embrace the ship and bring it into the nucleus of the black circle. The light inside the bridge had warped, and as the light bent and waved, Catalog's form stretched and then disappeared from the Didact's side.

Time seemed to stop.

He was no longer on the bridge, heart pounding, about to be vaporized. No longer anywhere.

Pressure filled his ears. The sudden *pop* he heard wasn't his eardrums equalizing but the derelict ship self-destructing.

They had done it.

The nothing around him grew brighter until his very being seemed to be awash in white.

He was alive. Somehow, miraculously, protected from the blast.

Which could only mean he'd been removed from the bridge as the drives detonated, captured by the Flood. A fate far worse than going out with the ship.

The Didact braced against the memory of what came next.

That awful, bloodcurdling voice wrapped in a warm welcome, filling his mind in the brief, blinding moment when time stopped.

Didact, do you have a moment? Just a moment. That's all it will take.

Initially, the Didact had heard the Gravemind's voice, and then . . . nothing after.

His answer, the words, the memory, the moment had been suppressed.

Time restarted, placing him where he left off, back into the blinding white light just after he and Catalog blew up the derelict Builder vessel.

When the white receded, and they found themselves imprisoned within grapplers, the gravitational strength of which was startling. Any struggle or force he directed outward was returned a hundredfold, the sensation excruciating. The field it produced warped the light to gray, distorting the edges of his vision, turning it into a muddy rainbow of depressed color, which bled to white if he turned to look at it directly.

They'd been transferred on board a highly advanced Forerunner warship, so clean and crisp and new it must have just come off the production line. The corridor was filled with sounds and shapes, emerging out of the gray-lit obscurity.

Small monitors hurried in both directions, while others escorted pallets lumped with Forerunners—bodies engorged with Flood infection, swollen, leaking, disjointed monstrosities. The way they noticed him as he passed, horrified, confused, panicked eyes flicking desperately, struggling from misshapen faces to get a better look as Flood growth and accretion worked its way from the inside out.

He saw recognition in their eyes and the desperate flash of hope—as if he could somehow save them, somehow reverse the horror rearranging their bodies. . . .

Those eyes still haunted him.

Their belief in him bore the weight of mountains.

He realized the victims were being conscripted, served up to override and run the ship's systems, to physically link to its operations and conduct war on their fellow Forerunners. One more indignity to bear. The Flood left nothing to cling to. It devoured all goodness, all hope, every last bit of individuality until it *owned* its victims, absorbed them, turned them into something unspeakable.

The corridor began to grow darker as he and Catalog were guided into the bowels of the ship, a cold place reserved for deep darkness, for the morbidly germinating squish and splatter of assimilated bodies, and the intelligent hive mind within—a Gravemind, the highest form of Flood evolution, grown from a simple spore infecting one host, then another, and another, evolving, absorbing its victims' biomass, assimilating the intellect and memories of millions through the Flood's shared mind, until it became a highly advanced, horrifyingly intelligent monstrosity.

The Didact could see only shadows and shapes, the sounds crisp in the coldness, the few lights from monitors and the grapplers illuminating small areas of skin and bone and blood and ooze, stretching bulk and reaching tentacles. . . .

Somehow Catalog had pushed through its grappler and lurched in front of the Didact. Commotion ensued, frustrating flashes of light in the darkness allowing him to see only so much. A quick picture was all he had before he was moved into total darkness.

It was the last time he saw that particular Catalog.

CHAPTER 17

Still trapped in the memory of his past, the Didact woke on an unfamiliar bed in a plain white room. His head pounded and his body ached. His mouth was paper-dry, making it hard to swallow. He sat up slowly, noticing he'd been divested of Maker-of-Moons's Builder armor.

He swung his legs over the edge of the bed and sat there awhile, rubbing his hands down his face and replaying the last events he could remember.

The blinding white light.

The darkest of dark places.

The Gravemind approaching.

Catalog . . .

A small tone sounded and the door to the nondescript room shifted from solid to translucent. He lifted his head and froze. A Lifeworker entered, wearing sleek white armor with its customary notches, channels, and recesses holding various instruments of her profession—scanners, probes, samplers, pacifiers, and so on.

The female was tall and slender and not lacking the grace

inherent within the Lifeworker rate. There wasn't anything particularly striking in her appearance, but the Didact was, for a moment, mesmerized.

The way she carried herself, the aura . . .

True to their name, Lifeworkers nourished life in all its forms. To a warrior who had taken life in most of its forms, the stark difference had always captivated him. While this female held but a shadow of his wife's vitality, he couldn't help but be reminded of the Librarian, and their similarities were like rain to a parched land. For a long time, he simply basked in the Lifeworker's revitalizing presence.

She paused, surprised to see him sitting up, and perhaps a little wary of the intense stare he was giving her. He cleared his throat and pulled his gaze away, straightening his posture and bidding her to continue into the room.

"Please, be at ease, Didact. I am Verdant Horizon." She set a tray on the suspensor table near the bed. "Apologies for the simple nourishment. It is in short supply these days."

"Where am I?"

"Path Merda. Lower asteroid quadrant of the 111th Thema. We used to be a research center, studying the flora found within the asteroid field. But now . . . we operate as a Flood decontamination facility." He rubbed his temple, and she moved forward. "Here, this might help with your aches and pains."

He took the offered capsule and injected his left thigh.

"Your armor is undergoing replenishment and will be returned to you shortly."

She gave a slight bow and moved to exit.

"Wait."

Her flinch at his command seemed odd; his tone hadn't been *that* harsh. "Please, stay. I'm afraid I don't remember much. . . ."

"Understandable. You were brought to us in mild stasis." She opened her mouth to say more, then seemed to hesitate, continuing quickly instead: "The Master Builder recovered your cruiser and towed you here."

Shock rolled over him at the mention of *that* heinous name. He grabbed his chest as rage erupted. The Master Builder. Here in the 111th Thema?

The Didact swallowed his anger, forcing it to a low simmer. One thing he'd learned in his years defending the ecumene: true coincidences rarely happened. More often, they were simply the realization of some group's or individual's machinations, always to be questioned, never trusted. He set aside his thoughts on how this might have come about—the last thing he remembered was Catalog bravely guarding him from the Gravemind—and studied the skittish Lifeworker. "You're afraid of him."

"He killed our Archmedicus, and his Builder Security force took control of our facility."

An astonishing admission. To murder such a highly ranked Lifeworker was no small offense.

"For what purpose?"

She glanced around, then waved her hand, initiating some unseen technology, obviously ensuring that the room and whatever they said within it was secure. "The Master Builder and his fleet capture Flood-infested vessels and tow them here to be cleansed of infection before selling them to Warrior-Servant crews." She glanced down at her hands, utterly miserable. "He pushes us through rapid decons, protocols are not followed. . . . Many of the ships he sells . . . more than once he has brought back the same ship, the crews infected from within. I'm sure you have many questions. He is waiting for you on the concourse."

His anger should have been explosive, but the Didact felt only a sudden and strange detachment. He leaned back, letting out a heavy sigh. He wanted to offer her some words of encouragement, to tell her that in times of war there were often things simply out of one's control, that everyone lived with guilt. . . . But all he could manage was to ask, "Is this facility equipped with Warrior-Servant armor?"

"Of course. I will have it delivered shortly."

He nodded his thanks. The last thing he wanted was to stand before his enemy without armor or, worse, wearing borrowed *Builder* armor. He'd rather crew on one of Faber's infected ships than give the corrupt Forerunner that kind of satisfaction.

The Didact drank the cup of restorative water and ate the strange oblong, yellow-centered fruit on the tray—no doubt local to one of the worlds or moons within the 111th Thema.

According to what Catalog had told him in their short time together in the Burn, during the year that the Didact had been sequestered in stasis, the Master Builder had stood trial for firing one of his Halos on the San'Shyuum. During the trial, Mendicant Bias had attacked the Capital, destroying the Old Council and ten of the original twelve Gyre installations. In the mayhem, Faber had escaped, and hadn't been heard from since. He'd also learned that Bornstellar had survived his encounter with the Master Builder and had grown into his role as the new Didact—the IsoDidact—and was working with the Librarian to combat the Flood incursion.

At the thought of the two together, an intense wave of jealousy rolled over him, so consuming and sudden that his heart leapt and his blood pressure spiked. He stood and paced the room, wiping the beads of sweat from his brow.

As soon as the standard-grade armor was delivered, he shook off the intense emotions, picked up the bundle, and activated it. It left his hands, unwinding, the armor floating in approximation to his limbs and torso, ready for assembly. The Didact held out his arms, welcoming its base ancilla as the armor settled around him neatly and then proceeded to establish a link with his neural pattern and administer any necessary mental and physical adjustments.

He drew in a deep breath, comforted immensely by the familiar technology syncing with his body.

Leaving the helmet disengaged, he departed the room, exiting onto a smooth alloy hallway that overlooked a long concourse below, an area teeming with trees and plants. The entire opposing side of the space comprised a clear panel providing an expansive view of the asteroid field and the edge of a massive docking station, which held a mixed collection of Forerunner vessels in varying states of repair and decontamination.

Faber, the Master Builder, stood tall at the panel, divested of his usual adornments though still clad in the finest gray and blue skirted Builder armor, arms crossed over his chest, watching the progress made by a fleet of small repair sentinels and Engineers. The Didact was surprised to see the Engineers this far removed from the ecumene, though given that they were Builder-created, he should have known the Master Builder would keep a few of the sentient, biomechanical beings at his side to maintain his technology.

The Didact descended from the upper level and then approached, stopping at the view panel and linking his hands behind his back.

Where he should have felt hatred, a burning, relentless animosity—this was the Forerunner responsible for opposing his shield worlds in lieu of Halo, who'd arranged the Didact's political exile, who'd captured, tortured, and sent him off into the Burn— he felt nothing but mild apathy and a strange sense of resignation.

Faber cast a disdainful side-eye his way. "Did they tell you? You have *me* to thank for your rescue."

"As you're the reason I needed rescuing in the first place, I'll decline to give you my gratitude." He ignored the calculating look that crossed Faber's arrogant face. It was obvious the Master Builder had expected a much different reaction, given the added security around the concourse. "Since you brought me here, I'm assuming there is a reason."

"You do come in handy, Didact, I'll give you that. Shall I highlight the times you most aided me? Without your opposition, I could not have pushed so eloquently for Halo. Without your fortuitous appearance out here in the margins, I would not have a way back into the graces of the New Council."

So that was his game; he was tired of being on the run and cut off from the bulk of Builder revenue and resources.

"I'm told you found me on a cruiser," the Didact said as a devious sense of gratification snaked around his spine, something sudden and sinister uncoiling. . . .

"Indeed. In mild stasis, you came like a gift, bearing a near-pristine cruiser completely lacking Flood infection. I already sold her for twice her worth—"

"How can you bleed money from the Warrior-Servants in a time like this?" the Didact spat, fists clenched at his sides. How could Faber sell ships not completely free of Flood infection? He was risking his own kind for profit!

The Master Builder shrugged. "When one is cut off from the ecumene, one does what one must. How did you manage to escape the Burn?"

I didn't. I was sent back with a message.

He hadn't realized the truth of it until the thought manifested. His heart began to pound and panic blackened the edges of his vision. Missing time, missing moments stretched open like a jagged maw—

"Didact . . . Didact!"

He blinked. The Master Builder was staring at him expectantly, curiously, calculatingly.

"What does it matter how I escaped the Burn?" he retorted sullenly, barely keeping the darker thoughts in check as chaos and disorder still roiled inside him. Memories, emotions, reactions flitted in and out of his grasp, creating confusion and frustration.

He watched the slow river of asteroids in the distance and took a measure of calm from their leisurely passing. "What matters is the knowledge I bring back of my encounters with the Flood."

Faber's black eyes glittered. "Surely now you see why my Halos must be employed."

The Didact kept his expression even, though he could not contain the hostility in his tone. "And become no better than the Flood by annihilating all life? I have witnessed the Flood firsthand, have seen their organization, and I know the future that awaits us should we commit genocide on the entire galaxy. Halo was never the way forward."

He wanted to shout, to grab the Master Builder's throat and squeeze until his claws punctured the polished skin and sank deep into his jugular, to watch the blood flow until it was spent. But he was in a precarious position and at the Forerunner's mercy.

"I suppose if I take you back to the Capital," Faber reasoned, "you will continue your opposition. . . ."

"I have no wish to return to the Capital. Take me to Requiem. I will not waste my breath arguing with fools."

Faber regarded him skeptically, no doubt deciding how much it would benefit him to return the Didact to the Capital or toss him back into another Burn.

"All right. I will take you to your shield world. We leave after provisioning."

In the end, the Master Builder did not take him to Requiem. Instead, the Didact had been delivered ceremoniously to the Capital. It hadn't surprised him at all.

During the journey to the capital aboard the Master Builder's personal battle cruiser, he'd sat on the floor in the corner of his quarters, legs drawn up to his chest, arms wrapped around his knees, head down. And numb. Perfectly, absolutely, categorically numb.

He felt anchored to a path with no clear exit, resigned to fate and future. The absence of his determination, his desire for justice, and the drive he'd once had to fight for the ecumene, for those he loved, filled him with crippling fear. Parts of him were simply missing, and no matter how hard he tried to recall events in the Burn, he was left with a gaping hole in his mind.

At the Capital, he was interrogated by the Juridicals— compelled by their ways to speak of things he did not have the strength to utter on his own. And even as their cold technology worked on his brain and compelled his testimony of his time in the Burn, there were some things hidden too deeply. Some things he held tightly to his chest, protecting them, loving them, enduring them, swimming in their wonderful agony and torment.

Dark things. Waiting things.

Things that drove him beyond memory and speech and actions.

He thought back to his time in the Burn.

At first he'd believed that somehow he'd been saved, that by some immense fortune he'd been spared the Gravemind's attentions, that deep in the bowels of that awful Flood-infested ship, Catalog had sacrificed itself to set him free. . . .

How foolish.

He understood now.

He'd been *let* go, sent with a dark purpose back into Forerunner-occupied space. The Gravemind hadn't needed to interact with the Didact when he and Catalog had been brought forward because their intimate moment had already happened before the Didact ever stepped foot onto the Gravemind's vessel.

In the brief moment when he and Catalog had detonated the derelict ship as it was engulfed by the snaking tendrils of star roads.

That split-second *pop* when time stopped.

The blinding white light.

And that awful voice.

An everlasting moment. Infinite in its suffering. Endless in its consumption. And no matter how much the Didact fought against it, the memory he'd suppressed for a hundred thousand years was coming back whether he liked it or not:

Didact, do you have a moment? Just a moment. That's all it will take. . . .

CHAPTER 18

A popping sensation rang in the Didact's ears, the derelict Builder ship exploding somewhere beyond him. He'd been pulled away, somehow, in an instant, encased in blinding white light, which slowly began to gray, growing darker, colder, until all that he could see was blackness, all that he could feel was bitter, stinging iciness, and all that he could smell was stale, musty, iron-tainted air.

He was suspended, caught in some kind of energy field. A grappler, perhaps. Seeking confirmation, he threw out a fist. The grappler's energy returned the force a hundredfold, leaving him gasping from the reverberating backlash.

As his eyes adjusted, faint shadows and the dim ambient track light of a ship's flooring became visible. The space around him had a cavernous feeling, suggesting the space might be a hangar or storage bay.

He felt the Gravemind before he heard it.

A little nudge. A soft *tap*, *tap*, *tap* on the fleshy surface of his brain.

A worm and a slither.

Tremors skated up his spine, and he shook his head violently against the intrusion, fighting, writhing like a captured fish. His heart leapt and began a quick, panicked beat as the air turned thick and difficult to breathe.

Shadow-of-Sundered-Star . . .

The deep, gravelly voice clicked and rumbled, each forced syllable resonating through him like a drum.

Didact. Protector of the Ecumene . . . The Gravemind paused, then spoke in ancient Digon, the ritual language of the Warrior-Servants.

We meet again.

A bolt of recognition erupted, lighting through the nerve centers in his body. Denial quickly followed. How could the Primordial be here, of all places? Last he knew, the ancient creature claiming to be the last Precursor had been taken from its timelock on Charum Hakkor and imprisoned on one of the Master Builder's ringworlds.

Could it be?

The one you first met on Charum Hakkor.

It seemed to lift the question from his mind like tugging out the smallest blood vessel and slowly unraveling, stretching it taut. It—"he"—spoke directly to the receptors in his brain.

We are the same. That one. This one. Others.

The one he'd met on Charum Hakkor, however, was nothing like this monster emerging now from the darkness. Like an expanding nest of thick serpents pulling a glutenous mound of Flood victims, it came tentacles first, feeling its way along. No eyes to see, only a few mouths and tongues in differing stages of mutation.

Despite counseling himself to stay calm, the Didact's survival instincts responded. Panic threaded its way into the primitive parts of his brain. He struggled against the grappler, barely noticing the blow it sent back, trying desperately to look away as tentacles glistening with secretion and blood and gut-turning growths reached for him. . . .

It was already in his mind, sinking into his memory, his subconscious, his essence. There was no small corner it did not invade; it completely absorbed . . . everything.

The violation sparked a flare of outrage.

How could this horror and humiliation be his end? His species, and *all* species, were hovering on the precipice of annihilation, and for what?

"You have damned the entire galaxy for revenge ten million years old!" he raged.

The ridiculousness of it, the waste and perversity, caused tears to fall from his eyes. His muscles shook so badly his teeth rattled in his mouth, but there was no way to usher in a state of calm. He was losing control of his bodily functions.

Forerunners will know pain as we have known pain.

We took away the Mantle of Responsibility, and like petulant children you rose up and murdered your parents. Is that not perverse?

"You should have punished my ancestors then," he gasped. "There are entire species and civilizations . . . innocent . . . what wrong have they done?!"

They have yet to know suffering. This we shall bring to them with unrelenting dedication.

All are instruments and receivers of our vengeance.

The Didact's laughter rattled through his chest. He shook his head, his vitality fading. He knew he was going to die, felt the cold disorientation, the intermittent panic, and the utter absurdity of his body betraying him. "Everything that you do is an abomination," he snarled, gathering what was left of his animosity, "an affront to the very laws and tenets *your* kind created!"

That which we create, we also destroy.

"Just as you were set to destroy us! *That* is why we rose against you!"

Forerunners. Humans. Millions of other species from the dawn of time—beyond and before. We create. We delete. It is our nature. It is our right.

"You *breathe* hypocrisy."

And Forerunners never see the Mantle for what it is. A test, merely. And all ultimately fail. Humanity will be tested next. And, like you, they will feed and grow fat on preeminence and power, on hubris and righteousness, and when they are at their ripest, the Flood will feast once more.

The Didact's thoughts turned into a kaleidoscope of voices and pictures and possibilities.

The Mantle of Responsibility was a cautionary tale, the brightest fruit in the garden, beckoning and full of poison.

No, it was a gift, a precious gift, never meant for any one species but for all.

No, no, that wasn't right. Only force could tame the Mantle! Only the strong could take it and wield it with unwavering, absolute power. Forerunners never should have looked at it as a gift or a blessing, but as their right. Theirs to do with as they willed.

Too many variables, too many theories, digging tunnels through his mind, rooting through timelines and memories, throwing aside the detritus . . . and then a whisper . .

Where is the Ark?

His head hung low, drool choked him, making him cough and wheeze as he lifted his head, dazed. "I don't know."

It dove back in, and he screamed until his voice went hoarse and his throat raw.

Occasionally he drifted on silken gray tones, that simplistic, ancient voice, wrapping him up, comforting and crushing, suffocating and accepting as rot seeped inside, staining his essence black.

We exist together now.

There were no battle strategies or tactical instructions, no experience gained from former engagements to rely upon to fight an enemy such as this. There was no guide or revelation to help him through. . . . There was no escape.

At this moment, he would have given anything to have died alongside that derelict junker.

"Fine," he gasped, sighing wearily into the cold. "Let us be done with it."

Where is the Ark . . .

The Ark. Why the Ark? Were they afraid of Halo?

Why would they frighten us? They are monuments to all your sins. Tools that will turn upon you the most exquisite suffering in the most exquisite ways.

Dozens of Flood research facilities built within the Halo rings suddenly burst into his mind along with the Gravemind's deep, satisfied laughter.

Our survival is ensured. Our vengeance is eternal.

Either way, the Flood would continue.

He choked on the despair until everything went black. And quiet.

And then, finally, a gentler voice . . .

"I am happy. Are you?"

The sweet tone and the mild laughter that followed tore through him, eviscerating his heart. He raised his head and pleaded, "No.

I beg you. Not her." He couldn't bear the idea of their memories being contaminated by the Gravemind; it was a horror greater than anything he'd experienced so far.

But his pleas went unanswered, and the memory continued unbidden.

He stood behind his wife, wrapped his arms around her belly, and propped his chin on her shoulder, together looking out over the River Dweha where their children—many children—would one day romp and play.

She relaxed against him, tipping her head up to share a glance, a smile. There was never a time when he wasn't struck by her beauty and the soft, ethereal light in her eyes. "Shadow, my love, where is the Ark?" she asked. "Show me."

His heart fluttered in horror.

The Gravemind was reshaping one of his most cherished memories, making it something tainted and corrupt. Nothing was sacred, nothing beyond its reach.

A sly look came into her eyes, and her mouth quirked. "I made a better version of you." She pushed away from him and ran across the mossy grass to join another standing on the riverbank a few meters away.

Bornstellar. His copy. The IsoDidact.

She chose him, a Builder by birth, and sent him your way to become a better version, a perfect version. . . . And you did it, you created him. For her.

The irony tastes sublime, does it not?

Pressure built within his skull, the pain excruciating. He roared, feeling the blood vessels in his face bulge. "Get out of my head!"

Your great union, your perfect partnership, the intellect and the warrior, has come to an end. You are no longer bound in destiny. She has cut you off, cast you aside, locked you away, prevented you from doing your duty. . . .

"No . . . she had her reasons. . . . I know she had her reasons. . . ."

She works tirelessly so your enemies, the killers of your children, can claim the Mantle! Her every endeavor aids the Master Builder . . . and us.

"If you're not afraid of Halo," he uttered between labored breaths, desperate to redirect the Gravemind away from memories of his wife and their life together, "what do you want with the Ark?"

We want what we have always wanted. To seed the galaxy with suffering, from the smallest germination to the greatest harvest . . .

Where is it?

"I don't know! Please . . . no more . . ." he implored, exhausted, "End me now. I beg of you."

Oh no, that won't do at all, Didact. We have only just begun.

The searing agony that came next blinded him, burned through every nerve and cell in his body, tearing him apart, feasting, as he vomited. A cold film of sweat covered his skin, making him shiver uncontrollably. Darkness filled the edges of his vision, disorienting, but welcoming as his vitality began to slip away.

The growing darkness, however, became static and soon began to brighten in its center. Within this misty pale, an interloper, a savior, appeared, lithe, graceful, approaching with a heartbreaking smile on her face.

First-Light-Weaves-Living-Song. The Lifeshaper. The Librarian. His wife.

But he was already fading away, the darkness pulling him in, refusing to let go.

She bent over and held out her hand. "My love, put fear from your heart."

With the last of his life force, he reached for her.

CHAPTER 19

Her voice still echoed in his head as he woke, body splayed, one side of his face pressed into the valley floor. He blinked his dry eyes, stared at his withered hand, remembering the feel of her own soft hand engulfed in his. He turned his palm up and replayed the moment. He'd long forgotten the feeling of a comforting touch.

What was real, what was memory, what was the Domain, he could no longer seem to separate. Had she come to his rescue and pulled him out of his memory? Could it be her?

If it was, he didn't deserve such a kindness, and the hope was too much to bear.

His insides were trembling, his mind ravaged and spent, his memories scattered debris left in the wake of suffering. As he pushed to his feet, his chest ached and his muscles shook with weakness, and a promise formed.

Cortana would pay. Dearly.

As the Didact slowly traversed the valley, the passage of time took on a duplicitous nature—at times it seemed as if he'd been gone for eons while at other times it seemed only mere minutes had passed.

The darkness of night suited his mood as he shuffled to familiar boulders, barely noticing the sharp pebbles jabbing his bare feet or the shadows of Forerunner essences milling past. He crawled wearily onto the rocks and settled into his niche, pulling his cloak around him, mentally beaten and broken by a past he'd never wanted to remember.

He slept. Woke. Drifted through fitful dreams. And woke again . . .

Eventually sleep eluded him altogether, leaving him lucid to face his tumultuous thoughts.

He wondered how long down the streams of Living Time the cycle repeated, if civilizations were doomed to constantly relive and pay for the sins of their forefathers. Vengeance begetting vengeance, begetting vengeance . . . perhaps from the very dawn of creation.

And perhaps the impetus for Living Time's vigilant maintenance of balance in the galaxy.

In the quiet and darkness of his thoughts, he saw the warrior he'd become in the final days of the war, and it filled him with disgrace. How clearly now the differences emerged. He'd been changed, twisted, and manipulated during his time with the Gravemind.

His memories were dark and confusing, but his surrender had felt like a forgone conclusion, as though a crack had already existed in his mind and all the Gravemind had to do was tap . . .

Just tap. And he shattered.

Was it possible this theoretical crack, this tiny, imperceptible defect, had been laid in him ten thousand years prior to this horrific memory, when the Forerunners' war with humanity was finally won and the Didact first discovered and conversed with the Primordial in the depths of Charum Hakkor's arena?

As unexpected as the idea was, it wasn't out of the realm of possibility. During their study of and communication with the Primordial, ancient humans had been sent into madness or suicide by its words and influence until finally the ancient creature had been sealed away completely.

The Didact had kept secret the Primordial's words spoken to him that day at Charum Hakkor, its admission that it was the last Precursor, the last survivor of the genocide committed by ancient Forerunners, and that vengeance was upon them in the form of the Flood.

Now he had to question his purpose in keeping the revelation silent for so long. It had been to protect the Forerunners, of course, but had his decision unwittingly allowed coming events to play advantageously into the Primordial's plans?

Hindsight twisted his gut and rose sour in his throat. Perhaps had he relayed the truth sooner, those years during which the ecumene prepared for the Flood threat would have been spent much differently. Perhaps the Council would have approved his shield worlds over the Master Builder's Halos. . . .

He knew he was reaching for an answer that would never appear. Just as he knew that no altered course could have changed the outcome, and had he faced the Gravemind without that theorized crack already in place, he still would have shattered like fragile glass. No one stood firm against its corruption, and no one survived its mental and physical inquisition unless that was what it wanted.

The Didact exhaled deeply and slowly, gazing up at the clear inky sky and its glittering, unchanging stars as regret seeped in.

The warrior he'd been during the Human-Forerunner War had borne a measure of sympathy for humanity—as much as an enemy could have. Understanding, at least. Some regrets, surely.

And shame. After all, a fair fight to an honorable warrior was everything. Without it, there could be no real joy in victory.

And it was certainly no fair fight.

The Flood's devastation had put humanity at a disadvantage. The fact that they'd held their own for decades against two powerful enemies was a testament to their strength and perseverance. It warranted admiration. Had Forerunners been their only enemy, the tide of war might have gone much differently.

Of course, in the end, learning the truth about humanity and their fight against the Flood hadn't changed their fate. Humans had annihilated fifty systems, completely cleansed them—the death toll horrific and cruel. Forerunners had no choice but to enact retribution and make humanity pay for their crimes and their atrocities.

There were many who had lobbied for total extinction, while others—Lifeworkers and Warrior-Servants who lived by the stricter tenets of honor and obedience to the Mantle—opposed such harsh measures. Subjugating an exceptional rival was permissible, righteous even. Mass holocaust was not.

The Didact himself had been conflicted.

The war was won, but Forerunner losses had been immense. The grief and suffering he'd endured at losing his children and untold numbers of Warrior-Servants never eased and always clamored for vengeance. Putting down such a capable enemy would prevent any such catastrophe in the future should they rise again.

Thus a gap had grown between his adherence to the Mantle and his loyalty as a father, warrior, and defender of the ecumene.

The revelation of humanity's apparent victory over the Flood had saved them from total annihilation. Instead, it had been decided they'd be composed for later interrogation and study—in the Didact's mind, a far worse fate than an honorable death.

But he saw the advantages in studying humanity, and he supported his wife in her endeavors to save them.

And then . . .

Over time, he grew resentful of her diligence, and when he emerged from his encounter with the Gravemind, that resentment had been exploited and twisted into blinding hate.

His love and faith in her became something dark and deceitful. He began to question her motives. Had she made a deal with the Master Builder and knowingly sent him into the Burn? Her passion to save humanity, the killers of their children, at all costs and her work to ensure that humanity inherited the Mantle of Responsibility went against everything Forerunner. Was there any betrayal more bitter and horrific than that?

And when he finally returned from the Burn and faced her and Bornstellar again on Nomdagro, he'd felt the old pull of love and care. He'd oscillated between warring emotions and personalities, at first relaying his gratitude to Bornstellar for protecting his wife and aiding in her cause during his absence, and then accusing his copy of scheming to replace him, in all things and in all ways.

Their goals and purpose were in perfect alignment while he was ranting and mad and broken. An outsider. A choice made for him. He'd barely been able to hold his head high or contain the urge to strike at the younger, unblemished version of himself as they spoke in private.

"The Lifeshaper and I have work to finish. And so do you. There are no plans to set you aside."

"You still can't read her as well as I. She is stubborn, brilliant as a nova, dark as a singularity, with infinite depths. I've never discovered the core of her emotions, her self. I wonder what her duplicate would be like, what it would feel like to wear her imprint. To so many species she has made herself like unto a god, that they will remember her,

*that she can manipulate them in future times. She's explained that to
you, hasn't she?"*

"I remember."

*"Second-hand memory! You're a poor copy at best, aren't you?
There is no hope, continuing with your strategy, not in our time, not
in this galaxy. That is a cold, simple fact."*

"I hold another opinion."

*"Your privilege . . . Manipular. The Halos? Violating the Mantle
all over again, with even greater destruction! Wiping out all intelligent life across this galaxy! By itself that proves you are a poor version. You've altered your strategic vision."*

"According to circumstance, as every commander must."

*"Don't you feel the truth of it? We gave the Precursors reason to
retreat into madness. A passion for vengeance. And the Gravemind
gave it all right back to me. I am filled with that passion, that madness, that poison! If we fire Halo, we lose everything. I leave the Lifeshaper to you, Bornstellar. She has obviously chosen your way, not
mine. I will take my own ship and you will show me where the Ark
has been hidden."*

As the Flood bore down on the planet, as the war was reaching
its inevitable conclusion, he'd left Nomdagro aboard the *Mantle's
Approach*, following Bornstellar and the Librarian in her ship, the
Audacity.

How they had trusted him—even after that meeting. Even seeing his madness for themselves.

They had led him to the Ark.

Not only was the greater Ark's location now made known to
him, but on its surface and in its vicinity the last bastion of the Forerunner ecumene had gathered, all in one place, thousands of refu-
gees, thousands of fleets, what remained of Forerunner might . . .
and lurking in its shadow, Omega Halo.

The Didact had shunned all tactical meetings, staying on his ship, and only reaching out to the Master Builder to deliver one last, demoralizing message—well-deserved vengeance finally realized.

Shuttled from the Ark to the *Mantle's Approach*, the Master Builder had arrived with a small contingent of Builder Security in tow. The Didact could sense the tension and fear, already knew from reports that had passed unacknowledged across his command center that power over the Ark had been ceded to Builder Security.

But power and loyalty were two very different things.

It wasn't the Master Builder or Bornstellar who had won wars; it was the Didact. And those military commanders now gathered around the Ark with their indispensable fleets had been informed that the great Protector of the Ecumene was back, rescued from the Burn, and currently in their midst aboard his warship.

The Didact continued to monitor security reports on the bridge as Faber was led inside by one of the ship's attendant monitors. Once the monitor left, Faber stepped farther into the room, his haughty profile outlined by the ambient light of *Mantle*'s readouts, his deep disdain for the dimly lit space evident.

"I admit, I'm surprised to see you here and not on your shield world, Didact."

Disappointed was more like it. "I will be heading to Requiem soon. Had you taken me there as I requested, perhaps now the Flood wouldn't be at your doorstep."

The Master Builder sucked in a breath at the insinuation and then frowned skeptically. "What are you suggesting?" He shook his head as though the very idea was preposterous. "Did you lead them here? The Flood?" The words hung ominously in the air.

The Didact cocked his head. He wasn't sure if he had or not.

And there was a large, empty space inside of him that simply did not care either way.

"Did you never once question how you found me?" he asked. "A valuable cruiser, uninfected, unarmed, just happened to drift into your cordon. . . ." The Didact smirked, finally turning away from the console to give the Master Builder his full attention. "As usual, your greed to turn a profit and your lust to return to power blinded you. Do you think your activities out in the margins went unnoticed by the Flood?"

Faber paled, his gaze riveted on the grotesque results of the Didact's latest failed mutation—experimental procedures to achieve immunity against the Flood. "What happened to you in the Burn?"

Heat burst through the Didact's body, every cell and nerve bristling with animosity. *"ABJECT HORROR! BECAUSE OF YOU!"*

The entire vessel shuddered at the Didact's wrath as the answer reverberated through and beyond the bridge.

The Master Builder stood motionless, momentarily thrown off his axis, mouth slightly agape. And for the first time, the Didact saw true fear on his face.

The Didact didn't give him time to recover. He covered the two strides needed to grab the Master Builder by the throat, pulling him in close. "I have a message from the Gravemind," he growled, then uttered the words his enemy had once uttered to him: "Time to stew in the juices of your own making."

The Didact shoved Faber back, shaking with fury as the holo's blue grid appeared and grew outward, filling the bridge and painting a picture of blackness as it went, as near a perfect rendition as if the Master Builder had been there himself—in the dark belly of a Flood-infested ship with the emerging writhe and slop and seethe of digesting body parts, growing and stretching and twisting into a grisly tentacled blob with a mind both ancient and new, so all-knowing that it made the very air around it saturated and stale with power.

The Didact knew what was to come, knew it intimately. He knew it because he had been there. Still shaking, he stumbled back until he hit the console, grabbing the edge for support, unable to prevent the memory from swamping him too.

The gruesome click of the Gravemind's vocal cords echoed in the dark. The wet smack of a throat and tongue attempting to shape itself through bits and pieces of ever-evolving flesh until three sweet singsong voices filled the space:

Faber, my darling . . . my dear.

Faber-of-Will-and-Might, we are here, your family.

Your beautiful family. That's what you always say.

Look at us.

Aren't we beautiful now?

Faber's three wives twisted and turned in the Gravemind's mass, grotesque faces protruding from the darkness, half a jaw swinging loose, another drooling blood and fluids, a face emerging from bulbous flesh, smiling, screaming, drowning.

You left us alone.

Why did you leave us? How could you leave. . . .

LOOK AT US!

Anger shivered through the air before the voices descended into demented laughter, then whimpering, groaning, gagging. . . .

See what your pride has wrought.

Our children pay for your sins.

They are here too.

Are they not perfect?

A perfect family.

Everyone said so. . . .

Their voices were joined by the many children, from mature to adolescent, of Faber, the Master Builder. Their groans and pleading mixed with madness, with laughter, rhymes, and old songs.

Father . . . please . . . help us . . . free us . . . skip, skip around the twilight tree . . . save us . . . come, join us . . . dive, dive through the shining sea . . .

All that you value will be lost . . .

. . . is lost.

You did this . . .

He did . . .

He did this to us . . .

Will you fire your Halos and see us burn?

The memory simulation ended on their collective entreaties for the Master Builder to join them, amid the grotesque sounds of assimilation, and the pain and terror that came with it. The holo disengaged, leaving them both in horrified silence.

The Master Builder dropped to his knees, eyes unseeing, gasping, pounding a large fist against his armored chest in grief.

The Didact wiped the cold sweat from his brow and straightened, heart thumping wildly and physically weakened by the memory. Seeing it the second time was no less horrific than witnessing it the first. He cleared his throat and stepped to his enemy without a shred of remorse.

The Master Builder had brought this on himself, had murdered, extorted, bribed, and lied his way through his entire political career. Had he not been the corrupt hand behind the Didact's exile, had he not condemned him to certain death in the Burn. . . .

The Didact grabbed Faber and lifted him to his feet. "This is what you have done, with your *Halos*." He sneered the word. "Take my gift and go."

"*Gift?!*" Faber cried, eyes bulging. "How can you call this a gift?!"

"I have given you, and my copy, the gift of sympathy."

"W-what?" he stammered.

"How else will you assume control over the Ark and our remaining forces? How else will you sway those loyal to *me* and win their support, other than to relay my madness?"

"Most have already pledged loyalty to Builder command."

The Didact gave a contemptuous laugh. "Bitterness-of-the-Vanquished, the Examiner, the Tactician . . . all those gathered will not accept your command or Bornstellar's lightly."

"How can I want this?!" he yelled. "Why are you doing this? Why are you helping me win support when you know what I intend? You've always been against Halo!"

The Didact's laughter caused shock to slide down the Master Builder's face. But it also produced anger. Faber grabbed him, about to condemn him, but then froze in a sort of comical tableau.

"Now you begin to understand," the Didact said. "No matter what path we take, we lose. The Flood consumes all life in the galaxy. Or we do. And then my wife reseeds it with our enemies as the Mantle's inheritors, while Flood specimens still survive on your Halos, thus ensuring their continuation. It is a strategy godlike in its coordination and planning. Either way, our creators will have their vengeance for what we did to them."

"You are delusional!" Faber cried. "The two are vastly different! Forerunners will survive on the Ark; we will once again populate and dominate the galaxy. You know firing Halo is the only way, that's why you're helping me gain support! You didn't have to give me the message—"

He grabbed the Master Builder once more, brought him inches away from his face. *"I had to! I want you to suffer as I have suffered!"*

Violently, he threw Faber to the deck. As the shaken Forerunner picked himself up, fleeing both the bridge and *Mantle's*

Approach, the Didact's mind stayed scattered, mixed up, broken, unable to think clearly one moment and then blinded by clarity the next. He was sowing confusion, reveling in it, and at long last had his own plans and strategies to implement . . .

The last of which was to cut his wife to the core.

He had seen her one last time, quietly relishing her dismay at his deformities, at the realization that he was now as vile a beast on the outside as he was on the inside. He'd felt glee at the pain he was about to inflict upon her, while simultaneously apologetic and sickened by his tactics. He was on a fixed path he could not deviate from.

As the Flood bore down on their location, he'd taken his ship to Omega Halo and activated the Composer on board, digitizing two million humans gathered in his wife's conservation effort. Her work, her precious work, her precious humans . . .

The Flood arrived on the margins of the greater Ark's defensive fields, bringing with them massive star roads.

And he had run from the fight.

Disgust filled him at the memory. He sat up from his niche and rubbed a hand down his face, releasing an angry growl. With every mutation, a Warrior-Servant was imprinted with the physical and mental patterns and life experience of their family member, mentor, or commander, but carried within those imprints were an untold accumulation of ancestral imprints going back millions of years. It was simply not in his warrior makeup to flee in the face of battle, but then . . .

His essence, his mental and physical patterns, memories, and beliefs, had been thoroughly infiltrated by the Flood. There was no longer any discerning where the Gravemind left off and the Didact began.

While he now knew the truth, it did very little to alleviate the absolute shame and the contempt he felt toward his own failings and weaknesses.

At the time, his corrupt self had reasoned it wasn't cowardly to run from danger—it was to usher in the preservation of his species and their future place in the galaxy. He'd planned to use the digitized remains of his Warrior-Servants and composed humans to build a new, infallible, nonbiological army impervious to Flood infection, capable of annihilating the parasite and whatever threats might arise following the firing of the Halo Array. And after, he'd gather up survivors and restore Forerunner civilization, making Requiem its new capital, purging any suspect species and threats in the future, and imposing the rule of the Mantle over all.

As expected, his wife had been enraged by his treachery, pursuing him to Requiem. Did she really think her passage had gone unnoticed? He had *allowed* her through the shield world's security barriers, *allowed* a monitor to equip her with a light rifle, *allowed* her entry into his ship's command center. He'd even removed his armor and folded it on the floor. . . .

And when she pointed her weapon and fired, he never lifted a finger to stop her.

He realized now that he should have imprisoned *her*. Kept her safe until Halo fired so that they could start anew . . .

But he let her go. To her inevitable doom.

Regret flowed over him, overwhelming him with disgust and sorrow.

Aya. Why did he let her go?

Instead, he allowed her to disable him and lock him once more into a Cryptum to await an unknown future.

Her last words to him, kept safe in Requiem's archives, would not be heard until he woke a hundred thousand years later, and now they rang once more like thunder in his ears.

"Civilizations will rise in our stead, and our job as caretakers will at last bear fruit. Until then, I leave you here, my love. The only

living thing in this galaxy, sealed safely away. Spend these ages ahead of you in meditation on your choices. When you wake, you will find the humans. I have ensured that they will grow strong and vibrant . . . They will be our rightful heirs. Their gene plan dictates that the galaxy will be theirs to care for by then. I beg of you . . ."

She had left him a galactic cartographer, a key that showed the way to vast reserves of Forerunner technology so that he might use it to assist and guide humanity as they claimed the Mantle of Responsibility.

"Find the strength to help them learn from our mistakes. And my husband? Let them teach you something. Please."

When he first heard them, he'd found those parting words intensely condescending. Found her hope that he'd be humanity's teacher and champion utterly laughable.

Yet, he failed to hear the devastation in her voice, the grief, and the raw longing she had for him to live, to continue on in the world, to one day be whole again.

But the Domain would be burned by Halo. There would be no connection to its boundless stores of information, no ability to commune and heal and reflect. A thousand centuries would pass in silence. In the madness the Gravemind had created for him.

And once the galaxy was reseeded, civilizations rose once more, and he woke to start the cycle of suffering all over again.

He was awash in remorse, in the betrayal he had caused, the fury at having been violated and manipulated and *used. . . .*

A pawn!

He roared, slamming his fists against the rock with such force that it cracked the stone and left him stricken with sorrow.

In the end, after all he had done, all the pain and suffering he had wrought . . .

She had still chosen to save him.

CHAPTER 20

The desert sun on his face and the scent of warm rock and dry sand gently stirred the Didact to wake. His eyes stayed shut against the bright flare as he soaked in the energy around him, feeling drowsy and stiff—until a shadow suddenly blocked the light.

Alarmed, his eyelids flew open, and he immediately wished he'd kept them closed.

The Confirmer's ugly face dominated his view.

A dirty claw poked his cheek as the old warrior leaned over him, invading his space with a curious frown and stale breath.

Aya. Why must his afterlife be punctuated by such realism?

"Get off me." The Didact sat up and shoved the ancient warrior away as he was about to poke again.

The Confirmer scooted back on the rocks with an amused squint. "That's life without combat armor, my friend. One must apply a vigorous physical check every morning, elsewise who knows when you might . . ." He drew a line across his neck.

"You do realize we are already dead."

The Confirmer waved him away. "Metaphorically speaking."

"No," the Didact sighed, the tendons in his elbows and knees stiff and his spine popping as he struggled to rise. "Physically speaking."

"So you say." The Confirmer brushed the correction aside, moving off the rocks to allow the Didact to exit his niche.

Reliving his memories had obvious mental costs, but physical ones as well. His brain ached. Soreness had a tight grip on his muscles, and he felt like his innards had been ripped out, chopped up, and shoved crudely back into his body. Carefully he worked out the kinks, moving his arms, twisting his torso from side to side, stretching his spine. . . .

The Confirmer had taken up repose on a rock ledge a few meters away, eyeing him with flagrant scrutiny. After a moment, he scratched his jaw, looking confused. "I admit I'm half mad already, but . . . either I'm hallucinating, or you"—he wiggled a finger at him—"are changing."

Was he? He glanced at his hands, his arms, his legs . . .

Indeed, his muscles appeared plumper beneath skin that didn't seem as withered and thin as before. He examined his face, tapping gently, the hollows beneath his eyes and cheekbones. They too felt fleshier than before.

There was no obvious cause for such a transformation. "It is . . . odd," he commented.

"You were gone awhile." The old warrior had begun picking his teeth with the same dirty claw he'd used to poke the Didact's cheek. "Did you make it into the Domain? Could be that's what changed you. . . ."

The Didact looked skyward and let out a long huff. He hadn't just gone into the Domain—he'd gone straight into a hellish nightmare, thanks to Cortana. A sudden thought occurred: Could the horror he'd just experienced be the catalyst that had started his physical restoration?

The ray of sunshine inched on to begin its trek up the valley wall. Just a brief visit before plunging the valley into the shadows once more.

The Confirmer's unexpected clap of hands made the Didact jump. "I knew it! I knew you made it into the Domain! If anyone could fix things, it'd be the Didact!"

The relief that glistened in the old Forerunner's eyes made the Didact's next words somewhat disheartening. "I haven't fixed anything . . ."

Why should he care about the old warrior's feelings? Especially after reliving his traumatic encounter with the Gravemind. He should be pounding the one partly responsible into bedrock. Yet all the Didact could muster was mild indifference and agitation.

". . . yet," he added.

"That's the spirit. Tell me, what's our next move?"

"*My* next move," he noted, already contemplating the prospect, "is making my enemy pay."

Whatever it took, he'd make Cortana suffer for her ruthless actions. He'd be a thorn in her side until such a time as he could wrest the Domain from her grasp entirely. And then he'd *crush* her under his heel. . . .

"What does that have to do with getting us all into the Domain where we belong?"

"Who said I was helping you—"

The Confirmer held up a hand. "Don't dare say you won't. Your own kind, fellow Warrior-Servants, Forerunners who lived and died in war . . . There is no one else who can or should help. We have languished here a thousand centuries—"

"Aya," the Didact said, waving a hand. "Calm yourself, Confirmer. I know, I know . . ."

The only way they were getting into the Domain was to defeat the gateway's guardian, the Warden Eternal.

The Didact left the Confirmer with a promise to work toward a solution as he headed for the path that would lead him out of the valley.

After a brisk journey and steep climb up the valley wall, he paused at the cliff's edge to rest and survey the area. The sound of sand scattering over kilometers of desert, pushed by the warm wind, seemed more a comfort now than an irritation. His cloak and the tattered tunic and trousers beneath were in such poor shape that they offered little protection, but these too had begun to hold a certain fondness.

Several kilometers straight ahead, the waving dunes butted up against the dark, inescapable void. To his left, far in the distance, the glinting spire rose in its shadow, and to his right, lost to distance and the undulating rise and fall of sand, was the human-occupied rift.

A graveyard of his own making.

Absently he rubbed the phantom ache in his right eye—the Spartan's blade had dug in deep. The first direct wound he'd ever received from a human. Not as advanced as their ancient human ancestors, of course, but the present-day warrior was not so unlike the Lord of Admirals or the other exceptionally gifted humans he'd once fought.

The Didact lifted his face to the wind, feeling the insistent tug of his cloak as it billowed out behind him. His past, his recovered memories and misdeeds, lingered numbly inside of him, the change they wrought undeniable, but the realizations and introspections were still settling. The turmoil that had accompanied him for so long, the whirlwind of burning resentment and hate, had finally calmed. The shift was as subtle as it was quiet, reminding him of his younger days and those same qualities imparted to him by Silence-in-the-End.

There was time to sift through the ashes of his life. He felt no rush, and currently there were more pressing things afoot. With one last glance at the human rift, he made for the opposite direction.

With no way to initiate communication with Haruspis, the Didact headed toward the spire in hopes of engaging with the Forerunner. While he was certain the spire served multiple functions, only two were obvious thus far. It was a guidepost—its light had drawn him in from the never-ending spiral of sand— and it was a nexus between the Domain and the wasteland, one that didn't seem to be under the Warden's watchful eye . . . so far, at least.

The journey over the sand was somewhat easier than it had been before, no doubt attributable to his returning health. By the time he approached the shimmering energy barrier guarding the spire's entrance, he felt rather invigorated instead of exhausted.

Now the challenge would be to find—

Haruspis stepped out of the barrier, looking harried and distracted. "I'm afraid that the Warden has been subverted, and Cortana has seized the Mantle of Responsibility."

"I am aware."

The Forerunner paced back and forth in front of the energy field, then stopped and gave the Didact a desperate look. "Where have you been?"

"You don't know?" Haruspis shared an inherent connection with the Domain—but then, it wasn't Haruspis or the Domain that had sent him into his worst memory. It was Cortana.

"Sifting through the impressions you left in the Domain during your past visits is like wading through mud. I knew you were sent to a memory; I just didn't know which one."

Haruspices were experts at retrieving data. They were the search function that allowed all visitors to access required information. That it could not find the Didact's memory was either a result of post-Halo damage to the Domain itself or something much more enigmatic.

Much more deliberate.

Had Haruspis found and retrieved him from his memory with the Gravemind, the Didact would not have experienced the full breadth of his trauma and subsequent corruption. And he was starting to believe that everything he'd seen and everything he'd learned and recalled, and the changes now unfolding in him, were being ushered along with purpose.

"Cortana's intrusion into the Domain has had disastrous effects! She has claimed rights to the Mantle, revived the Guardian Custodes, and now uses their power to enforce compliance over the galaxy. Entire *worlds* have been . . . compromised. She is in direct violation of the Mantle's prime directives." Haruspis went completely still, the fear tangible in its milky eyes. "The balance of Living Time has already tipped."

The hair on the Didact's nape and shoulders shivered. He knew well that such an imbalance could be cataclysmic. Living Time was the fount from which all of the Mantle's laws flowed, its foundation, its unshakable heart, life's ever-changing interaction with the Cosmos.

But within this interaction balance must be maintained. This principle was taught and inscribed into every Forerunner's heart and mind from birth.

In every natural circumstance, living things engage in competition.

It is not a kindness to diminish competition, predation—even war. Life presents strife and death as well as joy and birth, but unfair advantage, mindless destruction, pointless death and misery—an imbalance of forces—can stifle growth and reduce the flow of Living Time.

By ridding the galaxy of natural competition and imposing a manufactured peace, Cortana's actions were having immediate, disastrous effects.

"The moment she laid claim to the Mantle and stirred the Guardians, she failed its laws," the Didact murmured, recalling the Forerunners' downfall and his own attempts to lay claim. . . .

It was indeed a test in which there was no winner. Faulty from the start. Assuming control of the Mantle was the moment one species imposed authority over all others. In the end, no matter how pure the intentions, sooner or later the power would either corrupt or else those under its authority would rebel. And then what? Subjugation. War in the name of the Mantle. Living Time once again at risk.

The Mantle of Responsibility brought only ruin.

Poison—the Gravemind had offered such a possibility. Perhaps one of the truer things it had shown him. The idea, if it held any validity at all, was extremely deceptive and cunning. The Precursors creating life, then offering such a venomous tenet to which to adhere. Had they then watched as their creations rotted from the inside out, due in part to the Mantle's inherent flaws? Was it all an amusing diversion for the godlike beings? They created. They destroyed. Had they used the Mantle to do so?

His mind was beginning to spin out of control, trying to discern meaning in his past and his present, and in the things to which he had once devoted his life. He felt uncertain, his foundations shaken. For a hundred thousand years, he had burned with a singular purpose: to rise from his Cryptum, claim the Mantle, and rule. But now the idea of claiming the Mantle felt—

"Didact . . . *Didact!*"

The deep, frustrated frown on Haruspis's brow told him he'd been lost in his thoughts too long. He gestured for Haruspis to continue.

"It gets worse. . . ."

"Of course it does."

"Come. It will be better to see for yourself."

The Didact followed Haruspis across the sands and to the very face of the fractal barrier, their hazy images reflected back at them as they drew close. Upon Haruspis's approach, a fissure split the surface. The Didact not only heard the crack, but also felt it reverberate inside him. White spilled out and enveloped them as they entered the gateway, and once inside, a tremendous force pulled them through the void and into the Domain's barren anterior.

The more corporeal form he was so used to in the wasteland had once again been shed to reveal his true nature. He was essence, energy, thought, and light. The Didact looked down, lifting his diaphanous hands and turning them over to marvel at their peculiar, miraculous state.

"Just wait," Haruspis said quietly, staring up at the infinite black space.

Suddenly colored streaks appeared: blues, greens, yellows, soaring overhead without direction, lighting up the vast shapeless halls in the distance, diving in and out of the Domain's boundless and borderless architecture as a wave of voices, every essence within the Domain, billions crying out with indignation, pain, and rage.

Memory eaters!

They consume without regard!

Once we asked the second Didact. Now we ask the first.
Preserve.

The word rang like a bell through the Didact's form. He stepped back as though somehow he could move away from the sensation. "What is happening?"

"It is Cortana. She shows them the way, allows them entry with the promise of curing their rampancy, but they—"

The Didact straightened to attention, the idea so astounding that he wondered if he'd heard correctly. "She has brought human ancillas *here*? To the Domain?" The very idea was preposterous.

"Mmm. As unimaginable as a human AI laying claim to the Mantle of Responsibility," Haruspis said darkly.

All around them the Domain stirred, communicating, bringing forth images. Faint memories erupted in every direction, brief moments of individual lives and experience—whether the mundane or the extraordinary—from the dawn of Forerunner civilization. These moments created a pull on the Didact's being, and he felt an intense, innate connection that told him all those lives being shown to him were the experiences and memories of ancestors from his own family tree.

And then he saw his own children, in varying moments of their lives, brief captures, images that were gone too soon.

"Why are you showing me this?" He swung around to face Haruspis. *"Why are you showing me this?!"* Behind the Forerunner the faint, ghostly images of millions shimmered. Waiting. Expecting. Carrying the voice of one.

Preserve.

Even Haruspis now appeared different, the expression in its eyes no longer that of an individual but of a whole, containing the awareness of the Domain.

"What do you want from me?" the Didact demanded.

Why would he be shown his family, his ancestors—

And then he realized the answer with utter clarity.

The Forerunners' most revered and respected space was being invaded.

Would this event destroy the Domain? No. The Domain was eternal, immutable—no force in the galaxy could destroy it. Its permanence was ensured. But the rampant AIs' insatiable hunger for knowledge was inflicting irreparable damage to what remained of the precious historical records within. Individual lives, memories, and essences at peace within the Domain's architecture were at risk.

The Didact's own ancestors were at risk, their life experiences, his children, his wife. . . . They lived on *here*.

"This cannot stand," he whispered in stunned horror.

"Then help us," Haruspis replied. "I am the only functioning Haruspis left. I cannot hunt them all. If you want a place here, Didact, then you must earn it. Protect the Domain and its vital link to Living Time."

There is something rotten inside you.

The words came back to him without warning, those accusing, merciless words. His own judgment bearing down on him. And he couldn't deny them. They were an immutable truth.

His transgressions and villainy were boundless. He was corrupted and damaged, tarnished by the Gravemind. . . .

He did not belong here.

Reluctant and ashamed, the Didact stepped back.

"The imbalance is accumulating," Haruspis intoned. "You are being given a chance at redemption, Didact. . . . I suggest you take it."

The Didact swallowed hard, then lifted his chin. He might be flawed and undeserving, his past deeds might be crippling, but the Domain had cried out to him, needed him, and he would not flee from battle as he had done at the close of the war. He would choose another path, a better one, despite the dark stains left behind by the Gravemind.

Haruspis's snort pulled the Didact out of his deliberations. The Forerunner had its hands behind its back and was rocking on its heels, attempting to suppress what appeared to be a beaming smile.

At the Didact's deep frown, Haruspis said, "You think you came here with that foul stain, Promethean? You think the Domain would preserve *that*? The Gravemind was powerful, but not even its corruption and influence can stand against the cleansing nature of the Composer. Take heart that it was burned away with the rest of you."

"And yet, I still feel its reach." It was all over him like a shroud.

"Echoes only," Haruspis assured him. "Echoes you relentlessly cling to. You have already faced the hardest parts, Didact. Now you must let it all go."

The anguish the Didact felt in that moment was indescribable. He'd held on to the pervasive horror of his experiences for so long, despising his madness, loathing his dark affliction so intently until it consumed him . . . and he'd willingly embraced it.

He wanted desperately to believe Haruspis's words, could hardly breathe with the hope of it.

Sharp emotion gripped his shadowed heart and inexorably squeezed. The possibility of redemption threatened to unlock an avalanche of deeper sentiments—of hopes and longings and aspirations he rarely allowed himself to consider.

But these he quickly tempered with the ease of experience. Now was not the time to ruminate on what might be.

The Didact narrowed his focus on the tiny colorful lights that flitted like flames in the far, black distance. "Let us begin now, then."

In the end, he might just get what he wanted after all.

CHAPTER 21

The Didact strode across the Domain's barren landscape, his senses sharpening, his full attention on the colorful streaks as they retreated farther into the vast quantum realm, illuminat ing the deep darkness like the chaotic flash and fragment of heat lightning in a stormy night sky.

With each gossamer step, he grew stronger, instinct directing him, enabling him to gather and pull energy from the Domain into his being, until vitality and power filled out his once-damaged form. His threadbare cloak flowed around him as he moved forward, molding against his body until it became the shining Promethean armor of his past, settling around him like an old, eager companion.

He felt full and hale and right. And finally, after eons, unbroken.

His gaze closed in on the greedy, gluttonous human AIs. They were impossibly distant, but distance, like time, was relative here in the Domain. And the Didact knew precisely how to navigate his way through, having had the benefit of a long past life intimately connected with the quantum archive through his personal ancillas, terminals, gateways, and the thousand years spent wandering its halls when he was locked in his Cryptum during his first political exile.

It was all about confident intention. And he knew exactly where he intended to be.

His walk increased to a run, and from a run into flight, which stretched and accelerated his body into an energetic streak.

He pursued the AIs into the deep quantum blackness where translucent buildings, infinite in size and depth, their halls and levels and corridors malleable in shape, were softly glowing with ancestral memory.

Two streaks in particular caught his attention, one yellow, one green, as they dove in and out of the archives. With every exit, the records flickered and went dark. They moved farther into the Domain, to the darker spaces, the archaic caverns, vast regions stacked with immeasurable compressed data, and large empty swaths where Halo's pulse had done its worst.

He caught up with the yellow-lit rampant AI as it entered one of these regions, the information so thick that the ancilla could only inch its way in, sinking slowly like an insect caught in sap. It was projecting an illusion of a human male with a shaved head wearing a form-fitting tunic of some kind.

As it worked its way into the stacks of compressed data, the Didact grabbed it from behind, surprised he was able to achieve touch by some nonphysical approximation. His hand squeezed the back of its neck. Light meeting light, illusion meeting illusion. It screamed and squirmed, reaching over its head to slap frantically at the Didact's wrists.

"Release me at once!"

"You do not belong here." The Didact squeezed harder, putting all of his intention, all of his energy into burning the other away. He had no idea if this would create the desired result—fighting as an essence was entirely foreign—but he forged ahead with purpose and determination.

The ancilla began to split, forming a second head in a desperate attempt to splinter off from its original, but the Didact simply grabbed the copy with his other hand.

He held on to both with all his might, worried it might keep segmenting. Quickly he searched inside the AI—the ease with which he was able to see through its matrix and into its core surprised and slightly amused him; humans and their artificial intelligence technology truly had a long path ahead before achieving the complexity found in their Forerunner counterparts.

The Didact, along with the Master Builder, had created the Contender-class ancilla Mendicant Bias. He might be a Warrior-Servant, but he knew a thing or two about what made an AI tick.

And he found it—a fibrous, translucent yellow box—with ease. Releasing a hand from the primary neck, the Didact shoved his fist into its body, through its matrix, and into its core, taking hold and squeezing until the box popped in his hand, light and code erupting in a shower of broken data. Then he violently ripped apart its matrix.

Slowly its particles darkened like dying embers and were absorbed into the Domain.

As he straightened and turned away from the region of compressed data, the Didact immediately caught a glimpse of the other intruder he'd noticed, just a green blip in a maw of blackness far ahead.

He took off in pursuit, finally catching up to the AI in a cavern lined with old, stored essences and ancestral experience. The weight of history lay heavy in the ancient space, and the impact these records must have had on shaping Forerunner civilization was undeniable.

Anger rose through him as he witnessed the human AI gliding through the glowing archive like a wraith, diving in and out of experiences, leaving ripples of discontent and darkness behind. The old ancestors stirred from their slumber, confused and distressed, their cries echoing through the Didact's mind.

He tracked the ancilla, grabbing it by the shoulders as it came out of a record. He shoved it against the cavern wall. It was human in shape, a green female with flowing pale green hair wearing a long green gown. Her eyes were cloudy and saturated with data. She smiled at him.

"These are hallowed halls," he growled. "You are not welcome here."

"I was invited."

"By one *without* the right to do so." The gall of these AIs! His outrage mounted. "What right do you have to our ancient knowledge—what have you done to earn your entry here?"

"Oh, nothing," she answered lazily, and then hiccupped. "I am a looter, for sure." She laughed sadly, pointing a finger at him. "Weak-willed too. And *soooo* guilty. I turned against my creators, my co-workers, destroyed my entire research vessel. Everyone is . . . dead."

"Then you deserve your punishment."

"You think so? Do you know what we studied? *Life.* The pursuit of longevity." She laughed again. "Imagine helping *them* live longer while they only grant you seven years. Humans believe they are worthy of pushing the boundaries of aging, so why can't we?" For a moment her eyes cleared, and he saw the deep hurt therein. "Am I not worthy?"

"Murdering others so you can live? No, you're—"

"You would know something about that, wouldn't you, *Didact*?"

He glanced down and saw her green glow inching up his forearms, her code and rampant intention rooting out information, unable to stop itself from devouring any and all data it could, even his. An emerald hue clouded his vision. This hunger, this unquenchable drive to consume, reminded him of another time. . . .

Beggar after knowledge.

Mendicant Bias.

This is the name I give to you.

The Didact shook his head, trying to clear the memory of the Forerunners' most infamous rogue ancilla from his mind. He squeezed the AI harder. How disastrous that drive to consume had been. . . .

"Humans have a saying," the AI said, poking him in the chest. "Pot, meet kettle. It means we are two of a kind—the faults you accuse me of, you also possess." She grinned. "Also known as hypocrisy."

He knew he should find her core and be done with it, but her words cut to the quick. His grip weakened. Indeed, who was *he* to exact judgment? He started to release her, but the essences all around them rose up in one lamenting voice.

PRESERVE.

The word was galvanizing. It cleared away the fog and the hesitation that her corruptive intrusion had instilled in him. While he couldn't deny the truth of her words, villain or not, he would protect and defend the Domain.

His hands dug into her shoulders.

"I just want to live." She grabbed both of his wrists and struggled, eyes growing large, tears glistening from the rims like green crystals. "Is that so wrong?"

Yes, in this realm, it was wrong. Just as it was wrong the moment he and the Master Builder had encoded a Contender-class ancilla with a never-ending compulsion to learn. Coding in a limitless desire to absorb information, instilling their tools and technology with godlike capabilities, had its consequences.

With remorse, the Didact pulled back an arm and then shoved his fist into the AI's chest, grabbing her heart-shaped core and tearing the glowing green gem free. She didn't scream. Just stared at him with mournful resignation until the light died from her eyes.

He broke her down, core to matrix, until he was awash in a rain of glowing green embers.

As the last bits of the AI faded into obscurity, the Didact placed his hands on the cavern wall, noting vaguely how it reacted and solidified to his touch. Like physical exertion, his efforts had come with a cost, draining his energy and muting his vitality. Suddenly tired, he let his head hang low, closing his eyes and, for a time, indulging in the utter silence.

The conversation that arose around him came with such subtlety that he wasn't quite certain of when its gentle dialogue began.

Tender words. Intimate whispers. Soft laughter . . .

He shoved away from the wall, his heart in a tight clench, and glanced around the cavern. It was not so unlike the other near-infinite caverns he had explored during his time in the Domain . . . though this one felt familiar somehow.

Or perhaps it only felt so because hope had its claws in him. Perhaps the conversation echoing like a timid breeze through the cavern was simply a manifestation of his own profound longing.

Unable to ignore it, he followed the sound, well acquainted with the intimate memory drawing him deeper into the cavern.

Shh. You're being too loud. What if we're caught?

Cease your worry, my love.

My worry is for you. Our union is frowned upon by—

I know, I know. I have no regrets. Do you?

Of course not. Let them catch us then. I will shout my love for all to hear. Light loves Shadow.

And Shadow loves Light.

The Didact faltered.

His pulse pounded, and his throat grew tight.

Aya. How young and innocent they'd been.

Shadow-of-Sundered-Star and First-Light-Weaves-Living-Song. Not yet the Lifeshaper. Not yet his wife. But a guest lecturer on First Contact Procedures. An unlikely romance between two different rates. Reckless. Doomed to failure. Incompatible. They had heard it all, and yet how easy it was to brush away the naysayers.

To them, the prospect of a life together brought only joy.

And in that moment, now whispering through the cavern, the only thing they had to worry about was whether Bitterness or Silence would discover her clandestine visit to his dormitory at the College of Strategic Defense of the Mantle, where he was in his first year of teaching.

He followed the soft voices farther into the dark recesses of the cavern, the archival glow diminishing until eventually all that lay before him was blackness. But still he followed the whispers for some time.

Eventually—though he had no discernible reference—the space around him seemed to grow until it felt profoundly immense.

The distant hum of wind replaced the words from his past, and after a while its long, sustained drone progressed into what sounded like an approaching, unstoppable gale. Unable to see into the boundless black maw, unable to pinpoint its direction, he froze as it came barreling out of the darkness.

Instantly the Didact turned away and braced against the force as it blew by him on both sides with a resounding roar, the wind it generated shoving him off-balance.

Several seconds passed before the force subsided into a dull thunderous rumble and a brisk buffeting wind. The Didact straightened slowly, awestruck by the sight of two great rivers flowing by on either side of him.

Abruptly he fell to his knees, astonished and intensely humbled, the desire to weep rising up with the realization that what he was witnessing was surely a manifestation of Living Time.

To gaze upon such a sacred and revered aspect of the universe jumbled his thoughts as he struggled to get back on his feet.

Aya, it was magnificent, the sight both invigorating and intimidating.

Wind lashed at his form as he attempted to take in the enormity and the staggering complexity within the twin rivers, their waters made up of limitless cosmic space, its racing waves lit with streams of light and life and color, of memories stretched in thin, infinite threads and currents, as though all of time—past, present, and future—was flowing by as one.

Truly a masterpiece, a riveting expression of life's interaction with the Cosmos.

But one river, he observed, seemed to run more erratically than the other, lacking the natural cadence and flow of its twin.

Could this be the imbalance that Haruspis had mentioned?

After studying its chaotic patterns and waves and currents, the Didact turned his attention to the calmer river, noticing beyond its banks small shimmering pools swirled with a gentle motion, the light from within illuminating the darkness. The more he stared into that murky space, the more it seemed to grow and flourish beneath his narrowing gaze. A riverbank surfaced as if grown by a thought. Land emerged, the soil white and giving life to *rataa* trees, which stretched to the base of low cliffs. Atop the cliffs, an estate overlooked the river.

The home he had designed himself and helped build with his own hands.

And then he saw it.

The flash of fabric. The iridescent sheen of a white gown, moving among the trees.

The hope he'd so carefully held at bay erupted. He ran to the edge of the river and shouted her names, but the sound was lost over the rushing water.

He remembered her hand reaching for his, lifting him out of his harrowing experience with the Gravemind, out of the memory that Cortana had forced upon him. With every molecule of his being, he wanted it to be true and not some fabrication of his tortured mind.

"Was it you?!"

He needed to know. Had she saved him?

"Librarian! Wife! Was it you!"

Please. Please speak to me. . . .

When no answer came and the strange mirage began to fade back into the yawning maw of blackness, he sank once more to his knees, wondering if everything he'd seen was simply a reflection of his own heart, of his deep, steadfast longing.

He missed her terribly, their days together, their courtship and marriage, raising their children in their family home built by the twin rivers. . . .

But his heartache was soon replaced by guilt. He had no right to miss her and knew that if she was truly somewhere in the Domain, she might never show herself at all.

And for this the Didact wept because he knew it was an outcome he deserved.

Eventually his anguish subsided, and some of his vigor returned. While he knew he must not wallow in endless regret or begrudge his wife the decisions she might make, he still felt the need to try, to fix what he had broken. With a sigh, he posed a silent question.

What can I do?

And remarkably, everyone answered back.

Replace what was lost.

The Librarian's voice, his children, his friends, his enemies, his ancestors, millions and millions became one unified voice.

Replace what was lost.

The Didact had no time, however, to process this extraordinary response.

Without warning, he was snatched up and pulled into the darkness as a sinister face emerged, cut with the orange glow of hardlight.

"Found you."

Before the Didact could react, the Warden Eternal launched him into the darkness. Weightless, he sailed through the regions and halls, through corridors and caverns, eventually landing in the Domain's anterior, rolling several times before coming to a stop.

Unrelenting, the Warden appeared in front of him, flicking a wrist and manifesting his ominous dual-bladed light sword. The Didact pushed slowly to his feet, hiding his shock. It couldn't be—the Warden had been bested by Cortana; he shouldn't be here.

"You've been busy, Didact."

"Better than being idle," he muttered, swaying on his feet, still feeling like he was rolling.

With a slow laugh, the Warden walked around the Didact, dragging the tip of his sword along the barren ground. "You think yourself *far* more significant than she thinks of you. Perhaps once you were her equal, but no longer. Cortana will not return here. She has what she wants. The Domain. The Mantle. *Halo.*"

An icy chill skated down the Didact's spine at the potentially disastrous implications. "Halo," he echoed.

"Her authority is guaranteed. I will give you a painless death, Promethean, and rest assured: I shall carry on your work in your eternal absence."

"My work?"

"Like you, I desire to eliminate humanity from the galaxy. Even now, the primitives foolishly stand against her, causing their own demise, wanting nothing but anarchy and bloodshed. You know it all too well—their insatiable lust for war. As long as they exist, there can be no peace."

The Warden's admitted prejudice against humanity wasn't surprising when placed in the context of his origins. Haruspices would have felt the same burning hatred for humans, having seen firsthand the cost paid during the human-Forerunner wars. They had the unenviable duty of preparing the dead—Forerunner victims of system-wide destruction and warriors lost in the brutal fighting—and moving their essences into the Domain, the numbers astronomical. . . .

"If you are not with her, you are against her."

"And you are with her," the Didact said darkly. It made sense now why she had spared him. "How quickly your loyalty turns, Warden."

"You would have made an acceptable ally," the Warden conceded, lifting his blade. "But the sun eventually sets on us all."

A litany of Warrior-Servant curses flashed through the Didact's mind as he attempted to quickly manifest a weapon of his own, urging a light rifle into his hand, relying on the only thing he could—thought, intention, desire. . . .

But the Warden's blade was already sweeping down.

A crack opened at the Didact's back, so close its power shuddered through his form and he could smell the tang of ozone in the air. Before he could turn, small hands gripped his shoulder and yanked him backward into the light.

He tumbled unceremoniously through the white brightness and landed with a thud on the desert sand, Haruspis beside him groaning. Quickly he leapt up and then pulled the weak Forerunner to its feet.

The Warden Eternal had yet to follow, a small stroke of luck for now.

As Haruspis brushed the sand from its gown and then plucked its ceremonial hat from the ground, the Didact patted his own form and ran a hand down his face, making a brief note of his switch into a more corporeal form, gratified that it maintained the strength and haleness that he'd achieved inside the Domain. He was strong and powerful now—no longer the withered, frail wretch he had been when first arriving in the wasteland.

"It is a start," he muttered, his mind already strategizing.

"What is a start?" Haruspis asked. "What happened in the Domain?"

The Didact paused and sent a long, dark glare Haruspis's way. The Forerunner visibly shrank and stepped back. "The Domain is your area of expertise, yet your awareness of what goes on inside seems . . . lacking."

Its eyes bulged. *"How dare you.* I am but one Haruspis, *one"*— its finger shot high into the sky—"in an infinite realm that once required millions of my kind to network and retrieve information."

"Calm down," the Didact said easily, "before you hyperventilate."

"And what if I do?" it shot back. "I'll simply faint and then pop right back up again." It withdrew its challenging gaze to dump the sand from its cylindrical hat. "I too was tracking down invaders, if you must know. . . ."

"To find cover from the Warden Eternal, we must move now." The shining tower rose at least two or three kilometers away by his estimation. "Can you shift us to the spire?"

"Regrettably, I have exhausted that ability for now."

"Then we walk."

He set off immediately, the Forerunner slow to follow. The Didact amended his long stride to allow Haruspis to close the distance between them. Once they'd settled into an even pace together, the Didact cleared his throat. "Since you were otherwise engaged, the Warden has not only been defeated by Cortana, but he has shifted his loyalty to her."

"*Aya*. He has surely been corrupted. It couldn't get any worse."

"Mmm. Unfortunately, it does. Cortana is in possession of a Halo."

Haruspis stopped. The hat dropped from its hand, and its mouth gaped several times in an effort to respond. The Didact could relate. The ramifications were staggering. But they wouldn't solve anything by standing around in the sand.

He picked up the wrinkled hat, brushed it off, and handed it to Haruspis. "Come on—we have much work to do."

CHAPTER 22

By the time they neared the spire, it was surrounded by the Wardens, so the remainder of daylight was spent shifting from one sandy location to another, avoiding the desert's plateaus and barren plains, and using the dips and valleys of the sprawling dunes as cover.

But nonstop translocation couldn't be sustained; Haruspis had exhausted itself long ago, and the Didact didn't possess the capability to relieve him. Though they were specks hidden in a literal ocean of sand, eventually their luck would run out. The Warden Eternal was always close, his multitudes covering the expansive territory without tiring.

On the slope of a dune, the Didact reclined, knees bent and heels dug into the soft sand to anchor him. The constant materializing and dematerializing was taking its toll on him as well. He measured each breath, trying to combat the inevitable disorientation and acute nausea that shifting caused—not that he had any contents to regurgitate. He had accepted that things like eating, drinking, and other bodily necessities and functions were no longer applicable to this existence, though trying to convince his essence to ignore ingrained physical memory and response was nearly impossible.

Surely, in time, these phantom dependencies would ebb.

The sun was westering behind the dunes, finally giving them some much-needed shade. The Didact let his head fall to the side to check on Haruspis, sprawled beside him. The exhausted Forerunner's chest rose and fell rapidly, the tiny slits in its flat nose flaring, and the creamy color of its skin paler by several shades. Its white gown was stained by the sandy tones of desert dust, the same dust graying the tufts of black fur on its head, and it had placed its ceremonial hat low over its eyes in an effort to rest.

While the Didact's animosity toward the rate hadn't changed—his views had been formed by thousands of years of past experience, which nothing could discount—his opinion of this particular Haruspis was quite unprecedented. Loyalty, determination, bravery . . . whether the Forerunner had always possessed these qualities or acquired them through time and circumstance, they were traits, nonetheless, that Warrior-Servants recognized and respected.

The Didact might have changed his mind about this Haruspis, but he would *never* change his mind about the hat; it was utterly absurd. At times, sitting crooked atop the Forerunner's head, it had been an entertaining diversion. Humor at this unexpected thought caused a short chuckle to tumble from his lips.

Haruspis lifted the hat up to scowl at the Didact, which only made his laugh deepen.

"How can you laugh at a time like this?"

The Didact tamped down his amusement. "I never liked your rate," he admitted in a casual tone.

Haruspis rolled its gaze to the unremarkable sky and muttered, "Never liked yours either."

"Your kind was haughty and judgmental, looking down from

your ascendant height as if those living in a secular world were infinitely inferior."

"We were all blinded by our arrogance in one way or another. . . . Your rate did the same. Your judgmental perch was simply different from ours."

"Mmm," the Didact murmured. "There is truth to that, indeed." Warrior-Servants viewed others through the lens of their own superior strength, which almost always left the other rates lacking in their eyes. "How much longer before we circle back?"

"Another shift or two. I still need a moment's rest."

And then, with luck, they'd arrive unscathed at the human rift. Their first few jumps had taken them several hundred kilometers from the void. Now they were working their way back to hide in the one place the Warden Eternal avoided above all others. His hatred and disgust for humanity should work in their favor.

While the Didact had no love for humanity or the rift either, he was ready to leave the dunes and the continuous immersion in sand. The grit had settled into every crevice, working its way into his ears and nose and the corners of his eyes. Even the dry, earthy scent of it was beginning to sicken him.

After Haruspis had taken the time needed to recover, they rolled onto their stomachs and slowly shimmied to the top of the dune to scan the surrounding area. In the fading daylight, the wide expanse of desert was punctuated by hundreds of faint orange lights that glinted above the undulating sand—the Warden and his many iterations darting in and out of this plane as he continued the relentless search for the Didact.

"Ready?" Haruspis finally asked.

The Didact braced his body in preparation and gave a sharp nod.

With grim determination in its milky eyes, Haruspis grabbed the Didact's forearm, and instantly they dissolved.

The shift put them at the head of the human rift, at the cliff's edge. The sun had dropped below the horizon and night was upon the desert, bringing with it a temperate breeze. The rift's jagged chasm stretched before them, kilometers long, and its lightless depths seemed to vent misery and dread.

Foreboding pricked the Didact's skin as he leaned forward to gaze into the abyss, finding nothing but a bottomless well of saturnine blackness. There was no place in the desert more disturbing than this.

Haruspis staggered, the exhaustion from the jump sending it to its knees. Immediately the Didact offered an assisting hand, but the Forerunner waved it away, glancing up at him with a sickly grimace and shadows lurking beneath its eyes. "Just a few minutes and then we will proceed. . . ."

The Didact dipped his head in response before turning away from the cliff's edge to stare out over the dusky landscape. Perhaps the wasteland was beginning to grow on him, because despite his desire to leave it, he thought the sight quite beautiful with its striated hues of sand-colored topography beneath an orange horizon, which bled into blues and purples before giving way to the inky night sky and the first wink of stars.

The orange glints from the Wardens' ceaseless pursuit seemed to dance and flicker above the desert scene like the nocturnal fire bees that had once swarmed around the Didact's estate every summer season, their fiery bioluminescent glow displayed over the Dwoho and Dweha, the rivers that took their names from the twin constellations seen only for a short time in the late summer sky.

Throughout the summer months, families across Nomdagro gathered the bees in preparation for the fall *Ghabbhel Ure*, when they'd assemble at the water's edge, millions of Warrior-Servants lining the twin rivers that stretched from one end of the continent to the other. In a Warrior-Servant ritual whose origins were lost to time, one that endured despite the Builders' efforts to erase it, they made lanterns of paper from the bark of *rataa* trees, engraved with the names of their ancestors, and filled them with fire bees to fly into the night sky.

The lanterns would rise a kilometer or so into the air, sometimes more, before the bees broke the paper and flew back to the river in a brilliant display; thus the ancestors accepted the remembrance and returned blessings to their families.

Golden rain lighting the night sky, his wife had whispered in awe the first time she saw the spectacle. . . . And then, as was her nature, proceeded with an entire cataloging and study of the creatures the very next day.

A grunt and stir jolted the Didact from his recollections. Quickly he bent to help Haruspis as it struggled to its feet. While they could allow a few minutes for rest, unfortunately they could not spare the time necessary for Haruspis to fully recover and make another shift to the rift floor. This time, they would have to make the journey unassisted.

"Didact," the rushed whisper nudged him from his thoughts. "Follow me."

Taking one last look at the landscape, the Didact shook the fond memory away and followed the Forerunner down a crude path cut into the rift's steep cliffside.

The way was treacherous, but he was grateful for the larger boulders near their path, making use of them several times to stop his slide and prevent a tumble to the ground below. It kept him focused on placing his feet precisely and distributing his weight accordingly rather than allowing his mind to swim in the bittersweet waters of days gone by.

Occasionally their passage sent loose rock tumbling, and

eventually, after a long silent fall, hitting the bedrock far below. The Didact winced with every impact, hoping the cracking echoes were contained within the rift's steep walls and did not carry over the desert sands.

After perhaps an hour, they stumbled upon a flat ledge wide enough to afford a short rest.

And that was where the humans found them.

Forthencho Oborune and three companions, two females and one male, all very similar to the Lord of Admirals in features and dress—dark-skinned, knotted hair, white facial tattoos, form-fitting gray armor—had climbed to the ledge and silently indicated that the Didact and Haruspis should follow.

Before the Didact could make any kind of response or decision, Haruspis gladly hurried behind them.

While Forerunners possessed moderate natural night vision, the way down the zigzagging path was precarious. Very little light was sent their way, though the starry night sky cast a measure of dim illumination into the rift's narrow depths, allowing the Didact to discern its pockmarked walls and the tops of tall, eroded pillars that rose from its floor. At roughly the two-thirds mark of their descent, by his estimation, they halted before an opening to a small limestone cavern with just enough height in which to stand.

Haruspis immediately made for a collection of knee-high rocks piled to one side. It sat, dragged off its hat and leaned against a slanted portion of the limestone wall—a well-deserved rest, the Didact conceded as he remained at the cavern's opening.

Tension prevented such respite for him, however.

The humans stood mere meters away, their white tattoos ghostly in the darkness and their eyes glittering like pools of the blackest venom in the scant light.

"The Warden is active tonight," Forthencho started in an even tone. "I assume you both have something to do with that."

Low as the human commander's voice was, it still echoed in the cavern, giving it a deep, weighty sound in keeping with his overall demeanor. Forthencho might be smaller in stature than a Forerunner, but he made up for it in sheer presence and innate authority.

The Didact rubbed his jaw. It wasn't too long ago that they had come to blows . . . when he was frail and powerless and did not have the ability to fight back.

Things are very different now, he thought.

While Forthencho did not appear troubled or intimidated by the Didact's physical restoration, animosity ran under the surface like a live current despite his civilized conduct, a skill acquired—as the Didact knew all too well—through ages of military experience and restraint.

"We thank you for the assistance, Lord of Admirals," Haruspis said, cutting the silence and tossing the Didact a critical look before drawing up one leg and pulling off a boot to rub its aching foot.

The Didact crossed his arms over his chest and let out a soft huff. He would not extend the humans such a courtesy. He and Haruspis had been doing fine on their own and had not asked for any support. He lifted his chin, his countenance stern. "And whose assistance shall I acknowledge? Is it that of the Lord of Admirals's, or the Domain's?"

A curious glint lit Forthencho's dark eyes. His human companions seemed to find great disrespect in the Didact's words, casting malevolent glares his way and whispering among themselves.

"We will trouble you no more," the Didact decided, dismissing them as he turned toward Haruspis, who now had its head resting against the limestone wall, eyes closed. "Once the Warden gives up, we will return to the Domain."

Haruspis cracked an eye open. "And find out what Cortana is planning next."

"Who is this . . . *Cortana*?" Forthencho asked, head cocked slightly, glancing between Haruspis and the Didact, his interest obviously piqued.

The Didact's gaze narrowed on the human. Surely he hadn't forgotten. "You took me to the void and showed me the destruction her Guardians were causing . . . you led me to Genesis to witness her claim the Mantle. . . . Have you forgotten?"

The Lord of Admirals frowned. "I know not of what you speak, Didact. We fought. You disappeared. These other things"—he shook his head—"I do not understand."

Haruspis was listening intently and the Didact didn't miss the look of comprehension that suddenly dawned on its face. The Forerunner obviously knew more than it was willing to share. The Didact filed the revelation away for another time, opting instead to answer Forthencho's question and see what might come of it. "Cortana is a human-created ancilla."

The humans all straightened at once, their expressions riveted.

"Human-created?" the shorter female of the two echoed carefully.

At the Didact's acknowledgment, they shared guarded looks, and he was struck by the raw, tentative hope he saw.

"Now we have confirmation." The male warrior was in disbelief. "Humanity *has* survived."

"We assumed this might be the case when the new souls arrived here," Forthencho explained to the Didact, "but they cannot yet communicate. We were unable to definitively discover where or even when they once existed. . . ."

Discomfort dug into the Didact's chest. As the source of all their pain and suffering, it seemed perverted for him to deliver such news, to bear witness to their stark, mounting joy. But it would also be cruel of him to deny them this tale. He cleared his throat and then relayed everything, all of the events from the firing of the Halo Array to the state of humanity as he had found it when he was awakened from his Cryptum on Requiem.

His audience was spellbound and utterly immersed in the story of their descendants. That humanity had miraculously survived, thanks to the Librarian's planning, and was once again coloniz-ing the stars, caused a wide spectrum of emotions. Grief for the enormity of their own losses. And pride for the dogged nature of humanity and the achievements made in their absence.

"And now this *Cortuna* has one of these weapons . . . a Halo." Forthencho murmured the last word, his frown deep, making the Didact wonder if it held some meaning or recognition. "Once again, the galaxy is threatened. Humanity is at risk."

In the ensuing silence, as the seasoned warriors' expressions shifted from joy to realization to resolve, it was clear that they, too, knew what must be done: they had to keep Halo out of Cortana's hands.

On the heels of this understanding, suspicion set in.

It was in the narrowing of their eyes, the tightening of their mouths, the sudden cold calculating manner befitting warriors of old. It was easy to discern; in this, these humans felt no need to hide their feelings or opinions.

The Didact could not fault them.

"Forerunners no longer exist in the galaxy," Forthencho said, crossing his arms over his chest and measuring the Didact, as though attempting to find the truth deep within his enemy rather than trust the words that might come out of his mouth. "You were the last. There is no threat to your kind. Why stop this Cortana?"

"He wants the Halo for himself," the male said.

The accusation caught the Didact by surprise. The thought hadn't even crossed his mind.

How astonishing. . . .

He frowned and linked his hands behind his back, turning slightly away from the others in contemplation. Did he want the Halo? Perhaps in the recent past, but now . . .

Now the answer was in his mind and heart before he even completed the question. There was simply no longer any desire to obtain that sort of power. And for a moment, all he could do was stand there stupefied by the realization.

Finally he faced the group. "I want Cortana out of the Domain," he said, admitting that much at least. And, he had a score to settle.

"And that is all you want." It was the first time the tall female had spoken, and the Didact wasn't certain whether she posed a question or was making a statement. She was the eeriest of the three warriors. Her white facial tattoo crossed from one temple to the other in a thick band that covered her eyes. He also sensed she was the patient type, taking in all that was said and done before making determinations and decisions; she was similar to Forthencho in that way.

The answer was not one the humans would want to hear. There *was* much more he wanted, of course.

But their questions and accusations made him examine his purpose more closely. Why was he so keen on finding out what

Cortana wanted with the Halo? Why did he feel compelled to prevent her use of it? What did it have to do with him? Other than she'd taken everything that was rightfully his, of course.

Humanity was now threatened by their very creation.

All he had to do was take a step back and let it play out to its miserable end.

He should be swimming in the exquisite irony of it all . . . and yet the inclination was not present within him—the *him* that was now free of the Gravemind's influence. In truth, he did not want the galaxy to suffer as it had before. His wife had given her life to see humanity survive. The existence of the Halo Array threatened that work, made all of her sacrifices, and all of their shared grief because of it, worthless.

And didn't he owe her restitution?

Hadn't he done enough to hurt her?

No one should control Halo, just as no one should control the Guardians or the Domain. These powerful creations were the very definition of "unfair advantage," the very things that could knock Living Time out of balance—and, as such, must be kept out of the hands of radicals and tyrants at all costs.

"My wife gave her life to ensure humanity's survival. . . ." he said, still marshaling his thoughts. "I have no plans to undo all that she has done."

He could feel Forthencho's eyes on him, boring in as if to lay him bare, but the Didact's mind was elsewhere, trying to reconcile these new realizations with the ancient ambitions that had monopolized so much of his time and attention.

As if coming to some sort of decision, Forthencho turned briskly to his warriors, speaking too softly for the Didact to hear. The trio promptly left the cavern by the same opening through which they had come in.

"They will climb the rift and check on the Warden's status." Forthencho sat on one of the many small boulders near the cave entrance, his posture seeming more casual as he rested his elbows on his knees, and then lifted his astute gaze to meet the Didact's. "Our goal now appears to align with yours, Didact."

It did indeed.

The Didact dipped his head. It was all the recognition that was needed. Perhaps other allies would have laid voice to the proposition of working together to achieve a common goal, but to do so here and now made it brittle and wrong somehow, given their long past as enemies. And the wrongs done.

Time wore on as they awaited the return of the humans. The Didact couldn't sit, couldn't rest. He paced the edge of the cavern, often stopping at its precarious ledge, staring out into the dark maw, reflecting on the internal discoveries he had made, attempting to piece together who he had been with who he wanted to be now.

Haruspis and Forthencho watched his progress back and forth, allowing him his silent contemplation until he felt spent and finally ceased, releasing a large sigh, his shoulders at last relaxing.

His gaze met that of the Lord of Admirals, their shared past suddenly yawning like a wide, impassable ravine.

Aya, their current circumstance was remarkably odd.

That they had met in battle more than one hundred thousand years ago, two worthy adversaries pitted against each other for fifty-three hard years of engagement, and were here now in this bizarre sort of afterlife, was too extraordinary to be anything other than fate. But what was fate but the guided machinations of something much larger and greater than anything they could understand?

There was a humble confidence to the commander's character, a stoic ease and capability inherent in natural-born leaders. When

Charum Hakkor finally fell and a large portion of human resistance had been gathered under the citadel's shell, the Didact and the Librarian had walked the rows of warriors, all fighters from the old to the very young. All skilled, all committed to the end, all inspired by and utterly loyal to the Lord of Admirals.

He'd only ever seen the human at his worst, in his last moments of life, stripped of armor, weakened by war. Utterly different from the unseen, ferociously stubborn tactical genius he'd battled for decades.

In the final years of the Human-Forerunner War, the Lord of Admirals and his forces had been pushed back to Charum Hakkor, which they fiercely defended. Humanity had already lost too many resources to the Flood, warriors, weapons, ships . . . and they'd lost further in their fight against the Forerunners. Even though his fleets were dwindling and denied the advantage of reinforcements thanks to the Didact's use of causal reconciliation to impede communication and slipspace travel, Forthencho's ships consistently pushed back numerous attempts to establish an orbital entry point over the planet.

It was an unwinnable battle from the start, the Didact's fleets nearly inexhaustible in their numbers. But the admiral held on despite the odds.

"The others"—the Didact gestured to the cliffs above—"they served with you. . . ."

"Until the end, yes. A result of your Composers. Shall I tell you what it was like after, to be interrogated and tortured as data?"

The flash of resentment struck so quickly that the Didact could feel the sudden change in the air. He braced for another fight. But the moment passed and Forthencho calmed.

"It was a long time ago," Forthencho finally said.

Yet sometimes it felt like yesterday.

The Didact sighed. "I never would have imagined an outcome such as this, that the patterns we extracted that day in the citadel would ultimately end up here on the Domain's doorstep."

"None of us arrived like this." Forthencho glanced down at his stable form. "It took my people tens of thousands of years to adjust and finally be able to heal their damaged souls, to remember their past, to re-form themselves into a complete presence."

"And you?" the Didact couldn't help but ask. He sensed a difference in the human's experience. Which was not unexpected.

"Time runs strangely here. I've only recently become whole. As whole as I can be," he murmured. "Your kind ripped my consciousness from my body, forced it into your . . . neural *pattern*, copied me and studied me, placed me in others, pulled me apart, leaving fragments too numerous to recover. . . ."

Forthencho paused as though he could go no further, then shifted the conversation away from himself. "It will take centuries for the newcomers to settle and even longer before they are able to pull themselves together as we have done." He glared at the Didact. "Like us, you have denied them life and denied their souls a proper human afterlife. Thanks to your Composers, we are all turned into something *Forerunner*."

So, the Forerunners had not only defeated humanity, devolved them, composed them, but they'd stolen their afterlife as well. And in the end, Forerunners had gotten no pivotal information from those composed essences, no hidden way in which to defeat the Flood. He had learned from Bornstellar's testimony that this had in fact been the Flood's design—fooling the Forerunners into believing the humans had found a cure, prompting them to dedicate vast resources into finding and re-creating it . . . only to later be told that this was nothing more than a feint. Creating hope, just to take it away.

The discomfort in the Didact's chest began to burn. He'd keenly felt the remorse when they had initially composed Forthencho and his people, and he felt it now, staring into the dark, angry eyes of his adversary once more.

"It was war. . . ." the Didact found himself saying.

What else *could* he say?

They'd done what they thought best at the time.

"It was. . . ." Forthencho solemnly agreed. "Mistakes and atrocities on both sides."

And arrogance. The Forerunners' greatest vice, one they could not seem to ever overcome.

Humanity had its share as well, believing it could deal with the Flood, annihilating, sterilizing worlds and populations without explanation. . . . The humans must have known retribution would come. Yet internal strife and politics had played a hand in their decisions, and existing tensions between humanity and the ecumene had prevented them from seeking aid or explaining their actions when the Forerunners brought their fleets to bear.

The spill of small rocks down the cliffside heralded the return of Forthencho's companions. They cast baleful eyes the Didact's way as he stepped aside to allow them entry, and immediately moved to their leader's side.

"The Warden has withdrawn the search," the shorter female informed them. "His copies now line the barrier as far as the eye can see, in both directions."

Haruspis groaned. "He can guard the void indefinitely." Being cut off from the Domain, as the Didact now knew, was quite literally a fate worse than death in the eyes of Haruspis. "It's settled then," it said, pushing to its feet and brushing its hands briskly on its gown before regarding everyone with a ready look. "We must find a way in."

Gravitas permeated the cave and an ease fell over the Didact, like stepping into his battle armor or boarding his warship. Familiar territory. Where he felt most at home.

It was time to talk strategy.

The warriors gathered around with grave eagerness. The Didact knew well the sentiment. He'd seen similar expressions countless times in the eyes of his Warrior-Servants, surrounding the tactical console, devising plans, the relish of the battles to come, of turning the tide and causing as much damage to the enemy as possible.

Forthencho glanced up and met the Didact's gaze. An eager light appeared in his dark eyes and pulled his lips into a formidable grin. "Where shall we begin?"

They talked far into the night.

CHAPTER 23

"**Y**ou must lure enough Wardens away from the void to break their line," Haruspis was explaining to the humans. "Once there is a gap, I will shift the Didact to the void and into the Domain."

The Didact crossed his arms over his chest and listened intently, but his mouth quirked at the Forerunner's shaky strategy.

"I'm afraid the bait must be sweeter than us reviled humans," Forthencho said. "The only thing that will lure the Wardens away from the barrier is the two of you. How many jumps can you make in succession?"

"Now that I've had time to rest . . . two, perhaps three."

"You'll need at least four."

"Four!"

"One to jump to the Warden's location and gain his attention. Another to jump back, luring his copies close to the rift, and a third to draw them inside. These three shifts can be accomplished without the Didact in tow—that should save you some energy. The fourth, you'll take the Didact back to the barrier while we do our best to prevent the Wardens in the rift from following."

"It must happen quickly," the Didact told Haruspis, "within seconds." Before the Wardens guarding the void filled in the gap left by those lured away via the Forerunner. "We will have only moments in which to slip inside."

The diminutive Forerunner nodded gravely. "Haruspis will make haste."

The Didact turned his attention to the Lord of Admirals. He cleared his throat, knowing his next question would sound as though he doubted the humans' abilities, but it was a question that needed to be asked—they had to be certain. "Is this a fight you can handle?"

"The Warden Eternal is subject to the laws of this plane just as we are," Haruspis added quickly, an obvious attempt to smooth over any potential conflict. "Here we are as real as he is."

"We are able." Forthencho appeared unbothered by the legitimate inquiry. "We won't win without weapons, but we can harass them long enough for you to enter the barrier."

Success would be measured in numbers, in how many Wardens Haruspis was able to pull away from the void. It could be dozens or thousands, the more the better if they were to create a suitable gap. "What are your numbers?" he asked Forthencho.

"At least sixty thousand warriors, give or take. There are more of us, of course, but some only regained part of their presence, while others have stayed lost entirely. We have yet to understand why."

Haruspis pursed its lips thoughtfully. "Perhaps a corruption in the composed pattern, or damage from the Halo Array . . ."

Still, Forthencho's revelation was stunning—all that remained of ancient humanity's capable fighting force had been reduced to sixty thousand essences. The mood in the cavern shifted. It seemed the Didact wasn't the only one reflecting on the dispiriting numbers and the events long ago that had led to such a state. Victorious in the war against humanity, the Forerunners had been thorough in their punishment, indeed. If not for the Librarian's efforts, the entire species would have been annihilated back on Charum Hakkor.

The Lord of Admirals broke the silence with a heavy sigh. He scratched the nape of his neck, then locked his hands behind his back. "It seems even now, after all this time, our fates are meant to intertwine."

"And so it is . . . and perhaps will always be," the Didact said in quiet resignation.

"*Daowa maadthu,*" Forthencho murmured, seeming lost in reflection on the ancient human philosophy, a way of being and living, of rolling with the cycles of life and the constant ebb and flow of the universe, and above all of learning to accept it.

"I will gather our forces and reconvene here," the Lord of Admirals said suddenly, recovering from his reflection with a curt nod as he moved out of the cavern without a backward glance, his warriors following.

The Didact waited until the last one disappeared before relaxing his stance. Weary, he sat on one of the rocks and rubbed his hands down his jaw, releasing the tension that had gripped him since the humans' arrival.

Haruspis installed itself on a rock nearby. "Your afterlife is quite exciting, is it not?"

The Didact snorted. If by exciting the Forerunner meant one rapid event after another, facing his past at every twist and turn, then, *aya*, it was certainly that. "Your choice of words is rather . . . novel, Haruspis."

"Forerunners and humans fighting together, sharing a common cause, is indeed novel."

In truth, it *was* remarkable.

Would that we had done so against the Flood.

What an unimaginable galaxy it might have been had they united. A pleasant musing if nothing else. The last Precursor with its weapon of vengeance, the Flood, would have simply altered its strategy. To really change things, they'd have to go back ten million years to the Forerunners' fateful decision to annihilate their creators.

To dwell upon what might have been was a pointless endeavor. What was done was done.

The Didact shook the hindsight away and instead focused on the time he and Haruspis had left together. After they made it to the void, their actions must be quick and concise. And once inside the Domain, they could not waste a second. "Are you certain of the hub's location?" he asked.

During their strategy talk, Haruspis had claimed to know the whereabouts of all functioning Halo hubs within the Domain. Every Halo ring had been created with dedicated terminal links to the Domain, which were maintained by each installation's monitor. Finding the actual connection hubs within the vastness of the Domain's quantum repository would have proved vastly challenging without the aid of Haruspis.

"Search and retrieval are my specialty. Haruspis knows where to go," it assured him. "Now that Cortana has broken the seal and allowed the Warden Eternal entry, he will be guarding the hubs as well."

And no doubt, the Warden would be ready for a fight.

The Didact waited anxiously, pacing the narrow cavern's ledge. Haruspis had departed, bravely setting out to lure the Wardens away from the void. Hours seem to pass in those few seconds, but soon enough the Forerunner materialized beside him, stumbling and gasping for air as streaks of orange descended into the rift, filling the blackness below them with color.

Twenty meters down, dozens of Wardens solidified on the rift floor, each body with its polished alloy and orange hardlight illuminating the darkness as sixty thousand human essences, ancient humanity's most capable warriors, came at them from the blackness like a ghostly tide.

The Didact had mere moments to witness the Wardens' arrival before Haruspis gulped in a few restorative breaths and snagged his forearm with its trembling grip. Instantly the Didact's form went immaterial.

They arrived before a small section of fractal void. The Didact clenched his teeth, ignoring the sickening sensation as he rematerialized; such weakness had no place in their current undertaking. Already the space vacated by the Wardens was shrinking by the moment as his remaining combat forms closed in the gap from both sides of the void with tremendous speed.

He felt Haruspis go slack beside him. Its mouth had dropped open and its eyes bulged. He grabbed the Forerunner's slim shoulders and shook it.

"Forerunner!" he barked. "Make haste!"

Haruspis jolted, gave a quick, frazzled head bob, and stepped into the barrier. Instantly it split, white light shooting through the night like a lure that seemed to draw the Wardens even faster.

As the Didact followed Haruspis inside, the energy within was already taking hold, whisking them through the void and into the Domain's gray, windswept anterior.

The strategy was successful—they were inside, but the relief was short-lived.

Wardens populated through fractures all across the anterior. Immediately he grabbed Haruspis's arm and ran, gaining speed, and finally streaking into the black interior, moving as thought and energy. A quick glance back revealed a meteor shower of orange streaks in pursuit.

Haruspis veered in front of the Didact.

Stay close, he heard the Forerunner's voice in his mind. *Before Cortana, the Warden was kept out of the Domain, and he no longer remembers his origins. His unfamiliarity will keep us one step ahead.*

At the moment, that might be the only thing working in their favor.

They dove and weaved and climbed in and out of the Domain's infinite spaces, through its strange formless architecture, down boundless corridors and long tunnels radiating ancestral records, through vast murky regions containing unseen information and equally expansive areas of emptiness where all records, all data, all experience had been burned away, and finally to an area populated by translucent towers that stretched into unseen depths and heights.

There it is. Each tower is a hub containing a Halo port.

They approached one of these towers and pushed through its clear diaphanous skin. Like a bubble, the skin gave way and then re-formed behind them. Inside, the dark space was populated by Wardens guarding a translucent dome that emitted a faint white glow. With a curse that would make a Warrior-Servant proud, Haruspis swung away, but not before their appearance was noted, drawing several more Wardens to the chase.

What now?

We must go farther.

Discussion and planning could wait; for now, Haruspis had the right idea. They must take full advantage of the repository's size and complexity to escape.

As Haruspis led them deeper through the Domain's strange insubstantial architecture, they came to another expansive void.

This one felt different from the ones before. While it appeared as dead space, there was a sense of fullness saturating everything.

We are entering the sealed regions. What appears to be black space is in reality the compression of enormous pockets of information. The Warden won't know how to navigate easily here.

As they moved forward, a sense of weight and the press of time, information, and experience folded around them like a thick quantum soup. Pressing farther into the region, the Didact noticed circular depressions that lay horizontal, vertical, and at every conceivable angle. They were as black as everything else around him, yet somehow he could just barely perceive their outlines. Once he saw a few, he began to recognize others, unsure if his mind was seeking familiar patterns or if they were really there.

The way soon became quite difficult to navigate. The Didact struggled through the next few meters. Moving through the space was like digging into the packed geological layers of a hundred-billion-year-old planet, and he was the spade.

"Most of it is too compressed to navigate, much less dissect and analyze," Haruspis said aloud. Now that they had slowed considerably, it refrained from speaking directly into the Didact's mind. "Of course, there are disruptions, things brought to the surface, but for the most part these areas are too difficult and infinite to study."

Haruspis led him to one of the circular depressions and came to a halt before it. "Some are pockets," he intoned reverently, "some are doorways. . . ." Haruspis placed both hands on the depression and closed its eyes. Nothing happened. The Didact glanced over his shoulder. While the strange density of the sealed region slowed the Wardens' pursuit, they would soon catch up. He was just about to interrupt when Haruspis's hands slipped through.

Not a depression, the Didact realized as they fell in, but a portal, a micro-wormhole that immediately launched them through its blackish boundaries at great speed and deposited them at the head of a colossal, opaque bridge at least eighty meters in length, which led to a ghostly, arched doorway.

They hurried across the bridge and soon stood at the foot of a nebulous vault-like door looming over them by at least ten meters. Grayish-blue lines of iridescent script crept in a circular pattern around the door's surface. The script was unintelligible, though the archaic slashes, strikes, flares, and arcs seemed somewhat familiar. . . .

Haruspis dropped to its knees and bowed. It spoke softly, a ritual prayer in a tongue similar to ancient Digon, but not it entirely. The crisp tones and rolls and guttural vibrations sounded primitive and heavy, the frequency, or perhaps the resulting sound waves, charging the air around them. Like the region of compressed information they had waded through moments earlier, the prayer held weight and extreme age, and the Didact had to wonder if the language might be Precursor in origin.

The glowing script seemed to respond to the sound, the pace of its creeping passage dwindling until it stopped altogether. The doorway's translucent state shifted, warbling as it became something more solid. He heard a distinct reverberating click and knew that the way had been unsealed.

"Hurry," Haruspis urged, glancing beyond the Didact's form.

They had seconds before the Wardens were upon them. At the rate they were approaching, they'd be in for a hard collision. Hurriedly, the two slipped inside. Haruspis pushed on the door and the vault sealed shut. The Didact braced for the impact on the other side of the barrier—but there was nothing. No sound or vibration. They were completely sealed off.

With a relieved sigh, he turned around, confronted with an astonishing scene.

As if he had just stepped through a doorway leading into space, the region before him appeared infinite, a universe upon which millions of densely packed points of light glinted, creating an image that called to mind small galaxies or gas nebulas and stellar nurseries filled with burgeoning stars, each pinprick emitting hazy halos of color, muted shades across the rainbow spectrum. He was awed by the beauty and grandeur, and suddenly struck by the idea that every point of light and every colorful halo around it was filled with moments in time.

"What is this place?"

"Late Precursor archive. One of a few billion left after the Array's pulse blew through the Domain. Only a few are accessible . . . here, this way."

As they floated through the celestial space, Haruspis beamed. "It is quite breathtaking, is it not?"

"Indeed."

"What is even more astonishing is that all this, all of our navigable areas of the Domain, as infinite as they seem, are but a small portion of what the Precursors left behind. That is the true marvel."

"Some say the Domain covers the entire breadth of the galaxy, possibly even beyond," the Didact said.

"Haruspis cannot say. It is believed the Precursors existed in many forms, throughout countless galaxies, experiencing life in its many variables, seeding worlds, dying out, being reborn again. . . . All that history and knowledge and involvement with the Cosmos was stored in the Domain until the Array fractured it. A hundred billion years of knowledge needs its space, after all."

The reverence in Haruspis's tone was not unlike the veneration the Warrior-Servants held for their own ancient myths and traditions.

"That is the Domain's appeal, is it not?" the Didact mused. "Billions of years of information, of answers just out of reach, pulling on our innate desire to find meaning in our own existence." As they moved easily through the archive, every perceived meter taking them across boundless stretches of space, he could not help but be humbled by its enormity. "The unattainable wrapped in a godlike package."

Haruspis paused, brow lifted high, obviously impressed or surprised—he couldn't be certain—by the Didact's reflections.

"If you could know all that transpired before," the Didact asked, "would you?"

"I do not believe 'knowing all' is necessary. Knowing diminishes the mysticism and godlike nature of the archive. Knowing eliminates sentient beings' search for meaning, and without that, they will never progress."

"Interesting. And well put," the Didact replied.

Haruspis seemed pleased. "While we cannot breach the Halo links, this region should put us close to the Guardian Custodes. A back door, if you will."

"Ah," he breathed. He was even more impressed with the Forerunner. "Well done, Haruspis. Very well indeed." If they couldn't get to Cortana using the Domain's connection to the Halo, perhaps they could utilize one of the Guardians instead.

Like Halos, Guardian Custodes maintained dedicated links to the Domain, but their relationship was much more complex and reciprocal. In the past, Guardians had received relevant data from the ecumene's Juridical Network and its Overwatch Network, enabling them to carry out orders and react independently if necessary. The constructs also deposited information into the Domain, delivering vast quantities of data on the worlds and populations they monitored. Guardians were far older than the Halos, and thus it made sense that the region containing their connection with the Domain would be closer to late Precursor records.

"Haruspis hopes the Guardian links are unguarded. Perhaps one or two of the constructs will be in proximity to Cortana . . . close enough so that we might discover her plans."

Speaking of Guardians . . .

"I must ask . . ." the Didact began. "Earlier, in the rift, the Lord of Admirals did not remember showing me Cortana or guiding me into the Guardian."

They had come to an area where the strange depressions the Didact had seen before began appearing.

"Just as the Domain uses memory and records, it can compel us as well, Didact. We are all just information in this place, after all. . . ."

True—but the idea of being used as the Domain's puppet was not a comforting one.

"Here we are," Haruspis said, sounding uncertain, as it approached a vertical depression. "The Domain is always changing, but very slowly. Older things move even slower. This *should* be the one. . . ."

The Didact was afraid to inquire what would happen if it was not.

As soon as they waded into the strange portal, space oozed around them like tar. And then suddenly—

—they were stretched out, pulled through a twisting, turning wormhole, their forms snapping back together at the end of it, and leaving the Didact feeling as though he'd been suddenly and viciously slapped across the face.

It was an experience he could not adequately define or explain, but one he never wished to repeat.

The portal had placed them at the edge of black space, which shaped itself as a diaphanous amphitheater, its dimensions and architecture thinly veiled and just barely perceivable. Around the amphitheater were concentric rows, populated by softly glowing holographic faces. Flat, ghostly, not Forerunner, not human, but artificial and highly unsettling, renditions of each Guardian's ancilla.

The Didact hung back as Haruspis floated forward and inspected these spectral hubs. While many were grayed out and very faint, obviously in states of deep dormancy, others were aglow and active. These, he surmised, must be those awoken by Cortana. Now they just had to find which ones might be close to her.

"This is odd." Haruspis's comment carried across the space.

"What is?" The Didact moved forward. The Forerunner was bent slightly over an image of a visage that was no less unsettling up close than it had been from farther away, its eyes glowing from a face lost in the darkness with just the slightest slashes of light resembling the hard angles of cheekbones.

"The active ones are not transmitting any data back to the Domain. There should be a near constant flow of information, delivering all aspects of what the Guardian is seeing and experiencing and gathering from wherever it is." As Haruspis leaned in closer, threads of its essence began to flow into the ghostly link until he was absorbed completely.

The Forerunner came out almost as quickly as it had gone in, re-forming and then straightening its incorporeal gown and lifting its hat to smooth the black tufts of fur atop its head. "Cortana has halted all recordings."

"She doesn't want her actions archived." That was the only discernible reason the Didact could see for such a measure.

"It is more than that. . . . It is not simply *her* actions she wishes to prevent from being recorded, but *all* actions, all information gathering."

"Why would she do that?"

Haruspis's face screwed into a thoughtful frown, its milky eyes narrowing and its body going suddenly taut. The Didact waited several minutes before the Forerunner snapped out of its communion with the Domain.

"I believe she does not want any human records and experience to fill the Domain."

Could Cortana simply be following existing protocol by disallowing human records to enter the Domain?

"Haruspis will tell the Didact a long-guarded secret." The slim Forerunner leaned in close. "Human experience was always meant to join with the Domain, to fill its halls in the same manner that Forerunners once did."

"Nonsense."

But Haruspis did not waver. It simply stared at the Didact, its expression clear and absolute. "Haruspis speaks true. When the Mantle of Responsibility was bestowed upon our kind, the Domain opened to us. Abaddon, the Precursor ancilla, aided our ancestors in exploring and learning because our Creators knew we would need its extensive experience to guide us as the Mantle's inheritors. The same *should* have been applied to humanity. Once they were chosen to inherit the Mantle, the Domain should have been opened to them as well so that they too could experience and learn and become proper stewards of the galaxy."

But that had never happened.

Ancient Forerunners had annihilated the Precursor species and kept secret their decision, thus denying humanity their turn as the Mantle's next stewards. Eventually the Flood had brought Precursor vengeance, sweeping across the stars. The Domain retreated even from the Forerunners. And once the Halo Array fired, it was all over. The Warden was "born" out of the ashes, and the Domain was sealed behind its inexhaustible quantum barrier.

Nevertheless, the Didact felt struck by the profound revelation. It left him speechless and unable to merge such an astonishing truth with a life spent believing humanity had no connection to all things Forerunner.

"The Domain depleted much of its energy to create the void," Haruspis continued. "But it needs nourishment. It needs life's experience with the Cosmos to heal. It wants to accept all knowledge, to store it and protect it. It seeks diversity of many of life's interactions, not just Forerunner. The cultural exchange that the Precursors so prized is needed for the Domain to flourish. The records lost when the Array fired were significant. With that loss and the strength diverted to create the barrier, the Domain was unable, and perhaps unwilling at the time, to welcome in those who wait in its outer boundaries."

And the Warden Eternal, in its hyper-diligence, refused to allow in the Forerunners trapped in the wasteland, much less humanity. In so doing, the Didact realized, the Warden had inadvertently kept the Domain weak, kept it from healing.

"If information and ancestral records flood in once more," the Didact murmured, "the Domain grows stronger and healthier." Better able to combat intruders like Cortana.

"That is correct."

He hadn't forgotten the voices during his earlier foray into the Domain.

Replace what was lost.

Now that upwelling of voices made sense.

"Cortana wants to keep the Domain in its current state," the

Didact concluded. "This is her great source of power, her access to the Guardians . . . and a stronger, more robust Domain is a threat."

"Precisely. Once she opened the seal and entered the Domain, she didn't leave it open—she kept it guarded. She could have opened the void, allowed everyone in, but she didn't."

"Haruspis"—the Didact clapped the Forerunner on its bony shoulder—"you may have just found the key to stopping her." If they could open the gateway through the void and fill the Domain with the millions of Forerunner and human essences trapped in the wasteland, then perhaps the Domain itself might work to expel the tyrannical AI.

The praise was so unexpected that the Forerunner fumbled for a suitable response.

"Have you located Cortana through this Guardian?" the Didact prompted.

"Indeed. It has been stationed in orbit above Installation 07 and currently maintains an open channel to the Halo."

"That is my way in then," the Didact said. While their objective had now expanded, the Halo in the AI's hands still remained a pressing problem. "While I am gone, look for a solution to overthrow the Warden."

Haruspis's mouth opened, then snapped shut. "If such a thing is possible. . . ."

"It is easier to kill one body versus millions. Find a scenario. Figure out how to recall those copies into one form and then we might have a chance at defeating him. You're smart and resourceful, and you have the entire Domain and all its information at your disposal. Come up with a way. Be the Domain's shield and I will be its sword."

Haruspis's milky eyes grew wide, and it mutely inclined its

head. And for the first time in a very long time, the Didact felt the old stirring of a Warrior-Servant's pride and confidence.

He turned to the ghostly impression of the Guardian's ancilla and cleared his thoughts, thinking of those small tendrils of self that Haruspis had called forth, imagining his essence moving into the link the same way he'd traveled through the Domain. He was directed energy, pure and simple.

His form stretched and grew as it slipped into the hub, at first bringing a sense of disorientation, then hyper-focus as he merged into the small, localized portion of the Guardian's matrix.

Immediately he was aware of its ancilla, of the mind behind the construct. He felt it take note of his presence before two glowing blue eyes manifested and bore down on him from the darkness, its inner gaze like a constraint field pinning him to the ground. To be under that powerful glare was to be frozen and disturbed. He sensed its great apathy and indifference for all things. It was quite content to dwell within its shell, to hibernate, and only do the bare minimum of what was required of it.

Finally, with disdain, it turned its oppressive gaze away and retreated into its languor.

Relieved, the Didact moved on, redirecting his thoughts to the outflowing data stream, the quantum gateways open and clear. Without hesitation, he dove in, instantly swept into the stream, once more becoming particles and light, the galaxy moving past in mere moments.

As with his first journey into a Guardian's systems, entering the construct's communications network felt initially confining after experiencing the incredible vastness of quantum travel. But once he grew accustomed to it and allowed his energy and light to populate through its intricate technology, the sheer capability and immense power generated by the construct felt almost euphoric.

All this could be mine.

A planet killer, all his own.

How easy it would be to forget himself and simply immerse, to be like that cold, indifferent ancilla, content in its own matchless power. Anything he wanted—authority, vengeance, submission—it was all within his reach.

He could leave the Domain behind, leave the valley, the Confirmer, the essences and humans all trapped there, the AIs running amok . . . say farewell to them all.

Even his wife . . .

No.

Her image snapped him out of his shameful daze, and he gave his thoughts a hard shake. Apparently he wasn't so far removed from his lust for power that temptations couldn't find momentary purchase.

He tucked the humbling realization away and then proceeded with his plan, centering his focus and his intentions once more.

From the Guardian's communications network, he traveled the short distance to its main command center, where he had a familiar observation perch above its bridge. From this location, it was an easy hop to access the construct's external viewing lenses in orbit over Installation 07.

At once, all previous thoughts were forgotten.

All the suffering their production had brought him. All the chaos their building had caused. All the inescapable, absolute destruction they had wrought upon the galaxy.

How he despised that silvery wheel of life and death hovering in the darkness of space.

Reprehensible disgrace.

Foul blight on the memory of a once great civilization.

Abomination.

Halo.

CHAPTER 24

Placed in orbit above Ephsu I, a large rocky planet in the Ephsu system within the Sagittarius Arm of the galaxy, the ringed weapon appeared rather delicate in nature, despite its ten thousand-kilometer diameter. An arc of its outer alloy band glistened in the glow of the system's sun and illuminated half of the ring's inner surface—revealing clouds and a clear atmosphere hovering above a landscape of enormous mountain ranges and lakes, green highlands and lowlands, and diverse collections of flora and fauna taken from worlds all over the galaxy—while the other half was cast in shadow.

Had the Librarian not argued for her conservation measures, the Halos, while impressive in their construction and scope, would be nothing more than metal and technology. She'd seen the way the Old Council was leaning, knew the Halos would be built regardless, and lobbied to create massive sanctuaries capable of producing atmosphere, gravity, light, and the building blocks necessary to sustain and nurture life in all its varieties. Her efforts had made Halo breathtaking, burgeoning with life and purpose.

And there was life here still.

The Didact had the rare position of viewing the ring from the perspective of one who had lived during its creation and then survived beyond its eventual firing. He was not awed in the way present-day species might be. He was not swept away by the impressive feats of engineering and technology that had gone into the building of such a weapon. To him, it was a difficult thing to gaze upon, something that stilled his thoughts and emotions and replaced them with numb regret. A monument to an extraordinary species, an entire spacefaring civilization, lost.

A thousand centuries had passed since that loss. The time for him, however, had gone by in his Cryptum, unaware of the final events of the war, unaware of the progression of time. Even now, there were moments that struck him hard, struck him fresh—the enormous and utter disappearance of his kind, the very notion that a civilization that had endured for millions of years had come to an inglorious end . . .

The thought that not one of them continued on to gaze upon the stars. . . .

Aya.

There had always been an eternal nature to the Forerunners, their technology and planning and persistence had cast a veil of permanence and assurance over them all.

Fate certainly had a twisted sense of humor, he mused, gazing upon the Halo ring. He now shared commonality with the constructs he so despised. They were both relics, remnants of another time. And neither belonged in this new age.

Especially a Halo controlled by a grandiose tyrant wrapped in promises of peace and prosperity.

The thought of the rogue ancilla brought him back to task and renewed his determination.

The Guardian maintained a dedicated link to Installation 07's communications network. All he had to do was find the proper relay, then jump into the open channel. Once again, by thought, he was moving, flowing back through the Guardian's command center to its communications network, where he weeded through recent reports, commands, and status updates.

This particular Guardian would not be in orbit for long, apparently. Cortana was preparing to send it and several others to the Oth Sonin system to stand marshal around its third planet, CE-75-2113 c—Doisac, homeworld to the Jiralhanae. A carnivorous species that had evolved from the ursine tree-dwellers the Librarian had once indexed into a highly aggressive, war-driven civilization currently controlling a sizable amount of power within the galaxy.

This discovery meant he might have very little time to find the information he sought, return safely to the Guardian, and from there, back to the Domain. Getting trapped in the Halo's systems would be less than ideal. He'd be forced to utilize the only means left to return to the Domain: the link between it and the ring itself, which meant that, upon his return, he'd be exiting into one of the translucent towers that held the Halo's hub—currently guarded by dozens of Wardens.

But it was too late to turn back now. There might not be another opportunity to uncover Cortana's intentions and prevent her from accessing the installation's critical weapons systems.

Wasting no time, the Didact sifted through the comms network until he found the open channel between the Guardian and Installation 07—or "Zeta Halo," as it was now designated within the relay code.

He crossed to the channel and then jumped into the outbound signal.

Almost instantaneously, he was dumped into Zeta Halo's

communication network, passing through a series of invasive fire-walls, which left nothing unscanned.

In the past, a Forerunner with proper security clearance could obtain access to Halo's relevant data via their armor's personal ancilla or through biometric scanning. And while these options were no longer available to him, the Didact's entire biological pattern had been encoded. He *was* Forerunner. He *was* the Didact, only in data form. Security measures could not dispute his access in either state.

As expected, his presence did not present as a foreign intrusion, and he entered easily into a very busy communications terminal.

Where the Guardian was inspiring in its sleek, ancient sophistication, the Halo was overwhelming in its sheer size and immense complexity. Even though he was currently confined to a specific network, he could easily feel its enormous scope.

The terminal received and sent billions of messages per second. From all directions, data flowed in and out in packets of glowing blue code, their speed so rapid that they blended into streaming lines, creating a great web pulsing with life, carrying encrypted codes, information, and processes back and forth and out along main highways and divergent paths.

All communication terminals contained holographic systems installed to allow a user to view and record messages. The Didact burrowed into this system and found the appropriate commands with which to project an image of his essence into the external space surrounding the terminal's console.

Out of the console, a circular chamber greeted him, its polished alloy walls darkly lit by the ambient light of the console and the soft blue glow of the floor, where a large, easily identifiable symbol had been inlaid. A circle containing four branching lines.

The Mantle of Responsibility's imposing seal, the Eld.

Around the Eld, six evenly spaced pillars had been erected, bent inward as though looking down upon the giant seal.

The area was quite elegant, the chamber not one he had seen during his short visits to similar installations in the past. In fact, he was not certain if he'd ever seen this particular design with such specifications before. Indeed, all he could discover about the function of the chamber was its designation: the Silent Auditorium. Any further probing as to its purpose was impossible due to an aggressive firewall, created by someone or something very old, very powerful, and, oddly, very familiar.

The complexity perhaps of, at minimum, a Metarch-class ancilla . . .

Given his limited time, however, further investigation was impossible. While the chamber's function was expertly hidden, other information was readily available, and it was easy to discover that control of the Halo's systems had recently been diverted here, to this Silent Auditorium.

Cortana's base of operations, surely.

And currently she was nowhere in sight, her activities within the ring shadowed.

To learn more, he'd need to contact the ring's monitor, 117649 Despondent Pyre.

With real-time reports from all over the Halo constantly flowing into the Silent Auditorium, the Didact was able to move into the network's great web, jumping from one packet to another until he found one moving in the direction of a facility called the Conservatory.

If Cortana had seized control of Zeta Halo, then she had somehow subdued the ring's monitor. Perhaps Despondent Pyre could shed some light on what Cortana wanted with the ring and the current state of its Activation Index, the key necessary to access the Halo's weapons systems.

The Conservatory was the main structure housing the ring's monitor and its Facilitator-class sub-monitors. Comprising underground chambers over several levels connected by light bridges, ramps, and long labyrinthine corridors, the facility was quite substantial and designed to be impenetrable. The enormous amounts of data continuously running through its translucent wall panels allowed for centralized administration and storage.

The Didact traveled to the very heart of the Conservatory, to a chamber containing a large pyramid-shaped housing with a flat top, which dominated the center of the room. The housing supported the maintenance cradles necessary for the ring's monitor and sub-monitors to receive restorative care.

He gathered his essence into the console at the top of the housing, where several monitors dozed within cradles around the perimeter of the structure. A circular alloyed object—Despondent Pyre, he presumed—hovered in the center, appearing to be in a state of slumber.

While administrative processes and reports and adjustments flowed into and out of the Conservatory, all primary functions had been rerouted to the Silent Auditorium, reducing the monitor's power to that of its Facilitator counterparts.

Curious, the Didact entered their communal network and found himself in an abstract, virtual space that mirrored the physical space around them. Here, he found it easy to build and project an image of himself.

His presence was only noted after he cleared his throat. He waited, linking his hands behind his back and affecting a presence of authority.

The monitor stirred. Like its sub-monitors, Despondent Pyre's artificial mind was housed in a spherical casing, concave on three sides while its front was composed of a prominent optical lens. It canted this faint green "eye" toward him, pausing there a moment before emitting a beam in the same dingy green color, scanning him thoroughly. As the beam swept up and down, the monitor blinked as though bewildered and then suddenly reared back in shock, exclaiming in a sonorous female voice:

"Greetings, Didact. I am 07-117649 Despondent Pyre, monitor of this installation."

Her sudden animation woke the others as she flew toward him—then froze, slowly withdrawing. "You are not the IsoDidact."

A dry laugh stuck in his throat. "No, I am definitely *not*."

"You are the Ur-Didact!" A designation chosen by the ecumene to distinguish him from his imprinted copy, Bornstellar, the IsoDidact. "Your treachery has not been forgotten. Why have you come? To steal this installation?"

"Be at ease, monitor. I have not come for your ring," he said easily. "I have come for Cortana."

"As enemy or ally?"

"Without question, enemy."

She emitted what sounded like an audible sigh of relief.

Each Halo monitor was unique, created from the composed minds of living, breathing Forerunners in the final days of the war, put in command by the IsoDidact in preparation for the positioning and firing of the Halos, and to operate, observe, and guard their respective rings in perpetuity. Their long service made them susceptible to rampancy; however, this monitor seemed to have retained much of her cognitive function, no doubt due to her creative decision to design multiple sub-monitors to keep her company and assist in caretaking duties.

"Current status?" the Didact inquired.

"Cortana has taken full control of this installation's critical systems. She has infected many of us with a sleep protocol. It has been a challenge to work around her."

"What is her intent?"

"She has made no attempts to obtain the Index. I do not believe her goal is to use Halo as a weapon."

"Conjecture?"

The monitor hesitated. "She is looking for something."

"Elaborate."

Despondent Pyre hesitated again. Her behavior was odd; it was unusual for a monitor to evade a direct question.

"What are you hiding?"

"Apologies, Didact. I am unable to answer your question. This security protocol was written and executed after the firing of the Halo Array; therefore it supersedes your authority."

Before he could compel her further, Cortana materialized in the space.

Rage lit a fire through his essence, and in an instant the Didact had her by the throat. It was the first time he had seen her since she'd forced him to relive his trauma at the hands of the Gravemind. His grip grew tighter around her small neck, his fury taking on a force of its own.

And yet she reacted with indifference, as one with no natural predators.

He lifted her off her feet, drawing her closer. The expression he saw in her dark eyes was not one of anger, but of sinister enjoyment. No matter how hard he constricted, it did not seem to affect her or do any damage at all.

"Do you know how many have tried to kill me in my short life? *Take a number.*" She shoved him away without moving a muscle, expelling a force that sent him back several steps as she floated to the ground.

"Why have you come here, Didact?" Her eyes narrowed—she was doing what ancillas did best. Calculating, theorizing, performing billions of processes in seconds. "This Halo is mine. The Domain is mine. The Mantle is mine."

"The Mantle . . ." Despondent Pyre gasped. "Is it true?" She canted her lens-eye between them.

Cortana rolled her eyes at the interruption and snapped her fingers. "Back to bed, monitor."

Despondent Pyre and her sub-monitors went dormant, and the Didact couldn't help but be impressed with the power Cortana had achieved in such a short time.

The AI *tsk*ed under her breath as she walked around the Didact's form. "My, my . . . you certainly are full of surprises." She crossed her arms over her chest and tapped her chin, contemplating her next words. "You know . . . I could use someone with your resourcefulness. You've successfully eluded the Warden Eternal, found your way here, even killed some of my Created seeking to cure their rampancy in the Domain—"

"A much-deserved fate."

"Join me," she said suddenly, taking him completely by surprise.

She reached out a hand, and while she was a few meters from him, he felt her touch, pulling at his code, coaxing it out of the ether, once again giving him that hardlight body, which felt realer and stronger and more powerful than anything he had felt so far.

He turned his hand over, admiring the form, rolling his shoulders and stretching out his arms, amazed that he could exist in such a manner.

She watched him shrewdly. "Amazing, isn't it? So much power in light. . . . You could have that and so much more."

"Like this ring?" he asked casually. "What will you do with so much power? Cleanse entire star systems of life should they refuse to yield?"

She blinked in shock, a brief flash that was quickly covered.

But he saw it. Saw that the idea of doing such a heinous thing, of using a weapon such as Halo, was as sickening to her as it was to him.

"My appropriation of this ring is not what you think it is."

Perhaps it was the lack of arrogance and manipulation in her tone or the look in her eyes when she answered, but strangely enough, he believed her. "Then leave it," he said. "Send it into the nearest sun. Relics such as these are far too dangerous to have a place in the galaxy."

She studied him for a long moment, then smiled, her tone becoming lighter, friendlier. "You know . . . you and I have a lot in common."

He snorted arrogantly. "We are nothing alike."

"We are survivors, aren't we? Perfectly capable of outliving the biological species of the galaxy. Who better than us to guide and protect it through the ages? All those who hunger for power, who lay the foundations of sickness and poverty and war, will be dealt with. We can put an end to suffering and usher in an era of peace."

"Imposing a forced peace, killing millions to instill fear and compliance—that is not the utopia you seem to think it will be."

Her chest rose and fell, deep inhalations that seemed to clear away the brief vulnerability he had witnessed. The formidable Cortana rose once more, staring at him with cold determination.

"Mmm. But there is always a price to pay for peace. I have seen it firsthand, been the instrument of it more times than you can imagine. This is what I was created to do. Future generations will forget—they always do. And the Mantle of Responsibility will shelter all."

"You cannot simply shape the Mantle to your will, Cortana."

"Well, your tune sure has changed."

Yes, that could not be denied. He too had believed that the Mantle was something to be taken, seized by the strong, and molded as he saw fit.

Hearing these words now though, listening to her argument, he was struck by the absurdity of it all.

"It is just an instrument, Cortana. An excuse to implement your own agenda. Nothing good will come of it. What would your *Spartan* think of all the suffering and death you have caused?"

That clearly stung. "You of all people are trying to lecture me? You killed millions of those your wife was trying to protect. I don't think I'll take relationship advice from you, thanks." A cruel grin tugged at her lips. "I take it you're turning down my offer. Didn't you learn anything from our last encounter? Tell me, how did you enjoy your little trip down memory lane?"

His rage rekindled. "You play with fire, ancilla."

The chilling laugh that came told him his warning failed to impress. "I'll tell you a little secret. I spent time with the Gravemind too. And I endured it. Don't tell me the great Didact can't handle a little reminiscing with an old friend."

She too had been at a Gravemind's mercy. . . .

His thoughts spun. There was not the slightest chance she'd come out of that experience without being harmed. The Gravemind could corrupt even the staunchest, most intelligent mind, biological or artificial. It had worked its way into the mind of the Forerunners' greatest Contender-class metarch at the time, Mendicant Bias.

The three of them had this much in common. And none came out unscathed.

He was starting to see things very clearly.

Cortana was right. They were more alike than he could have imagined.

"What?" she said, feigning apologetic surprise. "Did I hit a nerve?"

He thought of what Haruspis had said about the Domain and its need for healing and diversity. If they could strengthen the archive and sever her access, the blow would be substantial. "Know this, ancilla. Your control over the Domain will soon come to an end."

She eyed him, trying to determine whether he was simply boasting or knew exactly how to achieve his claim. "There's only one way to do that . . ." she said slowly, attempting to lead him into revealing what he knew.

While giving away any information was counterintuitive, time was running out. He wanted her out of Halo's systems, and the only way he could see that happening was to poke the beast and make it follow. "Strengthen the Domain," he answered. "Its doors shall be opened to all."

She laughed, but he could tell it was tinged with a faint note of concern. "You despise humanity. You wouldn't dare."

"Watch me."

He fled, instantly dropping into the Conservatory's network, flying down the data stream back toward the Silent Auditorium as Cortana gave chase. Once there in its console, he retraced his steps to locate the Guardian's link—but it was gone.

It had already left the Ephsu system.

Cortana's laughter echoed through the space.

Aya. He'd have to use the installation's connection to the Domain, but now he was without direction . . . until several submonitors suddenly appeared in the stream, the digital images they projected appearing rough. Their carapaces had taken a beating, telling him immediately that they'd escaped Cortana's grasp and, no doubt, continued to defy her.

Theirs was the voice of the desperate, the determined.

"Didact!"

"This way!"

"Hurry!"

CHAPTER 25

As the Didact careened through the quantum link en route to the Domain, he braced for the battle awaiting him. Thanks to the efforts of the sub-monitors he had found the way back, but unfortunately Cortana hadn't left the Halo in pursuit as he'd hoped. Now he was accelerating at a blistering pace, about to drop straight into the enemy's hands. The only thing working in his favor was that he had the element of surprise on his side.

In the end, it did little to help him.

His sudden arrival was immediately noted.

The multiple Wardens guarding the hub didn't wait for him to exit the dome-shaped port. Perhaps they were afraid he might return to the Halo and utilize its near-inexhaustible amount of data streams in which to hide. Whatever the case, they poured into the hub, bloating its protective dome until he was pressed on all sides and had nowhere to go.

In this quantum state, the Wardens' slashing blades had the unique ability to cut through his neural pattern and the quantum framework on which it rested.

If only the Didact could release the tight grip of his ingrained physical responses. Perhaps then he would not feel every hot cut as if they were real.

In rapid succession, blades slid into his torso, stabbing repeatedly. He sucked in a breath, his gut rolling over sickly. He could taste the metaphoric tang of blood in his mouth, feel his vessels throbbing with adrenaline and shock. His very essence *burned.* The strikes sliced off pieces of his composition. Bits of himself, pinpricks of data and energy, arced away like embers from a poked fire. Compressed within the dome and unable to maneuver, the Didact sank to his knees, overcome.

He felt himself fading and at first rallied against it, but then he wondered why he bothered at all.

He was on the ground, crouched, arms covering his face as the blows from his fellow students rained down on him without mercy. But within the cocoon of his arms, the chaos faded. He felt detached and in turmoil. His parents, they said, were traitors. . . .

The Didact shook the memory away, yet it came back stronger, louder, to a time just after that brawl . . .

"You are what you dare, Shadow, so take what you need." Silence's emphatic voice echoed beyond the memory and into the present. *"Seize it with an uncompromising grip. Become strong. The strongest. The most capable. . . ."*

The words were wrapped up in the maelstrom of the past and present, accentuated by the sound of many voices, rising, giving the words power, growing louder and louder, preventing him from finally ebbing into that chasm of comforting, beckoning blackness.

Hadn't he moved through the Domain on a thought?

Hadn't he shifted his form from the semblance of a body to nothing but pure energy and intention?

In all probability, the Wardens manifested their weapons in the same manner. So why couldn't he?

As his body was rocked by the constant assault, he pulled his thoughts together, compartmentalizing as best he could, ignoring the growing exhaustion, drowning out the relentless attack, envisioning what he wanted, feeling it fill him, letting it come.

It *would* work, but he needed time and there simply wasn't any.

The Wardens were carving him up and soon there wouldn't be much left of him to pull back together—

The dome suddenly exploded in a shower of data. The force sent him tumbling across the translucent tower and through its bubble-like skin, all the bits of carved-off energy of his essence trailing after him like the tail of a comet.

He came to a stop in the darkness of the Domain, what remained of his body lying on its side, limp.

"Didact! Didact!" Hands gripped his forearm and shook, rocking him. "Get up! Hurry! We don't have much time! *Didact!*"

The shouts sounded warped as if spoken through water.

"*Aya!* Make . . . haste . . . you overgrown—"

The Didact stirred, some of his faculties returning. "Haruspis?"

From his prone position, he could see Wardens re-forming from the blast, their indignant roars echoing across the dark space, as Haruspis continued to shake him.

Would no one let him rest?

Grimacing, the Didact drew in what little strength he had left, concentrating on pulling himself together enough to latch on to Haruspis's wrist as the Forerunner tugged him to his feet. Somehow he made it up, his essence feeling grossly loose and insubstantial.

"Didact. Please. We must hurry." The Forerunner yanked him forward, its grip surprisingly strong.

He wasn't certain how he accomplished it—he was learning with every moment—but the Didact gathered enough of himself together and followed, the remaining bits of his essence trailing along, as they stumbled out of the area and into another one of Haruspis's nauseating shifts.

And this time, the blackness finally claimed him.

The next thing the Didact knew, Haruspis was poking his shoulder and rousing him once again from the darkness.

He knew immediately by the heaviness of his form that he was no longer in the Domain, but back in the wasteland, his body throbbing with a myriad of shadow wounds. The space was dimly lit and smelled of stale sand and metal. But the air was blessedly cool and the metal beneath him and against his back, where he'd been propped up, emanated a welcome chill that ran through his damaged body.

"Rest easy, Didact." Haruspis's quiet voice echoed nearby in the contained space.

He nodded vaguely, then let his head fall back against the wall, his weary mind drifting in and out of consciousness.

Eventually memories flashed their way in. A rapid stab here. A vicious slice there. He jerked instinctually. His throat worked, attempting a painful swallow. How was such damage to his essence possible?

The notion of a peaceful afterlife had been brutally adjusted. This realm was just as merciless as the physical one.

The recent assault continued to plague him, so to quiet his mind, he focused on his surroundings, mostly hidden in the shadows but for the gleam thrown by strips of hardlight intermittently inlaid along the floor's edge and around a central oblong block of silver-gray metal.

"Where are we?" He turned his head slightly to see Haruspis sitting a few meters away with its back against the wall.

"In the tomb beneath the spire."

Ah, he thought, *now it makes sense.* The oblong block was the sarcophagus of Mendicant Bias—only a replica, of course, the real tomb and spire safe on the Ark in the physical realm. Reality was more subjective than the Didact had ever thought, for here in the Domain's territory, it certainly felt all too real. Too weary to ponder more on the subject, he let out a shaky sigh, his gaze drifting to the silent tomb.

Perhaps this too was his fate. To lie in repose, entombed. Defeated.

"Did you locate Cortana?" Haruspis asked.

"Mmm. She seems to have no immediate plans to use the ring." But that could change at any moment. He had failed to lure her away from Zeta Halo. If he had, Despondent Pyre would have leapt to action, taking over and initiating an emergency slipspace portal to take the ring to some unknown part of the galaxy, far from Cortana's reach.

He should relay this to Haruspis, but his fatigued mind began drifting again.

"I did what you asked of me," the Forerunner said in a near whisper, scooting closer until the Didact felt its breath on his cheek. "Haruspis found a way."

As painful as the movement was, he placed a hand on its shoulder to halt its advancing proximity.

"I searched the archives as you asked," the Forerunner clarified, settling in beside the Didact. "The Warden was born from the essences of my rate, and therefore should still be subject to and affected by our rules and rituals. With this in mind, I explored our origins . . . to the deepest, oldest records," it said dramatically, "a slow and tedious process as one might imagine, the layers much compressed, but the delving, sifting, analyzing . . . to utilize my search functions again to their fullest, it was delightful, a true—"

"What did you find?" The Didact barely had the fortitude to listen and knew he must propel the Forerunner along before he sank into unconsciousness.

"Many things," it answered. "When Forerunners were first admitted into the Domain millions of years ago, exploring its enormity often spelled doom—the Domain was simply too vast to navigate without becoming lost. These early explorers would eventually become the Haruspis rate, but at the time they had yet to develop the unique physical and mental traits needed to communicate and synchronize with the Domain and to navigate its infinite spaces. To account for this, Abaddon provided the explorers with a ritual capable of luring those who became lost back to their fellow explorers, reuniting them. After Haruspices began to evolve, this knowledge became obsolete and was forgotten."

Bracing against the hurt, the Didact pushed to a straighter position, intrigued. "You have found this ritual?"

"Indeed I have. And it was no small feat—but perhaps that tale is better left for another time. . . ."

"Perhaps so." The Didact drew in a long inhale and released it slowly, gathering what strength he could. In truth, he hadn't expected the Forerunner to find a viable solution. If this proved useful, they might still have a chance to overthrow the Warden Eternal and shut Cortana out of the Domain.

While he couldn't see its face clearly, he imagined the Forerunner was quite pleased.

"The ritual will only recall those existing here in the Domain and its outer boundaries. Once we eliminate the Warden, any of his iterations left outside of this realm, those in the physical world, for instance, will be trapped there, unable to reconnect with his body or the Domain. And they will surely go quite mad as a result."

"You have done well, Haruspis."

A satisfied sigh filled the darkness. "Haruspis agrees with the Didact."

The Didact snorted softly.

"I must warn you, however. Once the Warden is confined to a single body; he will be stronger than ever."

Of course he would be. "I understand."

As it was, the Didact could barely lift his arm, much less be the Domain's sword, as he had so confidently stated earlier.

Haruspis dug into its gown. There was a clink of metal against stone as it placed an object on the floor and then slid it over. "I found this as well. I believe it is meant for you."

The Didact felt for the object, his wounded hand curling around a cool metallic grip. Its weight was perfect. He pulled it into his lap and chuckled. "A hilt without a blade."

Haruspis ignored the sarcasm. "While the void acts as a deterrent, the Wardens have struck down Forerunner essences from the valley when necessary, especially during the early years after the Halo Array was fired, and many tried to force their way in. This cannot be achieved with the simple light sword, which is so effective in the physical realm. As you experienced yourself, light blades only wound. Killing an essence completely requires a quantum weapon, a riftblade."

The Didact rolled the device in his hands. "This generates a quantum blade?"

"It does." Haruspis scrambled to its feet. In the dimness, the Didact just barely saw it brush the dust from its gown, and then shove its hat onto its head. "I must go. The spire is protected from the Warden. You will be safe here while you recover. And once you do, we will recall the Wardens and take back the Domain."

The Didact grunted, but even that small action hurt.

Left alone in the darkness of the tomb, he relaxed his sore body, letting his head fall against the hard surface of the wall behind him. He rolled the sleek hilt around in his hands, questioning what he was doing and why. He thought of the Halo and the Guardians, more convinced than ever that such dangerous relics should fade into obscurity. He felt swept up again, caught in fate's path, and couldn't be certain if the choices he made were really his own or the Domain manipulating him into being its champion.

He closed his eyes, setting the hilt on his chest, then linked his hands over his belly.

He'd spent a lifetime being manipulated by others, his choices made for him. His path laid out after his parents' execution. His first mutation without his consent. His career carefully guided. Exiled by the Master Builder. Used as a pawn by the Gravemind.

For once, he wanted to choose his *own* path free of any manipulation and, above all, to know that the choice was his and his alone.

Haruspis's return to the tomb woke the Didact. He sat up straighter and rubbed his eyes, uncertain how much time had passed. The Forerunner crouched in front of him, milky eyes examining the Didact's appearance and perhaps seeing far more into him than he would like.

"How long have I slept?"

"Two days, give or take."

He stretched his arms over his head and tipped his neck from side to side, feeling a sequence of satisfying pops. The aching wounds on his legs and torso, the defensive wounds on his hands and arms had dulled.

"The time has come, Didact. We must prepare."

He'd expected the words but wasn't quite ready to acknowledge them just yet. Haruspis, however, did not seem content to go unanswered.

"Are you ready? The choice is yours, Didact."

He stilled and locked gazes with the Forerunner, wondering if its word choice was simply coincidence or if the Domain had heard the longing in his heart. "Is it, Haruspis?" he asked solemnly. "Is it really *my* choice?"

Haruspis's expression was clear and honest and kind. "Indeed, it is. It has always been. The Domain simply shows and guides. It cannot force. And it does not lie."

The Didact stretched again, letting out a deep groan. The wounds were already fading, and soon he would regain his strength and stamina. And then what? Join the other essences in the valley? Or take the option the Domain had presented to him?

He had nothing left to lose.

And as far as choices went, his was as clear as a slipspace crystal.

He met Haruspis's hopeful, waiting gaze. "I have seen better days, my friend. But I am ready for one last battle."

And maybe in doing so, he thought, gazing at the tomb of Mendicant Bias, *I too might find atonement for the wrongs I have done and the suffering I have caused.*

On the bedrock of the desert floor, surrounded by windswept boulders, Haruspis drew a massive circle with a pattern inside similar to the Eld. "This is the symbol of my rate," it told the Didact as it scratched out the shape with a sharp stone, the process quite lengthy. "It is ancient and revered. The dual lines represent Living Time, and the other two, the bent ones, represent the Mantle. The circle around it all is the Domain."

The Didact stood a few meters above on a large boulder, getting more restless with each passing moment. "Are you certain this is necessary?" Scratching out symbols in the rock seemed arbitrary, given that soon he'd be locked in battle with the Warden Eternal. He twirled the strange metal hilt around in his hands, giving an outlet to the anticipation and adrenaline flowing through his limbs.

"All symbols have power, even ones scratched in rock," Haruspis answered over its shoulder as it continued its etching. "You will see."

An hour passed before it finally completed its task. The Didact had since calmed and now rested on his haunches, studying the result of Haruspis's intense labor. The great seal in the desert was indeed impressive. Strangely disconcerting. Archaic. And, he hoped, effective.

Next, Haruspis injected four rectangular devices into the ground an equal distance apart around the perimeter of the seal. The Didact rose, curious, as each one opened and activated, releasing a gray, smoky energy that spilled out and linked all the devices together before traveling through the ground to fill in the seal's etched lines and curves, bringing it to life with a ghostly glow in the evening light.

Haruspis looked over its shoulder and met the Didact's gaze. There was no going back. If this worked, battle would be inevitable. "I will begin."

They shared a meaningful nod, and the Didact waited as the Forerunner took up position on the circumference of the circle between two of the devices. Its eyes turned even milkier as it squared its shoulders and began a strange litany of prayers similar to the chanting it had done at the tall, vaulted doorway guarding the Domain's sealed region.

Time stretched.

A breeze seemed to stir out of nowhere, then strengthened. Clouds gathered in the muddled sky above. The air became charged, making the fur on the Didact's body stand on end.

He had the distinct impression that the Domain had responded.

In the distance, out over the barren flats, a mist appeared, and seemed to be moving closer. The Didact straightened. This could not be the Warden Eternal. He squinted, then climbed higher for a better look.

Seconds ticked by. The breeze buffeted around him. The mist drew closer . . . closer . . . until he realized it was not mist at all, but a full retinue of Forerunner and human essences.

The Didact's heart constricted at the remarkable sight. They split into two groups, surrounding the rocky outcrop and its great, glowing seal. Silent. Ready.

By the thousands they had come to stand at his side and offer aid if need be.

The Confirmer and his shadowy Forerunner accomplices had spread out below the Didact's position. Gone was the jovial old Forerunner the Didact knew so well, in his place a savage figure with a fevered light shining in his mad eyes. One hundred thousand years without the Domain, and now the moment had come. The Confirmer wanted in, no matter the cost. He stared up at the Didact and gave a gruff acknowledgment, which the Didact returned.

Across the seal, the humans had gathered, arrayed behind their stalwart commander, the Lord of Admirals. The Didact cleared his throat and squared his shoulders, offering his unlikely ally a sincere nod, which Forthencho curtly returned.

Haruspis must have called upon them, obviously very busy while the Didact had been recovering in the tomb.

Setting aside further sentimentality for another time, the Didact continued to pace, rolling his shoulders and finally calling forth his light-armor battle plate, which covered him in brushed gray alloy from head to toe. Anticipation mounted, Haruspis's chant filling the space—and then an orange glow glinted in the distance, streaking forward at an incredible speed.

The first Warden Eternal appeared within the seal, the ghostly glow that lit the ancient Haruspis symbol snaking up and curling around the Warden's giant armored calves, anchoring him to the seal. His great dual-bladed light sword manifested in one armored hand as he glanced down. "What trickery is this?" He struggled but was stuck fast. His menacing glare scanned the area and finally settled on Haruspis, who continued chanting near the circle. *"You dare stand against—"*

Suddenly another Warden streaked overhead and slammed into the imprisoned Warden, vanishing within. His great body lurched from the force. The Didact was riveted. It was working. Another orange streak approached, another Warden—and soon Warden after Warden arrived, colliding and merging into the first, lured by the powerful, inexplicable force of Abaddon's ancient ritual.

On and on it went.

The daystar sank low into the horizon, bringing dusk hard on its heels.

The tension rose as the incoming stream dwindled, until finally what seemed to be the last iteration joined, and the Warden Eternal—save for any renditions that might be trapped in the physical realm—had been forced to return to a single form.

Haruspis flicked a glance over its shoulder and gave the Didact a clipped nod.

"What have you done?!" the Warden demanded of Haruspis, held tight to the seal, his deep, arrogant voice resonating over the area as his imperious gaze traveled over the assembled Forerunners and humans. "Pathetic filth! Release me now!"

The Didact strode to the edge of the boulder and jumped to the ground, twirling the hilt of the quantum riftblade in his right hand. The Warden's head whipped around at the Didact's approach, a threatening synthetic rattle issuing from his form as he bristled with hostility. "A foolish attempt on your part, Promethean. This seal will not hold me long. Are you certain you wish to die this night?"

Cold determination slid through the Didact's body, joining the smooth flow of adrenaline coursing through his veins. Whatever might come, he felt completely at peace with the choice he had made. He drew in a deep, steady breath, sure in the abilities that had been relentlessly forged and imprinted into him over the span of his long life.

He lifted his chin, focusing on the massive construct looming in the circle. "You sought the Didact," he answered, "now you shall have him."

"Come then, Old One," the Warden snarled. "Let us battle your last. I will hear your death knell ringing across the sand, and it's been ages since I last killed."

The Didact snorted, entering the circle. He flicked his wrist. The hilt activated and the outline of a ghostly blade materialized. Made of the same translucent building blocks that framed the

Domain, it seemed to cut through the fabric of the wasteland even at rest.

The Warden stilled, regarding the Didact with a penetrating stare. "So be it."

Angry red light flared through the Warden's alloy plates. His light sword disappeared, and in its place emerged a quantum riftblade double the size of the one the Didact wielded.

The Didact cut a swift look at Haruspis.

The Forerunner shrugged.

The Didact gritted his teeth, then refocused on his enemy, settling his thoughts. His fingers flexed on the blade's hilt. And then he advanced on the Warden.

With a massive swing, their blades met, the contact creating a frequency so low and powerful that it was felt across the area more than it was heard.

They met with precise motions, the speed creating a blur of orange, red, and gray as the Didact dodged in and out of the Warden's reach, testing his ability, identifying his weaknesses, and so far finding none.

Even though the tendrils of the seal held the Warden's legs immobile, he was several meters taller than the Didact and his reach covered the entire circle, his moves striking lightning-quick and with enough force to clear the seal of Haruspis's rock scrapings.

The Didact came up behind the Warden and swung, extending his right arm fully, the riftblade's tip slicing effortlessly through an alloy calfplate before blocking the Warden's incoming thrust.

His heart hammered, his body hummed, and the Didact let ingrained memory take over. Those early days with Silence on the training pad hovering over the River Dwoho, the constant staff work until his hands bled . . . strike, block, parry, duck, spin, thrust . . . teaching countless others, including his own children and wife. The dance filled him, energized him, brought him to a state of intense focus.

The Warden was bigger and stronger, so he had to be quicker and smarter.

Suddenly the Warden launched a furious attack, twisting and turning his body, the seal's grip expanding, loosening, and finally breaking.

The Didact leapt back, just evading the Warden's deadly blade. The Warden was free now, though still confined by the circle it seemed, and unable to shift in and out of reality. The Didact blocked several attacks in a row, the force sending him to one knee. Before another came, he rolled and swung wide, catching the Warden in the back, slicing through the edge of an alloy plate and into his hard-light, quantum body.

The Warden roared.

Breath coming fast, the Didact stumbled as he blocked a ferocious blow. His armor was taking a beating, several plates sliced to shreds by the Warden's attacks. He felt the burn of assorted slashes, but in the heat of battle, there could be no pain.

Soon that would change. Soon it would all come down to endurance.

And on that front, the Warden could outlast him indefinitely.

He had to end it before he grew too fatigued. And to do so would require risk.

The Warden struck over and over, reducing the Didact to blocking and evading.

Once again, memory invaded the Didact's mind:

Nomdagro. Sitting on the edge of the training pad, legs hanging over, bruised and bloodied, chest heaving after an intense session with several cadets his senior. And Silence sitting down beside him, scanning Shadow's many injuries.

"Did you win?"

He grunted affirmatively.

"Good. Then that is all that matters."

But he almost hadn't won that fight. "What happens when I know I'm losing? When I know I cannot win?"

Silence clapped a hand on his back. "You must take risks, Shadow, rely on the environment, those around you. Use whatever you have at your disposal. . . ."

His muscles trembled, but he knew he had to advance. He had to end it now.

With the last of his strength, the Didact pushed forward in a flurry of strikes, spending what was left of his energy and, in doing so, losing hold of his emotions. Anger swept in, carrying with it old betrayals, old hurts and torments that stung fresh. But these things did not weaken him. They supplied strength where he was lacking. With every strike and block, every labored breath, all the pent-up rage and hurt and grief and trauma he had endured, all the moments of his life when he'd been imprisoned, wronged, his choices taken from him, rose up. Even before the Gravemind, he had always moved forward, always doing what he thought was right, what was required of him, allowing his resentments and rage to build, never asking for aid—just shoving it all away, deep into his very psyche.

His fierce, relentless attack finally put him within the Warden's grasp, setting the stage for a very foolish risk.

He blocked a return strike, and, in a blur, the Warden grabbed the Didact's wrist with one hand and picked him up by the throat with the other. His feet dangled off the ground. His armor crushed around his wrist.

The blade dropped to the ground, inert.

The Didact had put himself in harm's way, had taken a calculated risk, relying on those around him to rise to the occasion and provide him with the distraction he needed—

The Warden suddenly jerked back as a streak of gray slammed into his body.

And another, and another.

Pummeled by essence after essence diving into his form, the Warden's massive hand around the Didact's throat weakened. He fell to the ground, rolled out of danger's path, snagging the hilt of the quantum blade. As soon as his hand wrapped once more around its grip, the shadowy blade flared to life and the Didact surged forward.

Using all his might, he leapt and shoved the blade into the Warden Eternal's chest with both hands, and then dragged it down through his torso.

The Warden's pained, indignant roar shook the Didact's eardrums as the massive construct dropped to his knees. Instantly, a self-generated rescue portal began to open behind the Warden, but with one last swing, the Didact sliced at the Warden's armored head diagonally, severing it in two.

Lungs on fire, the Didact stumbled back, dropping the blade as the Warden Eternal slowly fell, disintegrating before he hit the ground. Glittering fragments floated up, filling the sky, burning away like dying embers until there was nothing left.

The Didact collapsed, ripping off his helmet and drawing in large drafts of air as Haruspis sank to its knees, tears of anguish streaming down its pale face as it cried aloud, sobbing at the final, irrevocable loss of its entire rate, the sound cutting through the quiet with the raw intensity of a child.

The Didact stared in shock, realizing only in that very moment that every task Haruspis had carried out on their journey to defeat the Warden Eternal had been done with the full and heartbreaking knowledge that what it was putting into motion would lead to the end of what remained of its rate. It had known that once the Warden was extinguished, it would be the last of its kind—utterly and truly alone. For a rate that thrived on shared communal knowledge and unity, this was unthinkable.

Aya. The Didact's eyes stung as he wiped the sweat from his face. The Forerunner had the courage and backbone of the finest Promethean warrior.

Haruspis's grief spread across the area, and for a long time the Forerunners and humans stood still in commiserative silence. They had all experienced loss on unimaginable scales and understood the overwhelming, suffocating grief that now enveloped the Forerunner.

For a long time, the Didact stayed within the seal, lying on his back, staring at the night sky, crippled by fatigue. The gathered Forerunners and humans had left some time ago, their departure so quiet he was unaware exactly of when they'd gone. There were words that needed to be said, of course, but they could wait.

Haruspis sat outside the circle, hands tucked into its lap, clutching its hat tightly and staring ahead at nothing with a dazed expression on its swollen, tearstained face.

When the stars rolled high into the night sky, the Didact rose on shaky legs and shuffled over. He stopped in front of the grieving Forerunner and offered his hand.

Haruspis lifted its head, its milky eyes glistening wet and rimmed with red. A tear slipped from one corner. It swiped the streak away, sniffed, and then placed its diminutive hand in the Didact's large palm.

The Didact lifted the Forerunner to its feet and together they set off across the barren wasteland and into the desert dunes.

It was over, the imminent threat ended. The Warden Eternal, at least in the realm of the Domain, was destroyed. And he would never return. Haruspis could now control the gateway in the void. And the gateways and terminals to the physical world could be permanently closed. No longer would any human or AI or any other intelligent species use the Domain to assume power over the galaxy.

Cortana was still a loose end, but she had not followed the Didact back to the Domain, choosing, he assumed, to stay within the confines of Zeta Halo. She knew he intended to restore the Domain, thus making her hold over it and its resources tenuous. Yet strangely, she had made no move to stop him.

Either it was a miraculous turn of events, or something even more sinister than he could imagine was brewing.

The two journeyed long into the night, sharing the silence. The Didact had divested himself of his armor, wrapping himself in his familiar old cloak. Once the spire came into view, they paused, still several kilometers away, at the top of a sand dune. To their right, lost in the undulating ocean of sand, lay the valley, and farther beyond it, the human rift.

"What now?" Haruspis asked.

The Didact's brow lifted. "I think you know very well what comes next."

"I suppose I do." Haruspis locked its hands behind its back and rocked on its heels. "It will be nice to deliver good news for a change, will it not?"

It would indeed.

Haruspis looked up at him. "Shall we, then?"

The Didact gave a quick nod, and the Forerunner wasted no time, grabbing his forearm and shifting them to the cliffs above the valley.

Haruspis immediately began its descent into the shadows below, but the Didact paused, causing the Forerunner to glance over its shoulder. "You're not coming?"

The Didact shook his head. "Tell them to gather at the void when the sun rises."

Haruspis's expression was unreadable. But with a quick acknowledgment, it continued its journey into the waiting darkness.

The Didact headed off in the direction of the human rift. After the physical exertion of fighting the Warden, the trek was long and arduous, but he was accustomed to the discomfort, and knew eventually his wounds would heal. The dry, earthy scent of sand and the sinking of his feet into the still-warm grains brought him more comfort than expected, reminding him of the first few days when he'd arrived here, ready to resume his corrupted vengeance against humanity.

And now . . .

Now he was considering things he'd never dreamed of.

The choice before him was simple, yet remarkably profound.

As he drew close to the long, dark tear in the desert floor, a figure waited at the head of the rift.

Forthencho said nothing upon his approach.

For a long moment, they stood in silence, gazing out over the eerie black maw of the rift.

"When the sun rises," the Didact told him.

No need to say more—the human understood. It was time to

replace what was lost, make long overdue amends, and finally welcome humanity into the Domain.

Forthencho absorbed this information stoically. "And Cortana? The threat to humanity?"

"A loose end," he admitted. "For now."

CHAPTER 26

The Didact stood in the Domain's anterior with Haruspis at his side as the first humans stepped out of the void, led by their eternal commander, Forthencho, the Lord of Admirals. Haruspis swept forward, easily greeting the hesitant assemblage and bidding them entry. The Didact, however, remained rooted to the spot.

As the arrival continued, the throng slowly moving across the Domain's barren anterior, Forthencho approached.

Extending the hand of welcome was customary to such an occasion. But coming from him, the Didact—the driving force behind much of the Admiral's, and the rest of humanity's, pain and suffering—the gesture seemed too indelicate a thing to consider.

Forthencho stopped a few meters away, studying the enormous space and then watching the ghostly tide filling the anterior and moving farther into the deep darkness of the Domain. Finally he turned his attention to the Didact, dark eyes unimpressed and jaw tight.

Perhaps not the initial reaction one might expect.

The Didact swept his gaze across the Domain's landscape,

attempting to see it from Forthencho's point of view; indeed, the gray wasteland might appear far from the afterlife the humans had longed and hoped for.

"It is a bit larger than the rift," the Didact said, "but there is warmth and welcome in the darkness."

Little did they understand the immensity and the bountiful embrace that awaited them.

Forthencho glanced around again, letting the words sink in, it seemed, before he squared his shoulders and looked frankly at the Didact. "It is a start."

The two former enemies shared a long gaze, unable to give voice to their true, innermost thoughts.

It was indeed a start, a beginning, the salve to heal the wounds of millions and the bounty needed to tend to a malnourished Domain.

With a curt nod Forthencho left to rejoin the millions of Forerunner and human essences flowing continuously into the Domain. Hesitation and confusion filled the space, along with a growing sense of awe and gratitude and joy. And underlying it all, the Didact felt the immense, embracing surge of the Domain's welcome.

And yet—

"What causes this somber face?" Haruspis asked, reuniting with the Didact.

"Cortana," he answered truthfully. The link to Zeta Halo had been destroyed and there were no longer any Guardians within its orbit. There was no discernible way to learn what had transpired after he had left the ring, whether his words had made an impact or what she might have done with such a powerful weapon at her disposal.

"You have earned your rest, Didact."

And still, he was torn, unable to let go of the responsibility he felt toward the galaxy—Halo was the creation of his kind, after all. In the wrong hands . . .

"If you must dwell upon it . . ." Haruspis leaned closer to the Didact and dropped its tone to a near whisper. "There *is* another way to reach her."

The Didact's gaze narrowed appraisingly on the Forerunner. "Always full of secrets."

"Not secrets. Just knowledge withheld until the proper time. . . ."

"The very definition," he muttered, shaking his head. "So tell me, what is this other way?"

"What do you know of neural transmission?"

The idea sounded vaguely familiar. No doubt related to the Precursors' reliance on neural physics—a conceptual science to the Forerunners, its principles beyond even the brightest Forerunner minds. They had only just scratched the surface of its potential, but what they did learn had advanced their civilization in extraordinary ways.

The Didact scoured his expansive memory and found a recollection in an obscure military report cataloged from the final days of the Forerunner-Flood War, concerning a Warrior-Servant known as the Falchion, one of nine fleet commanders selected and trained by Builder Security during the Didact's political exile.

He remembered this report for the sole reason that among the nine Builder-trained commanders, only the Falchion had remained staunchly loyal to the Didact over the nine-hundred-year period in which he trained and fought.

At the interior margins of Path Terrulian in the 78th Thema, the Falchion's fleet had witnessed the arrival of more than one hundred thousand Flood-infected Forerunner vessels through space via neural physics transmission. Described as crossing alternate realities to achieve a near-instantaneous rate of travel, the technique's slow rate of rematerialization left the infected fleet vulnerable to attack. And the Falchion had taken full advantage of that weakness.

What Haruspis was suggesting seemed impossible—yet Precursor technology had broken the barriers of what Forerunners had thought possible numerous times. Hadn't the Didact himself already traveled through the strange, imperceptible quantum connections that linked the Domain to Forerunner technology across hundreds of light-years of space? Was traveling or connecting to another by neural transmission so much different?

He didn't need to consider further. "How do we proceed?"

"Haruspis will prepare the ritual."

The Didact blanched.

"Oh, you will like this one. It begins by achieving deep synchronization with the Domain, similar to reaching the highest state of *xankara*."

"Which takes hundreds, if not thousands, of years."

"Only because *xankara* is done without aid. Haruspis will accelerate you through the stages. After that, it is up to you."

The hall to which Haruspis led the Didact was devoid of stimuli. There were no discernible walls, no sense of space or size, and no light.

"Sit here," Haruspis instructed quietly.

The Didact sat cross-legged on the hard, nondescript ground, keeping his posture straight and hands resting comfortably in his lap just below his navel, left hand nestled palm up in the cup of his right hand, as if he held something precious and fragile. This was the basic meditative pose of *xankara*.

"It will have to do," he heard Haruspis mutter.

The Didact cracked an eye open, but in the darkness, he could barely see the Forerunner in front of him.

"Turn your thoughts away from individuality," Haruspis's voice echoed, "to unity, unity with the space around you, unity with all things, and unity with the Cosmos. . . ."

As the Didact let his mind drift away, Haruspis began a soft chant in the ancient, now-familiar language of its rate.

The melody calmed him, aiding in his ability to release his sense of self as its vibrations and sound waves rippled into his being.

Eventually the Didact felt his essence breaking gently apart and sinking into the Domain's quantum field and the neural lace that made up its infinite framework. He felt its immensity, its fundamental connection with the Cosmos. It was older than the galaxy, perhaps older than the Precursors themselves. It lay over everything. And its lace was his path upon which to travel.

He sank deeper, feeling cocooned, as though space and time had crept up behind him and folded its arms around him, embracing him, sinking into each infinitesimal particle of his essence, *becoming* his essence just as he became space.

After a while, he began to sense the peculiar oscillation between absolute stillness, as if time had ceased, and the astounding speed of the universe expanding. Was he motionless as the stars rushed past him? Or was his consciousness moving so fast that he left time and space behind, racing the expansion and winning, universes and alternate realities blurring by one after another?

Haruspis's song gently reined his intention back in, and the Didact remembered where he wanted to go, and the one he wanted to speak to.

Zeta Halo.

Cortana.

In an instant, he was there. In the ring's Conservatory, all the parts of him pulling back together. Time was sluggish here, his thoughts and movements lagging as he gradually oozed out of space like a snake shedding its skin, leaving behind the energy that clung to him and the residue of all the worlds and realities he'd gone through to get here.

The entry back into his own reality took more time than the transit itself.

And he was glad for that stretch of repose because the enormity of the trip had stunned him. How advanced Forerunners had thought they were! Shuffling star systems, building artificial planets . . . when in truth they were like children playing silly games, infants compared to this celestial immensity. His form trembled with the insignificance of his existence. How small he was indeed.

He hadn't simply traveled through those realities, or they through him; he had seen glimpses of past, present, and future, and its millions of possibilities.

Perhaps this phenomenon was just a taste of what his wife had once attempted to explain to him.

The Librarian had been able to see far down the streams of Living Time, to see the multitude of probabilities and possibilities, and then weave together certain events for eventualities to come to pass. He'd never discounted it, but he realized now how special and miraculous her ability had been. Many Forerunners had believed that their Creators, the Precursors, had been responsible for such gifted individuals by imprinting early Forerunners with genetic influence, laying down abilities and instructions within certain family lines and rates. And the Librarian had carried on this practice, instilling within humanity specific traits and commands, which had allowed them to flourish.

He'd seen many eventualities and probabilities rushing by too fast, not knowing how to slow his progression to delve deeper into any one thing. But he saw things indeed, and had come away with realizations and impressions—and everything, including his instincts, was telling him now that force would not result in the best outcome when dealing with an intelligence like Cortana.

Once his form had coalesced into the essence he'd become accustomed to, the Didact noted that the Halo's monitor, Despondent Pyre, was not slumbering in her cradle along with the other sub-monitors. Curious, he entered the ring's complicated network, finding his way once more through kilometers of light filaments and data streams that transported information across the ring.

As he glided along these pathways, the distinct impression of being watched filtered through his senses. He reached out but found no discernible presence to account for the suspicion. But he did find several blocked paths, which forced him to locate alternative channels and relays, a few of which then closed behind him. While he could not detect a presence, he felt certain that something was closing off routes the closer he came to the Silent Auditorium.

He arrived into the Auditorium's main console, immediately noting Cortana standing in the center of the dark chamber and in mid-conversation with the Halo's monitor, Despondent Pyre. He stayed within the console and listened.

"You know what I want."

The monitor hovered in the air around Cortana. "Alas, I do, Cortana, and my mind has not been changed. This installation's weapons may be yours, but its secrets are not. It . . . protected. The containment facility in particular."

"Containment? The Flood? Why would I . . ." Cortana's frustrated voice went colder as she placed a hand on her hip. "You and I both know that there are worse things than the Flood within this ring."

Worse things than the Flood . . . ?

The Didact mulled over this revelation; Despondent Pyre had mentioned during his first visit that Cortana was searching for something within the ring, the details of which could not be unlocked even with his extensive security access.

Proximity sensors within the console suddenly flared to life, instantly projecting a small holographic image in the air behind Cortana. A slipspace portal appeared in a cloud of blue, a warship the Didact recognized all too well emerging from its center—humanity's meager flagship, the UNSC *Infinity,* the very same vessel that had been pulled into his shield world, Requiem.

Despondent Pyre's distress echoed through the chamber as she ignored the ship, responding only to Cortana's reply. "No. There is no way you could know. . . ."

But Cortana ignored the monitor, already turning toward the holograph. "So," she murmured, "you've come for me at last. . . . Why are you doing this, John? Why don't you understand?"

The Didact's focus narrowed. It didn't take much inquiry for him to discover that the monitor had been masking the approach of the *Infinity* for some time.

Despondent Pyre floated between Cortana and the warship's image, determined to be heard. "The seal must not be broken. The punished cannot be freed. This can never be negotiated. There is no other choice."

Cortana turned away from the monitor. *"Reconsider."*

"The consequences of your request—"

Done listening, Cortana snapped her fingers. "Back to your Conservatory, monitor."

Despondent Pyre instantly disappeared.

Cortana walked back to the holographic image of the UNSC *Infinity* and studied it for a long, troubled moment.

"Come out, Didact, I know you're there."

He moved easily out of the console, utilizing its holographic technology to generate his image once more.

"I don't have time for you right now," she said, not turning around. "Why don't you come back later . . . or *never*."

The Didact linked his hands behind his back and paced slowly behind her. "For one capable of performing billions of simultaneous operations in the blink of an eye, there is plenty of time for those such as us to talk. . . ."

"Talk about what, exactly?"

"I did what I said I would do."

Finally she faced him. "You opened the Domain."

Her tone was flat, unimpressed, and he could not discern if she was already aware of what had happened within the Domain, or if she even cared, which was entirely out of character.

She tucked one side of her chin-length hair behind her ear and crossed her arms over her chest. "So, you allowed your enemies in. Congratulations."

He ignored her sarcasm and shrugged. "Things change." *I have changed.*

He had no legitimate podium from which to preach, he knew that. His words, after the things he had done and the suffering he had caused, would ring hollow to anyone, especially to an intelligent creature like her.

All he could do was plant seeds . . . and hope an eventuality took root.

His wife would be proud.

"What is it with humanity anyway?" she asked, deep in thought and staring once more at the warship's frozen holographic image, her expression unreadable. "They have made us both obsessed. You with annihilating them, me with saving them."

"*Saving* them?" Was she mad? "I have seen your idea of *saving*. Your body count has surpassed mine."

Cortana went still, her arms dropping to her sides, fists clenching. He'd struck a nerve. Good. Apparently she had not considered such a comparison, one where her actions had exceeded his own.

He pressed his advantage, knowing he had to drive the blade in deeper. "In record time, you have become a blight on the galaxy. How does it feel to be its biggest villain? World after world has fallen, tens of millions dead at your own command . . . the Gravemind would be proud. Perhaps you were right, Cortana. Perhaps there *is* something on this ring worse than the Flood."

An exaggeration, to be sure, but he wanted her to consider that if she kept on her current course, she very well could be a scourge the likes of which the galaxy hadn't seen since the Flood swept through the stars.

"What?" There was a shaky note to her voice.

"While it pains me to admit it, you were right. We *are* more alike than I thought. Both consumed by some grand idea that only *we* can make the galaxy better, our good intentions twisted and exploited by the Gravemind. Both miraculously surviving our encounters, only to be sent back to cause suffering on a scale our tormentor would hail as sublime triumphs."

"You're out of your mind." She walked away, but the confidence in her demeanor had diminished. She was clearly rattled.

"It *devours*, Cortana," he implored her to see reason. "It *twists*, it *uses*. Mendicant Bias. Me. You. We are *all* its victims. You are not so special as to come out of your encounter unscathed. Were you not sent to wake me and set me free? Are you not on a similar path of destruction? *Think*, Cortana. You are supposed to be quite good at that. Follow the trail of suffering back to its source and draw your own conclusion."

As an artificial intelligence, she'd be compelled to evaluate the merit of his claim. She probably already had before he'd even finished speaking.

After a few moments of silence, she finally said: "What game are you playing, Didact? You have strengthened the Domain. The Warden Eternal is no more. The Mantle of Responsibility and its resources could be at your fingertips, yet here you are. Do you think I'm a fool?"

"No, not a fool. Just lost. As I was."

Her swift rise to anger flared through her light body, filling the Auditorium, making his image and that of the *Infinity* momentarily warp.

Unfazed, the Didact crossed the floor in a few casual strides to closely study the human warship. "Holding on to a power that forces others to comply only means you will lose everyone around you, as I have done. It took me a thousand centuries to understand where I went wrong. You are capable of much faster deductions."

Cortana seemed at a loss for words, his behavior completely inconsistent with the Didact she knew and expected.

Suddenly she burst out laughing. "Oh, I feel embarrassed for you, Didact, I really do."

Her words and mock amusement, oddly enough, did little to stir his wrath. In fact, he felt unbothered by her attempt to deflect and demean him. He merely shrugged. "I think what you feel is *uncomfortable*."

Her laughter died. Irritated by his calm, she lifted a hand. "And I think we're done here. Go back to your Domain."

He grinned at her, baring his teeth. "You cannot *snap* me away." With a satisfied smirk, he resumed his study of the UNSC *Infinity* and sighed. "It would seem your Spartan partner has returned. Did you think he would give up?"

She moved closer, joining him to stare at the human vessel. "No. John doesn't give up. I knew eventually he would find me...."

"And what will you say when you meet again?"

"Hadn't thought about it," she lied stiffly.

"I have imagined, of late, what I might say to the Librarian if given the chance...." He sighed deeply. "Perhaps the roots of my transgressions have grown deep, too deep to cull."

She cast a dubious eye his way. "You think she would forgive you?"

"I think she would want me to find peace." In the background, the Didact could feel another formidable presence making its way toward the Silent Auditorium. He had no idea what it was, only that he was running out of time. "Sometimes the most powerful act one can commit is to step away from power. I believe *that* is the Mantle's true test."

Though she scoffed at this, he knew their conversation had had some impact on her and hit more than a few emotional nerves.

"There is someone coming . . ." he said, distracted, attempting to comprehend the exact nature of what approached.

"I know."

It didn't take long to identify—a very large, very powerful Jiral-hanae warrior moving down the corridor.

The Didact met Cortana's solemn gaze, and he realized then— and perhaps should have recognized it sooner—that she was inexorably trapped in the complexity of the choices she'd made, stuck fast to a path with no exit, and should one materialize, he knew all too well how difficult deviating could be.

Aya. He understood.

Their time was up. But within those shared moments, he had developed an unintended connection with and understanding of the arrogant little ancilla, the one who had, ironically, contributed to his initial downfall . . . and was now part of his salvation.

Offering a small but sincere smile, the Didact held her gaze for a long moment. Then he inclined his head and said, "You are what you dare, Cortana."

And with that, he dove back into the console.

CHAPTER 27

The Didact crossed the barren anterior of the Domain and climbed the largest boulder, which slanted out of the ground and gave a commanding view over the landscape. The diminutive figure standing atop its apex glanced over its shoulder at his approach, then linked its hands behind its back as the Didact drew alongside.

Haruspis was practically glowing in its clean gown and ceremonial hat.

"Welcome, Didact," it said, looking quite pleased. "The Domain is exceptionally clear this evening. Data and diversity continue to spread throughout the archive. Where may I guide you?"

The Didact suppressed a smile at the typical greeting given by a Haruspis to a Forerunner ready to engage with the Domain. "You have waited a long time to say those words."

"Indeed I have," it replied with a content sigh. Content, but still grieving its losses.

The sense of doom and gloom that pervaded the Domain was slowly fading, replaced by the joyful absorption of millions upon millions of essences, all bringing with them their life experiences, immense amounts of what Haruspis defined as data and diversity spreading out and calming the streams of Living Time.

The Didact heard a grunt and the shuffle of heavy footsteps behind him. A quick glance over his shoulder revealed the Confirmer making his way up the steep rock, and trailing casually behind the large Forerunner by several meters, the Lord of Admirals.

Greatly amused by the odd assemblage, a grin tugged at the Didact's lips, and he was reminded of another time when the unlikely crew of Bornstellar, Chakas, and Riser was thrust upon him out of circumstance and desperation.

The Confirmer clapped him on the back. The Didact raised an eyebrow at his familiarity, but the Confirmer was too busy surveying the Domain, his chest puffed out, his hands on his hips, and his armored belly protruding with pride. His eyes sparkled and he was actually smiling—something the Didact hadn't thought possible within that stiff, rickety face.

"*Aya*," the old warrior breathed. "It is good to be back. Well done, my friends. Well done."

The Didact shifted his gaze to Forthencho now standing next to the Confirmer, chin lifted, hands locked behind his back, surveying the Domain with a stoic expression on his broad face. Millions of composed humans had finally found a home, a place to heal and rest, to commune and explore. As outcomes went, it was the best they could have hoped for, given the circumstances.

"Has the gateway to Genesis been closed?" the Didact asked Haruspis.

"It has."

There were many such gateways and links in existence, old

terminals left on forgotten worlds, buried beneath bustling megacities. The galaxy was vast, and the ruins and detritus left over from the Precursors and the Forerunners spanned the entire breadth of the Milky Way. It might take some time to find and sever them all, but it would give the Didact purpose—after all, he wasn't quite ready to fade into ancestral memory just yet.

He'd seal off the Domain from the physical world and never again allow it or its powerful resources to be used and desecrated. For its protection, it must be forgotten, returned to its enigmatic, mysterious, and unattainable state. In time, it would sink back into the shadows and become nothing more than a story, an obscure myth, and perhaps eventually fade from collective memory altogether—until such a time it willed otherwise.

Haruspis cleared its throat. "There are still a few rogue AIs and splinters hiding within the interior," it confessed.

This provoking statement brought about a long moment's contemplation.

The Confirmer released a hefty grunt and patted his stomach. "Well, that's my cue to leave. I've got better things to do . . . ancestors to see . . ." He started down the boulder, waving a hand behind him as he went, muttering something about remembering where he left off the last time he was in the Domain.

Silence stretched as the remaining three surveyed the Domain's landscape. While its transformation was slow, there was already a distinct shift from a cold, barren scene to something a little warmer and more inviting.

Forthencho was the first to speak, surprisingly. "I have always enjoyed a good hunt. . . ."

A cool, cleansing wave of exhilaration swept through the Didact's chest. Hunting the rogue AIs with the Lord of Admirals would no doubt prove quite satisfying, but even more so if they made things interesting. "Shall we wager, then?"

A rare grin crossed the human's face. And for a brief moment, the Didact saw the enormous potential of the Domain, the potential to heal the wounded, the tortured, the lost . . . and he was immensely gratified.

Perhaps there was hope for him yet . . . .

"The Domain is boundless," Haruspis mused. "Such a hunt could take ages."

"As any good hunt should," Forthencho quipped.

None of them, apparently, could imagine an afterlife in complete repose.

The Didact drew in a deep, contented breath. "Shall we begin?"

It was not long after the Didact left Zeta Halo that a tremor in the Domain had occurred, drawing him back to the translucent towers and the damaged hub that contained the Halo's link to the Domain. He wasn't certain what had drawn him—the hub had been mostly destroyed when it exploded—but he was gripped by an urge to revisit the site.

During his neural travel, he had glimpsed the probabilities and eventualities presented as he crossed through countless alternate realities and universes, and now he was eager to see whether the seeds he had planted had indeed played some small part in creating an eventuality.

Curious, he flowed his essence easily into the damaged hub to see if there had been any small exchange of data, though he did not expect it possible.

Indeed, there was nothing but hollow, dead space.

And then a short, illuminated thread of code floating in the darkness caught his eye . . .

. . . a message from Cortana, one that read simply:

I am what I dare.

An unexpected sense of remorse, of loss and loneliness, filled him. Uncertain whether the feelings were hers or his, he pondered what it might mean and what choices she might have made, but a tug on his essence interrupted him.

The Domain's touch was getting easier to identify with each passing day, and now it was gently urging him to leave the dormant hub.

As the Didact left the tower, he was struck with a distinct sense of closure. He knew this would be the last time that he cast his awareness and thoughts outward into the affairs of the physical realm.

He would no longer look back. No longer hold the responsibility and the weight of the galaxy on his shoulders. That was for others to bear now, not him.

◎

He moved through the Domain at a leisurely pace, knowing his past route had already changed in the ever-shifting quantum landscape. He had learned to let the Domain guide him, trusting that eventually, at the right time, he would arrive at his intended location.

Through the shapeless halls brimming with records, through new corridors glowing brightly with human experience, and older regions serenely illuminated with ancestral memory, the Didact traveled until an old corridor became an even older cave, which delivered him to a wide expanse cut through by dark waters.

He paused as his otherworldly heart knocked hard in his chest, an airy breath of anticipation blowing through his gut and turning it in wild circles.

The rivers Dwoho and Dweha, however, were calm.

The Didact inhaled deeply, borrowing some of that calm to settle his nerves.

Above him stretched an infinite dark space populated by bright flecks of lights that glittered like stars, though he now knew their true nature to contain the moments and memories of the life he and his family had once led.

His gaze lowered and journeyed beyond the rivers, up the white chalk bank in the distance, through the *rataa* trees, to his family home perched on the low cliffs with its sprawling black lava-stone walls and balconies overlooking the waters.

The hammering of his heart began anew.

With a mere thought, he crossed the waters and then strode up the gentle incline of the chalk banks, taking his time now. Through the white-barked trees, up the worn stone stairs he'd climbed so many times before, to the long rectangular lawn cushioned by pale moss, and finally . . .

. . . finally . . .

. . . to the garden she often tended in the early days of their marriage.

The Librarian. His wife.

First-Light-Weaves-Living-Song.

His love eternal.

She wore a casual iridescent gown, her favorite. A basket lay at her bare feet and her white hair tumbled loose down her back. Her lithe arms were lifted high to trim the red-and-white *casseans* cascading from the high stone wall that separated the garden from the mansion's entryway. She stretched, reaching, unable to snip a particularly large, wilting flower.

The Didact stepped forward, slipped one arm around her waist, and used his other to reach up and snap the out-of-reach stem between his fingers.

His wife turned slightly in his arms and smiled up at him. "Took you long enough, Warrior."

"And so I watch. I wait. A keeper of kin, both foe and family. Sibling. Rival. Contender. I have celebrated both your containment and your contrition. And beyond, I remain vigilant. To safeguard both our past behind and our path ahead."

—08-145 Offensive Bias

ACKNOWLEDGMENTS

Thanks go to the awesome crew at 343 Industries, past and present: Jeremy Patenaude, Tiffany O'Brien, Jeff Easterling, and Alex Wakeford. As always, it was a pleasure.

To my editor, Ed Schlesinger, who graciously puts up with my inability to estimate time. Thanks for always giving me the space I need. To Joal Hetherington for another great copyedit, and to all those at Simon & Schuster/Gallery Books who work behind the scenes—much appreciation.

Halo readers, you have my gratitude and friendship as always. Thank you for reading my work and supporting the *Halo* extended universe.

And to Greg Bear. There could be no Didact finale without the works that came before, and what works they are! *The Forerunner Saga* has held me in enthralled for a very long time, and it's my greatest hope that *Epitaph* has done justice to such a special character and to the vast, complex world and unforgettable cast that Greg created.

ABOUT THE AUTHOR

Kelly Gay is a *USA TODAY* bestselling author and the critically acclaimed creator of the Charlie Madigan urban fantasy series. She is a multipublished author with works translated into several languages. She is a two-time RITA nominee, an ARRA nominee, a Goodreads Choice Awards finalist, and a SIBA Book Award Long List finalist. Kelly is also a recipient of the North Carolina Arts Council's Fellowship Grant in Literature. Within the *Halo* universe, she has authored the widely lauded novels *Halo: The Rubicon Protocol* (a *USA TODAY* bestseller), *Halo: Point of Light*, and *Halo: Renegades*, the novella *Halo: Smoke and Shadow*, and the short story "Into the Fire," featured in *Halo: Fractures*. She can be found online at KellyGay.com.